After graduating with degr[ees in] political science, **Eva She[pherd]** [worked in] journalism and as an advertising copyw[riter]. She began writing historical romances because it combined her love of a happy ending with her passion for history. She lives in Christchurch, New Zealand, but spends her days immersed in the world of late Victorian England. Eva loves hearing from readers and can be reached via her website, evashepherd.com, and her Facebook page at Facebook.com/evashepherdromancewriter.

# A MISTLETOE MATCH FOR THE EARL

Eva Shepherd

MILLS & BOON

First published in Great Britain 2025
by Mills & Boon, an imprint of HarperCollins*Publishers* Ltd,
1 London Bridge Street, London, SE1 9GF

www.harpercollins.co.uk

HarperCollins*Publishers*, Macken House, 39/40 Mayor Street Upper,
Dublin 1, D01 C9W8, Ireland

ISBN: 978-0-263-34544-5

11/25

FSC
www.fsc.org

**MIX**
Paper | Supporting
responsible forestry
**FSC™ C007454**

This book contains FSC™ certified paper
and other controlled sources to ensure responsible forest management.

For more information visit www.harpercollins.co.uk/green.

Printed and Bound in the UK using 100% Renewable Electricity
at CPI Group (UK) Ltd, Croydon, CR0 4YY

To little Eva L de-W, welcome to the world.

# Chapter One

Cumberland, England, 1890

Alice Lambton never asked much of her older brother. She had not expected him to make one single contribution to organising the Christmas festivities. It had been Alice who had made sure they had more than enough food to feed everyone invited for Christmas Day. She had been the one to gather the ivy and holly and weave them around every wall in the house so Rosetree Manor was transformed into a colourful, festive home. She had been the one to convince the local estate manager to cut down the best fir for their Christmas tree, and under her direction he had even propped it up in a large tub in the corner of the drawing room and together they had adorned it with baubles and candles.

With the help of the servants she had woven colourful strings of paper chains and tinsel through every room, along with countless paper lanterns, so the house twinkled with inviting warmth and cheer.

She had also organised and rehearsed the church choir for the annual Christmas Eve carol singing. Under her guidance, the women of the Ladies Benevolent Society had bought or made and wrapped all the presents to be distributed to the needy on Boxing Day, and Alice had ensured preparations for the New Year's Eve Ball were well under way.

All that was expected of her brother, William, was for him to invite James Marlowe, the new Earl of Thornwood, to their home for Christmas dinner.

It wasn't as if he hadn't had ample opportunity. The two men had travelled together on the train from London to Carlisle, then on to the village of Ferndale. They had known each other since they were schoolboys and had once been the best of friends. How hard was it to ask him to come to Christmas dinner at a home where he had spent many hours as a child?

'I did ask,' William said with an infuriatingly dismissive shrug. 'He said no.'

'He was probably just being polite,' she responded with a sigh. 'Did you let him know just how pleased we all would be to see him again?'

William shrugged again and helped himself to a fruit mince pie.

'Don't eat all of them. They're for the carol singers.'

'I got the impression James wanted to spend Christmas on his own,' he said when he'd finished demolishing the pie in two bites.

Alice stared at her brother, unable to comprehend such nonsense. 'He couldn't possibly want to spend Christmas all alone in that enormous house. Of course he would want to spend Christmas with friends. He has to come.'

'Why?' William asked, drawing out that one word and narrowing his eyes.

'Because I've also invited Beatrice and her aunt,' she said, becoming exasperated with her brother, who never seemed to listen to anything she said.

'Who?'

'Beatrice, my friend. Lady Chigwell's niece. She's staying with her aunt for a few weeks over Christmas.'

'What are you up to, Ali?' he asked before eating another of the forbidden mince pies.

'I told you all about this in my last letter. Beatrice's father has informed her he does not wish for her to have a Social Season as promised but wants to marry her off to some businessman of his acquaintance.'

Her brother continued to stare at her uncomprehendingly. For a barrister who worked at a successful London law practice he could be decidedly dim-witted at times.

'It's imperative I find her a husband before the Season begins. James Marlowe is unmarried. He needs a wife. Beatrice needs a husband before she is forced to marry a man whose company she can hardly abide. If a wealthy earl offers for her hand instead, her father could hardly object, and Beatrice would make an excellent Countess of Thornwood.'

William went back to eating another pie as if none of this was any of his concern.

'But that is not going to happen if they never meet. That, my dear brother, is why I want to invite them both to spend Christmas Day with us.'

'Isn't Beatrice that strange little girl with the blonde plaits? The one who cried when James and I caught those tadpoles?' He gave an annoying laugh. 'She thought they'd miss their mother.'

'Oh, for goodness' sake. She was about eight at the time. She's twenty now and has grown into a beautiful, elegant young lady.'

William pulled a face as if he found that hard to believe. 'So you're going to marry her off to James, are you?'

'That had been the plan, but it required you to do one small task and invite him to spend Christmas Day with us.'

William looked at the diminishing pile of mince pies then thought better of it and turned to his sister. 'I know you mean well, Ali, but I'm not sure if that will be such a good idea. James… Well, he's not the same as he was when he headed off to America. He's changed.'

'Changed? How?'

'I don't know. He walks with a limp and uses a stick.'

Alice waited for him to continue. He didn't. 'That hardly matters, does it?' she said.

'No, I suppose not, but he's also got a scar down the side of his cheek.' William ran his finger from his hairline to his jaw.

Alice raised her hands, palms upward in disbelief. 'Beatrice is not so shallow as to care about something so superficial.'

'Hmm… Well, he was serious enough before he left for America, but he's even more so now.'

'Good,' Alice stated emphatically. 'I'd hate to think he was still behaving like an immature eighteen-year-old.'

She sent her brother a chastising look to suggest he too would do well to act with a bit more maturity now he was a man in his thirties. 'He's an earl now. He's got responsibilities and I imagine his travels in the Americas matured him.'

'Perhaps.'

She looked out the window at the grey sky and sighed. 'I suppose I'm going to have to walk over to Thornwood Hall myself and tell him he simply must spend Christmas Day with us. Perhaps I can even convince him to join Beatrice and me for carol singing.'

William snorted. 'Good luck with that.'

'Men,' Alice stated, that one word expressing so much. 'You'll never understand how important it is for a woman to make a suitable match. You just think it's all a big joke, don't you?'

'Hmm,' William repeated, now eyeing the sugar plums.

She swatted his arm, as much in annoyance at his lack of sensitivity to Beatrice's plight as to stop him from demolishing the sweets in the manner he had with the mince pies.

While men like her brother could laugh at the lengths women went to in order to secure a husband, they did not have to face the dire consequences that awaited many women if they did not marry.

Beatrice was facing the prospect of a loveless marriage to an elderly man who she could scarcely tolerate. Alice intended to do everything in her power to make sure that did not happen, and the best way to achieve her goal was to secure a better offer, and no offer would be better than one from a wealthy titled man.

'Maybe Beatrice doesn't want to marry?' her sadly misguided brother continued. 'You didn't.'

'No, I didn't, thank goodness,' she said with more conviction than she felt. 'But I am fortunate. I have options. Beatrice doesn't.'

Alice's first and only Season had been a disaster. It became immediately apparent from the moment she stepped into her first ballroom that a woman who was taller than most men, who was, to put it kindly, not reputed to be a great beauty, who was the daughter of the second son of the second son of an earl, and whose dowry was suspected to be modest, was not going to have a successful Season.

At that first ball she had found herself sitting in the corner while other young ladies were swirled around the dance floor by a succession of men. The only consolation for this humiliation was making friends with two other so-called wallflowers, Primrose Fairburn and Margaret Whitmore. The three young ladies spent each ball chattering together and their friendship had continued after the Season through regular correspondence.

But Alice was luckier than most young women. She had a widowed father who was more than happy for her to remain at home running the household, and a brother who she knew would always support her financially. In addition, Alice was now earning a respectable income from her children's books, an occupation that filled her with pride and a sense of satisfaction she was sure no marriage ever could. That, she told herself repeatedly, meant she could push aside any regrets she might harbour over missing out on love, marriage or the prospect of children.

'I'll just have to go over to Thornwood Hall and invite him myself,' she repeated, pushing the call button to summon a maid to fetch her cloak and gloves.

'You're not going to walk over to Thornwood Hall now, are you?' William said, putting down a gingerbread biscuit and looking out the window.

'Yes. I have to.'

'I don't like the look of those clouds. I think it might be going to rain.'

'A bit of rain never hurt anyone. And if it does start to rain, James will have to bring me home in his carriage. Then I'll be able to persuade him to accompany me and Beatrice when we go carol singing.'

William gave her a dubious look. 'Take the carriage, or perhaps I should accompany you.'

Alice resisted the temptation to roll her eyes. '*You've* already failed to get him to come to Christmas dinner. I'm sure *I'll* have better luck.'

'Then take your lady's maid. You should not visit a gentleman unaccompanied.'

'William, I am four and twenty. A spinster by all accounts. And it's James I'm visiting. I've known him since childhood. I do not need a chaperone.'

William's dubious look did not fade. 'Take the carriage, Ali. I want to make sure you arrive safely.'

Alice was about to argue but could see the concern on her brother's face. 'All right. The carriage can drop me off at the end of the driveway, then I'll walk the rest. That way if it does rain James can bring me home.'

'And when he gets here you can trap him in the basement until he agrees to marry this Beatrice creature.'

This time she did roll her eyes at her brother's attempt at humour.

'Then we can let nature take its course.' Although Alice had every intention of helping nature along, so it took the best course for all concerned.

James Marlowe, the ninth Earl of Thornwood, stared out the large sash windows at a landscape as bleak as his mood. Grey clouds shrouded the sky. Equally grey trees, stripped of their foliage, merged into the dim winter light, and the barren flower beds had a melancholy appearance, as if they had no expectation of spring ever returning.

As a child Thornwood Hall had seemed enormous, full of cavernous rooms. Now it loomed even larger, even quieter. And this three-storey, two-hundred-room monstrosity, which had been in his family since the time of Queen Anne, was now his. That was as unlikely an outcome as his return from America, and even more unwanted.

If his older brother had done his duty by marrying and siring an heir, instead of spending all his time carousing in London, then dying suddenly and unexpectedly, nothing would have got James back to this godforsaken home.

He gave a bitter, joyless laugh. Although, if he'd inherited the title and all that went with it just a few months earlier, he might now be a married man. The accident that had left him scarred and crippled might not have happened. He might have returned from America with the beautiful, charming and much desired heiress Clara Waverly on his arm, and this outlook might not appear so desolate.

He shook his head slowly at his own stupidity for ever harbouring such a dream.

For a brief moment he had thought he could be like other people. That he too could have contentment and happiness, and all thanks to being in love with a beautiful woman, a woman he had never deserved.

More fool him.

Reality and dreams seldom had anything in common, and thank goodness he had finally learned that cruel lesson, but that awareness did nothing to ease the crushing sensation that surrounded his heart every time he thought of Clara. The only bright light, if it could be described thus, was he had this private retreat to hide in while he recovered from his pain and humiliation.

The image of an injured dog slinking away to lick his wounds came to mind, and he could now see why animals chose to recover in solitude.

Another joyless laugh escaped. Thornwood Hall did have one other unintended consolation: he had plenty of work to keep him occupied and his mind busy.

His brother had neglected the estate, preferring to spend his time in the more exciting surrounds of London. His late father had also avoided his responsibilities, choosing instead to haunt this house like a miserable, restless ghost.

James had much to put right.

He would not be an absentee landowner as they had been. He had every intention of making the estate profitable again. It would provide him with a much-needed diversion, and he owed it to the tenants, servants and people living in the surrounding villages who depended on Thornwood Hall. It was up to him to make sure the estate flourished and brought in revenue to the area.

He looked over at the pile of ledgers sitting on the table, determined to make a start on the tasks he had set for himself, then turned back to stare at the dreary view outside his window.

He leaned forward and peered more closely. At the end of the long driveway, between the leafless linden trees, he could make out a small figure dressed in a bright red cloak, stark against the monochrome landscape.

James emitted a low groan.

A visitor.

He tapped his walking stick against his leg in annoyance. The last thing he wanted was company and he certainly was in no mood for entertaining.

He would leave the servants to deal with this busybody and send her on her way with the knowledge that the new earl was not receiving callers. Not now. Not ever.

The small red figure grew bigger, and like a prisoner in his own home, he moved back from the window lest she spied him watching her.

He might have known word of the new earl's arrival would spread through the village faster than frost on a cold morning. Being isolated up in Cumbria had its advantages. It was unlikely anyone from Society would bother to travel this far from London, but it meant everyone in the local area knew everyone else and they all knew each other's business.

Despite the closeness of the community, he would not have expected the gossip mill to have sprung into action quite this quickly. He'd hoped to at least be safe until after Christmas, preferably even well into the New Year.

The only person who knew of his return, apart from his servants, was his childhood friend William Lambton. James would not have suspected him of being a gossip. But it had been a long time since they had been friends, and people did change.

It had been a surprise to see William on the train,

though not an entirely welcome one. He had always liked William and they had spent many enjoyable times together when young. He'd also enjoyed spending time at William's home, which had always seemed small and cosy after Thornwood Hall, but was actually a substantial manor house that had been built in the Tudor period.

But those days were over. William had said he was only up in Ferndale for the Christmas break, having a busy legal practice in London to return to the moment the holiday season was over. It was unlikely the two men would have a chance to resume their friendship, which suited James perfectly.

And if this red-cloaked figure was here because William had spread word of his return, then all the more reason to avoid the companionship of his childhood friend. He did not want company, and he most certainly did not want people inquiring, talking about or speculating on his time in America or discussing it with all and sundry in the village marketplace.

He moved over to the wall, his injured knee aching more than usual, and rang for a footman.

'There's someone heading towards the house,' he informed the man the moment he entered. 'If she is here to see me then please inform her I am not home to visitors and send her on her way as quickly as possible.'

'Very good, my lord,' the man said with a polite bow.

The size of the house meant there was no likelihood of hearing the exchange on the doorstep, but James returned to the windows wishing to see her walk back down the stone stairs and away from the house.

Nothing happened. He waited. And waited.

Just as he was about to call for the footman to discover the fate of the intruder, the drawing room door opened. Instead of his footman, the unwanted visitor bustled in, minus the cloak, as if she had every right to do so.

James stared at her in disbelief. How on earth did she get past his servants? Before he had a chance to push the bell again and get the answer to this question, she approached him, her arms outstretched as if she intended to embrace him.

'James, how wonderful to see you again,' she exclaimed. 'Although I suppose I should now call you my lord,' she added with a laugh.

'Who are you?' he all but snapped, having no intention of being polite to this uninvited interloper who had somehow managed to evade his servants.

'You don't recognise me, do you?' she continued, still smiling, those arms remaining outstretched as she ignored his scowl. 'It's Alice, Alice Lambton, William's little sister, although I'm not so little anymore.'

She pulled a face, then laughed, as if her maturity was a source of great amusement.

He did remember William's tomboy of a little sister. She was correct in that she was no longer little. He stood a few inches over six foot and she was almost as tall as him, five foot eleven, he'd guess. He also remembered those grey eyes that were always full of mischief, that wide mouth that was always smiling and laughing. Her light brown hair was the same, although it was no longer tied in messy plaits but pulled into an equally untidy bun at the back of her neck.

One thing hadn't changed though. She was still as annoying as she had always been, and her company was as wanted now as it had been when he and William were boys and had tried to avoid the sister who refused to go away.

'How do you do, Miss Lambton?' he said with reluctant politeness. 'Or is it still Miss?' What would she be now, in her mid-twenties? She had been about ten or eleven when he left for America, aged eighteen. Presumably she was now married with a herd of equally irritating children.

'No, it's still Miss.' Her smile faltered briefly before returning just as brightly. 'But as you always called me Alice then, you can continue to do so.'

She tilted her head in expectation. Was he expected to inform her she should call him James? He had no intention of getting on such familiar terms with a woman who had not been invited to his home and whom he wanted to leave as soon as possible.

'William was supposed to invite you to join us for Christmas Day,' she continued, apparently not taking offence. 'We've got so much planned and it's going to be lots of fun.' She looked around the drawing room. 'You don't want to be alone over Christmas, do you? And we are so looking forward to spending the day with you.'

'William did invite me and I informed him I would not be attending,' he said, hoping that would be the end of things.

'Oh, nonsense.' She brushed her hand in the air as if wiping away his statement. 'Please do join us. I've invited several other people and they are all so eager to reacquaint themselves with you, and some to meet you for the first time.'

'I don't wish to be rude, Miss Lambton, but—'

'Alice,' she said raising one finger in admonition, but still smiling.

'I don't mean to be rude, but—'

'I'm sure you don't,' she interrupted again, flouncing down into the nearest chair. 'It's such a long walk over here and I really could do with a nice cup of tea before I set off back home.'

James swallowed a sigh and walked over to the bell press and rang for a servant.

When the footman arrived, James sent him a questioning look. The man coloured slightly, looked over at Miss Lambton, then back at him. That quick glance said it all. Stopping the indomitable Miss Lambton from entering the house would be like trying to stop a cavalry charge by politely asking the horses to halt their progress.

But where his footmen failed, James would succeed. Miss Lambton would be on her way as soon as she'd had her tea. He asked the footman for the tea tray and the man scurried out.

'Oh, those clouds are even darker now than when I left home,' she said, looking out the window. 'I think it might even be going to snow.'

'Then perhaps you should leave. Now. I'll arrange for a carriage to take you home.'

'No, you've already called for tea. It would be rude to make the servants go to all that trouble and not actually drink it.'

'I'm sure they'll cope.'

She laughed as if he was joking. He wasn't. Still smiling, she settled back into the chair, making it obvious she had every intention of staying.

'I was sorry to hear about your brother,' she said, that ceaseless smile finally leaving her lips.

'Yes, a tragedy,' he responded, without emotion.

His brother's sudden death at such a young age was indeed a tragedy, but it would be insincere of him to pretend he mourned his passing. It would be like mourning the death of a stranger. Giles had been twelve when James was born. He was away at school and rarely came home, even for the holidays. When he did make the occasional appearance at Thornwood Hall, he was inevitably in the company of friends and had no interest in getting to know his little brother. By the time James went off to boarding school, Giles was living the life of a young aristocrat in London, biding his time until he inherited the title and the estate.

As the second son, James knew he would inherit nothing, so had headed off to America at the age of eighteen, determined to make his own way in the world and to have the adventures that would be denied to him if he had been born the first son.

At the time of his sudden death from pneumonia, Giles had not married and produced an heir, presumably assuming that at the age of forty-four there was plenty of time to perform that particular duty.

'We didn't really see as much of the former earl as we would have liked,' she continued, that smile returning. 'But I'm sure everyone in the village will be delighted to hear that Thornwood Hall is occupied once again. And you must be so pleased to be home, where you belong.'

James did not answer that, unsure if he belonged anywhere now. He also did not like the sound of the entire district being excited by his return. One excitable, uninvited guest was more than enough.

'You must tell me all about your adventures in America.'

Was she staring at his scar when she asked that? If she was, she would not be hearing how he came to feel the cut of metal into his skin, and the even deeper pain he felt when he recovered from the carriage accident and discovered everything between himself and Clara had changed.

He rubbed his hand along his scar, trying not to focus on either event.

The maid entered with the tea tray and he was grateful for the diversion. She bobbed a small curtsey before placing it on the table, and smiled at Miss Lambton, who of course beamed a smile back.

'How are you, Mary?' she asked, with a surprising level of familiarity towards one of his servants.

'Very well, thank you, miss.'

'And your mother? Has she got over that terrible cold?'

'Yes, miss, and thank you so much for all that soup you sent over. It was much appreciated.'

'Oh, no, it's my cook you should be thanking. All I did was arrange for its delivery. I can't take any of the credit,' she continued as if they were having a pleasant chat in the market square and James was not present. 'Tell her I'll visit soon. Cook has baked far too many Christmas mince pies and I'm sure you'll brothers and sisters will be able to do them justice.'

The maid's smile grew wider. 'I'm sure they will.'

'Thank you, Mary,' James said, using the maid's name, which he'd only just learned.

She stopped smiling and appeared to remember her duties. 'Would you like me to pour the tea?' she said, looking at Miss Lambton, not him, and placing a plate of unrequested biscuits beside his guest.

'No, that's all right, Mary. I can do it,' Miss Lambton answered for him.

'And please ask the coachman to ready the carriage,' he said. 'Miss Lambton will be returning home once she has finished her tea.'

'Yes, my lord.' Mary bobbed another quick curtsey and departed.

Once the door closed, Miss Lambton poured the tea. 'Mary is one of thirteen children. Can you believe it?'

James neither believed it nor doubted it nor cared particularly.

'The poor mother, she works her fingers to the bone. But it's good that Mary has found employment here at the hall, and has a regular wage coming in. And now that you are in residence her job is secure.' She looked up, a teacup extended towards him, and, of course, still smiling. 'I'm assuming you are here to stay?'

James gave a nod. Although if he was going to be inundated with visitors he might have to reconsider that decision.

'It must be quite a change from living in New York,

but I'm sure you won't be bored. There's always plenty going on in the village, and in summer we get lots of visitors, with people wanting to walk in our glorious scenery. It can get quite hectic at times.'

He took a seat, placed his tea on a side table and silently urged her to drink quickly, rather than waste time trying to make conversation with him.

'Not that I know what New York is like, but I imagine it's quite exciting.' She placed two shortbreads on her plate, and he stifled a sigh. She really did look like she planned to stay for the remainder of the afternoon.

'It is not much different from London,' he answered tersely.

'We're all looking forward to hearing about your travels. You can regale us with your adventures during Christmas dinner.'

He could remind her he had not accepted her invitation, and add he would not be regaling anybody with any tales, but suspected it would fall on deaf ears. He ran his finger along his scar. He had no desire to talk about or even think about his time in New York.

His silence, as expected, had no effect on her and he was forced to listen to her own tales regarding everyone she had invited to this infernal Christmas lunch, along with details of seemingly every one of his servants and their families.

'Oh, it's starting to snow,' she exclaimed, looking

towards the windows. 'It's always so magical when it snows at Christmas time, don't you think?

She now had his interest. He turned to the windows, panic welling up inside. Memories of another night, another unexpected snowstorm, hit him with more force than he would have expected.

'You need to leave. Right now.' He stood and crossed the room as quickly as his injured leg would allow and pushed the bell to summon a servant. 'If you stay any longer the roads will become dangerous.'

He waited, anxiously watching the flakes drift down like white feathers threatening to smother all beneath them.

The footman entered and all three stared out the windows. The few flutters of snow had rapidly turned into a thick blanket.

Damn it all. It seemed she had lost her opportunity to leave. James knew better than anyone the risk of sending a carriage out in such conditions and would not endanger the safety of his driver or the exasperating Miss Lambton, even if he was desperate to be free of her.

'Tell the coachman to be prepared to take Miss Lambton home the moment there is a break in the weather,' he told the footman.

The man bowed and departed.

James continued to stare out the window, praying that the weather would clear before he lost all patience with Miss Lambton, forgot his manners and told her exactly what he thought of women who arrived uninvited and unwanted at a man's home.

## Chapter Two

William was right and he was wrong when he said James had changed.

The Earl of Thornwood was somewhat more serious, but he was still good-looking, just as he had been in his youth. Alice had to confess to having a tiny childhood crush on her brother's dark-haired, dark-eyed friend. Although perhaps his looks *had* changed. You could no longer just call him good-looking. Handsome was more applicable. Breathtakingly handsome, so handsome that behaving in a normal manner in his company was proving to be quite the strain. Alice's nerves were jumping in a most peculiar manner, and she couldn't help smiling incessantly, like some sort of ninny.

She supposed a certain amount of change was to be expected. He had been not much more than a boy when he left, but William had not warned her that James had matured into a tall, lean and muscular man who simply exuded confident masculinity. His eyes were still brown, his hair black, obviously, but there was now a brooding intensity to those dark eyes that was decidedly unsettling, and his slightly long, slightly curling black hair gave him an almost piratical look. As did the dark stubble on his strong, angular jawline.

She doubted she had ever seen a more handsome, more muscular, more, well, masculine man. No, that was not correct. She had *never* seen a man who more admirably embodied those qualities.

And every minute she spent in his company she became more aware of her own shortcomings.

Since retreating from that one disastrous Season, she had all but forgotten she was not the most beautiful of women, to say the least, nor was she the most accomplished in social graces.

In James's company it was impossible to forget that the most flattering thing any man, excluding male relatives, had ever said about her was that her face had character.

But none of that mattered. She was not here to impress him with her wit, charm or beauty, thank goodness, because if she was, she'd fail miserably. She was here to put James in the company of Beatrice, a woman who *did* possess an abundance of beauty, charm and wit.

And she only had just under two weeks to do so before Beatrice returned to her home so there was no point getting distracted by his appearance or her own feelings of inadequacy.

'With the weather being so inclement it might be better if you came back to Rosetree Manor with me,' she said, adopting what she hoped was an unflappable tone. 'Then you won't have to worry about taking the horses out again on Christmas Day, and you can spend this evening reacquainting yourself with William.'

*And meeting Beatrice.*

He sent her a look as stormy as the weather. 'Judging by this snow it is unlikely anyone will be going anywhere any time soon.'

She followed his gaze. The snow was now falling faster and heavier, turning the large windows a misty white.

This was a disaster. He was right. They would be going nowhere anytime soon.

'Oh, no. This is awful. We're going to miss the carol singing,' she said as much to herself as to James.

His frown suggested he questioned the sharpness of her mind. 'I doubt if even the most dedicated carol singers would venture out in this weather, and if they did, their voices would be lost in the wind.'

Alice was well aware that would be the case. She wasn't entirely stupid. If the carol singers couldn't walk around the village spreading their good tidings, everyone would gather in the village hall to enjoy the Christmas cheer. She had been hoping to encourage

James to join them and provide yet another opportunity for him to meet Beatrice, but it seemed like that opportunity was well and truly lost.

She looked over at the morose man staring out the windows, and had to admit William was right to snort when she'd suggested James join them for carol singing. She had difficulty picturing him holding a candle and singing his heart out for the entertainment of the villagers. She suppressed her own snort of amusement at this unlikely image.

William had also unfortunately not exaggerated when he said James was even more serious now than he had been when he sailed off for America. If the Earl continued to behave in this sombre manner there was a danger the light-hearted Beatrice would not fall in love with him. And that would never do.

Her mother had always been able to make the young James smile. Surely Alice was capable of doing the same so he would become exactly the sort of man her friend should marry.

She took a sip of her now-cold tea, looked out at the falling snow and contemplated how she was going to achieve this goal.

Perhaps it was time to put into practice the lessons in conversation she'd been forced to take in preparation for the Season. She had been assured at the time of their effectiveness in putting men at their ease and facilitating smooth social interactions.

That was what she needed to do now. Put James at his ease and draw him into a pleasant conversation. But how did one do that?

The weather had already been discussed. She'd asked about his family. She'd brought him up to date with all the goings-on in the village. She'd even tried to discuss his recent adventures, but all those topics had fallen flat, just as they had when she'd attempted to engage men in conversation during the Season.

That left making compliments. She would certainly not be mentioning his appearance; the mere thought of his manly looks made her tongue-tied.

She would have to say something complimentary about her surroundings. She gazed around the drawing room, which bore none of the festive cheer that adorned every room of Rosetree Manor.

'Did you not inform your servants you would be returning for Christmas?' she said, at a loss to find anything to compliment.

'Yes, I sent them a telegram last night,' he replied, his back still to her as he continued staring out at the falling snow.

'That must explain it.'

He turned to face her. 'Explain what?'

'Why there are no Christmas decorations. No holly, no garlands of ivy, no Christmas tree. I'm sure if the servants had received sufficient warning they would have made the house more festive.'

'Hmm' was all he said as his attention returned to the scene outside the windows.

'At least they've made a nice fire, and is that pine I smell?' She inhaled deeply. 'Yes, I do believe they've put pine cones on the fire to give it that lovely Christmassy smell.'

'I hadn't noticed,' he said absently.

She took another sip of her tea, discovered the cup was empty and racked her brains for another topic of conversation.

'So how do they celebrate Christmas in America?'

'In much the same way they do in England,' he said, not looking away from the windows.

'What? By staying alone in a miserable, undecorated house?' She gave a small laugh to let him know this was a joke.

He looked at her over his shoulder, not smiling. 'If this snow does not let up, I'm afraid you too might be spending Christmas in a miserable, undecorated house.'

She looked towards the windows and feared he might be right. Unless the snow stopped soon, the road would not be passable until men had been called out to clear it. It would be unreasonable to expect anyone to do so this late in the day unless it was an emergency. Although given the way he was looking at her, she suspected he would class getting rid of her as an emergency.

That meant there was every possibility she might have to stay the night.

Panic inexplicably welled up inside her. Why on earth should she be feeling panicky? She trusted James implicitly. He had been her brother's good friend when they were children. He'd spent endless amounts of time at their home, and always treated her like a little sister. That is, he always ignored her the way older brothers did with little sisters. And she had always thought of him almost as another member of the family.

But he was not that young man anymore. Far from it. He was now an adult male. One who was scarred, and she did not just mean the white line that ran down the side of his face from his forehead to his jawline, nor the cane with which he walked. There was an inner scarring, a dark, silent intensity about this new James that was deeply disconcerting.

Although that could not entirely explain her reaction to him, or the way, since she'd walked into this room, she had become strangely, profoundly aware of herself as a woman.

None of the men she had met during the Season evoked anything resembling that reaction from her. When those men had looked at her, she had been all but indifferent to their gazes. She knew they were assessing her, in a similar manner as someone weighs up the goods on offer at a market stall, with a calculating appraisal. She'd also been aware she had been quickly dismissed by those cursory gazes, before the men moved on to more-attractive prospects.

While those reactions had been offensive, she had been able to shake them off. When James's dark eyes met hers, she reacted on a strange, visceral level, fully aware of her body, of her heartbeat, of her rapid breathing.

She forced a little laugh and attempted to push those thoughts out of her mind. 'I'm sure it will just be a small, passing storm,' she said with more hope than she felt. 'In the meantime, I suppose we just have to make the best of things,' she added. It was a phrase she often used when one of her plans did not go exactly as she had imagined.

'Perhaps you are right.' He moved over to the sideboard and lifted the brandy decanter and raised his dark eyebrows in question.

'No, thank you.'

The last thing she needed was a glass of brandy. She was unsettled enough without becoming further befuddled by alcohol.

He poured the amber liquid into a brandy balloon, took his seat and crossed one long leg over the other. Had he always been so tall? He must have been, but she'd never realised before just how long his legs were. Nor had she noticed before the muscles in his thighs, which she could now see delineated under the fabric of his trousers.

Men of her class were rarely, if ever, so built. Had he achieved such a fine form when he was working in the Americas? An image of him toiling in the fields came to her mind, of his muscles slick from perspiration as he laboured under a bright sun.

She swallowed as heat rushed up her body. She took a tentative look in his direction, hoping he had not noticed her embarrassment.

He was watching her over the rim of his glass.

Had he realised she was looking at his legs? That would be beyond mortifying.

'So, as we have time to pass, perhaps you can now entertain me by telling me tales of America rather than saving them for the guests on Christmas Day,' she said, grasping at something, anything, to cover her embarrassment. *But do not mention working in the fields with your shirt off.*

He took an agonisingly slow sip of his brandy while she tried to maintain her smile and hoped he would assume her burning cheeks were caused by the blazing fire in the hearth.

'Or perhaps you can entertain me.'

She stared at him in shock, momentarily lost for words as she fought to decipher what he meant, before reining in her wild imaginings.

'I'm afraid my piano playing and singing are nothing to write home about,' she said with an embarrassed laugh.

That was among the many other shortcomings she had displayed during the Season. Other young ladies had been so accomplished and had performed with such skill and confidence they had reduced her own playing to barely adequate.

Not that anyone complained when she played for the children at the local school or during theatrical performances and other entertainment at the village hall. But they were happy occasions where everyone was out to enjoy themselves, not stressful events where one's very future as a married woman was at stake.

No, she would not be displaying further deficiencies to James. He had undoubtably heard many a debutante displaying her accomplishments and she was loath for him to see yet another of her inadequacies.

'I meant if you are so desperate to hear about my past, perhaps you can share something about yours first,' he countered.

She shrugged. 'I'm a female.' *In case you haven't noticed, which you probably haven't.* 'We don't have pasts.'

His lips curled at the edges in something resembling a smile. Well, almost, but even the resemblance of a smile was a glorious sight. It gave her a hint that the young James she had once known was in there somewhere. The happy James his mother could always bring to life.

'You presumably had a Social Season,' he continued. 'That surely constitutes a past.'

Alice couldn't help it. She rolled her eyes, even though she knew it was a most unladylike thing to do.

'I take it from that reaction there are tales worth telling.'

'I'm not sure if I'd say that. My Season was not a success, shall we say, as you can tell from my single status.'

'I had assumed that was your choice,' he said, and Alice had to give him credit for his diplomacy. 'You strike me as an intelligent woman. I assumed you could see the folly in surrendering to a state of wedlock.'

While being referred to as intelligent was rarely seen as a compliment for a young lady and had often been used against her in the past, that was not the most concerning thing about his response.

He saw marriage as a folly, something you surrendered to. Even the word *wedlock* did not sound like it was something he was seeking. That too would have to change. Hopefully, all that would be required would be for him to meet the delightful Beatrice and to see marriage as wedded bliss not imprisoned in wedlock.

'So tell me, why was your Season not a roaring success?'

She gave a little shudder, which wasn't entirely for effect. 'I don't think men will ever know what an ordeal the Season is for a woman,' she said. 'All a man has to do is attend a few balls, assess what's on offer, make a choice and that's that.'

'It's not quite as simple as that. And surely for a woman, all she has to do is look pretty, be charming, and try and attract the wealthiest man with the grandest title.'

Did Alice detect a hint of bitterness in his voice? Why should he be bitter? He was wealthy. He did have a title. And on top of that he was handsome, perhaps even dangerously so.

'And *I* could also say, it's not quite as simple as that.' For Alice it would more accurately be described as complicated, if not downright impossible.

'Let me guess. You didn't play the game the way a debutante is supposed to?'

'Yes, your guess is correct.'

*Why play a game when you know you are doomed to lose?*

He continued to watch her and she could see a fuller explanation was expected.

'It's all so unfair,' she said, those few words holding a wealth of discontent. 'The young ladies are expected to outshine each other and compete for male attention, while the men all behave as if they are fabulous prizes any young lady would be lucky to win, particularly those with titles.'

Indignation bubbled up inside her. 'And it was my experience that the wealthier the man, the grander his title, the more self-important and odious he was.' Her hand flew to cover her mouth as soon as those words had escaped, but that wry smile that had curled the edges of his lips returned. He was not offended; thank goodness for that. Alice had a habit of offending men but had no wish to do so with this particular man.

'Not that I'm condemning the women who had to compete to get the best man available,' she rushed on, feeling somewhat disloyal to those young women who did have a successful Season. The ones who did not find themselves all but ignored.

'You don't?'

'No, they're often being forced to do so by their parents, and if you're beautiful, dazzling and sought after, then perhaps the Season would be a lot of fun.'

That look of wry amusement disappeared as quickly as it had appeared. 'Even if it is all superficial and meaningless.'

Once again she heard that hint of bitterness. Intriguing.

'Do they have a Social Season in America?' she asked, fairly certain she knew the answer.

'Yes,' he answered with one clipped word.

'And did you attend this Season?' she probed.

'Yes,' came another terse answer.

'But you did not marry?' she asked, again knowing the answer, but curious to know why a man as eligible as him would not have his pick of potential brides.

'Obviously.'

'So we are both left on the shelf,' she said with a laugh, even if such a thing could never be said about a man, especially an earl.

He raised his glass in a mock toast. 'And in my case, determined to remain that way.'

*He didn't want to marry? That was not good.*

'But surely,' she said, trying to keep her voice light, 'you will need to marry eventually and provide an heir?'

'Are you volunteering?'

Heat once again exploded on her cheeks. Hotter than before, blazing down her chest and seemingly engulfing her entire body.

'No, no, of course not,' she said, stumbling for words. 'I'm happy to remain a spinster. And, well, I just meant, well, it's what's expected, isn't it?'

'Just as marriage is expected of young ladies, but you appear to be happy to flout expectations.'

'Well, yes, I suppose, but, well, it's different. You have your duty, your lineage, all that.'

He huffed out a laugh that did not sound amused. 'I intend to live for a lot longer, so there is no immediate danger, and when I do finally pop my clogs, I have cousins who I am sure will be happy to inherit this estate and the title.'

'So you don't want to marry?' she asked quietly.

'No.'

'What if you met the right young woman? What if you fell in love?'

He frowned at her, as if she was saying something absurd. 'And what do you know of love, Miss Lambton?'

Heat once again consumed her. 'Well, nothing, but, well, isn't that what everyone hopes, that they will marry for love?'

'Is it?'

Alice drew in a deep breath and plunged on before nerves, embarrassment and basic common sense stopped her. 'Have you ever been in love?'

He emptied his brandy glass in one swallow, stood up, crossed the room, refilled it, then sat down, all the time ignoring her question, but his harsh expression was all the answer she needed.

He *had* been in love.

Was that the reason for the change in him? If it was, surely all he really needed was to love again, and surely Beatrice would be the ideal woman to mend his broken heart.

## Chapter Three

Love?

That was the last thing James wanted to discuss with this relentlessly cheerful woman. That and the New York Social Season. He did not wish to think back to his time with Clara, of dancing the night away with the most beautiful, most captivating woman he had ever met. Even if she hadn't been such an exquisite gem, being the daughter of a railroad baron would still have made her the toast of New York Society. And she had chosen him, until his accident ruined everything and she had married the Duke of Brimley.

He swirled his drink around in the brandy balloon before taking another sip, trying to force images of her beautiful face and alluring body out of his mind.

'You promised to entertain me with tales of your Season,' he said as much to get his mind off his despondent thoughts as to listen to anything she had to say.

'Do you want to hear every excruciating detail?' she asked, smiling as if about to impart a gleeful tale.

'I believe we are going to have all evening.'

They both looked towards the windows, where the whiteness of the falling snow had been replaced by the sudden darkness of an early midwinter evening.

'All right then.' She sat up as if about to tell an intriguing tale. 'I suspect like most young women, I had been led to believe the Season would be a delight, even something magical. I should have known better.'

She paused and shook her head.

'On the first night, I found myself standing on the edge of the ballroom waiting for someone, anyone, to ask me to dance.'

She said this with a smile, but James flinched. She might be telling it as a funny tale, but he suspected she was not actually amused by this humiliation, but was unwilling to admit how much it hurt, perhaps even to herself.

'That happened at the next ball as well, so I just gave up, found a comfortable place to sit, next to a potted fern, which became my constant companion for the rest of the Season.' She laughed as if such a rejection was all jolly good fun.

'I'm sorry,' he murmured, not sure if he was sorry for her experience or sorry that he had asked and caused her to relive what he was sure must have been a harrowing ordeal, despite her attempt to paint it otherwise.

'Don't be. Two other young women soon joined me beside the fern and we all became wonderful friends. Well, not with the fern of course. It was a terrible conversationalist, unlike my fellow wallflowers. I believe we ended up having the most fun, chatting and laughing more than anyone else at the ball, and we were probably the only ones laughing at things that were genuinely funny, rather than having to titter and flitter at what passes for wit among the self-satisfied men.'

He nodded his head, suspecting she was right.

'But I didn't actually make it to the end of the Season,' she continued.

'No?'

'I had what perhaps could most politely be described as a mild altercation with Baron Hogmore.'

'A mild altercation?' This was starting to sound interesting and he lifted his eyebrows to encourage her to continue.

'I overheard a conversation he was having about me and the other young ladies at the ball and thought he needed to be put in his place.'

She sat up straighter and her face adopted the expression of a schoolmarm about to give a reprobate child a good telling-off. 'I heard him say "They're a bit of a rum lot all round this Season".'

This was said with affected loftiness, her nose tilted

upward, her lips pursed. Despite the insult, James was amused by her accurate rendition of the pompous bore who had unfortunately attended the same school as James.

'"But Miss Lambton has to be the least attractive of a bad lot",' she continued in the same arrogant tone. 'No dowry, no connections and not even a modicum of beauty to recommend her."'

'The swine.'

'Yes, exactly,' she said, unaccountably still smiling. 'All the other men laughed as if Baron Hogmore had the wit of Oscar Wilde. So I marched up to him, looked him up and down and said,' she continued and raised an admonishing finger. '"Baron Hogmore, no decency, no intelligence, and not even a modicum of charm to recommend him. Definitely the least attractive of a decidedly rum lot available this Season." Then I walked out and it was the last ball I attended.'

'Good for you. Although it's nowhere near what the man deserves.'

She shrugged one shoulder. 'But he made me realise one thing, they were all a "rum lot" and even if none of them wanted to marry me, the feeling was mutual. I could not imagine myself tied to any of those boorish oafs for the rest of my life.'

She feigned a little shudder then smiled. 'So I returned to Ferndale and this is where I am happy to remain.'

He doubted any woman could really shrug off such a public humiliation so easily and wondered if that was why she had supposedly accepted becoming a spinster, a fate which most women would move heaven and earth to avoid.

'And you still have no wish to marry?' he asked.

Her smile became slightly strained, and James suspected she wasn't quite as content with her unmarried status as she so flippantly claimed. If she hadn't turned up dressed in a plain brown dress with her hair tied back in a practical bun and lacking any adornment, he would suspect she had set her sights on becoming the next Countess of Thornwood. But Miss Lambton appeared to be without artifice, which was perhaps another reason why she had such an unsuccessful Season.

'No, and fortunately my father has no objection to supporting his unwed daughter. In fact, I think he's quite pleased that I have continued to live with him and manage the household.'

She looked down at her hands folded in her lap. He remembered that the mother of Miss Lambton and William had died while he had been in America. She must have been about fourteen at the time. She had presumably taken on the role of managing the home since then and was now expected to continue doing so, as was often the role assigned to a spinster.

It was something they now had in common. His

mother had also died when he was young and it had torn the family apart. His father, not the most gregarious man at the best of times, became increasingly morose, and Giles chose to spend even less time at Thornwood Hall.

If he hadn't had the warm-hearted Mrs Lambton in his life he hated to think how miserable his childhood would have been. She had been more than happy to gather up her son's friend and treat him as if he was part of the family.

'I was so sorry to hear of your mother's passing,' he said. 'I would have returned from America for the funeral but word did not reach me until sometime later.'

'Thank you,' she said with a sad smile.

'She was a wonderful woman,' he added as much to himself as to her. He looked up. 'How did your father cope without her in his life?'

'Oh, he became rather melancholy at first, as one would expect. Theirs truly was a love match.'

She looked back down at her hands clasped in her lap. 'They were so lucky to have found each other,' she said quietly, then looked up at him and smile again. 'That saying must be right, that time is a great healer, as he's now back to his old self.' That had not been the case with his father, whose mood got worse and worse as the years passed, until he eventually died a miserable and lonely old man.

'Father's even courting a widow from a nearby village and we suspect there will be wedding bells in the family soon.'

James stared at her in surprise. He could not imagine anyone replacing Mrs Lambton in her husband's life.

'If he marries her then what will your role in the household be?' he asked, suddenly concerned for her future. 'A new wife might not want the unmarried daughter in her home.' Surely that had to be a worry for her.

'I doubt that very much. Widow Harcourt is a delight, but what will be will be and I'm sure I won't be thrown out into the cold.'

He admired her optimism, even if it was possibly misguided.

'And William is also more than happy to support me,' she continued. 'And now, well, with the money coming in from my books I am a woman of independent means.' This last statement was accompanied with a small self-deprecating laugh.

'Books?'

'Yes, I write and illustrate children's books. I've had two published already to some success and I'm writing a third at the moment.' He could hear the pride in her voice, and rightly so.

'That is most impressive.'

'Thank you,' she said, still smiling. He had to admit, it was rather a nice smile. There was nothing coquettish about it. It wasn't designed to flatter or impress him, but was an unguarded expression of happiness, which caused her grey eyes to sparkle and her cheeks to glow.

'I've always loved writing and drawing, so it's wonderful to turn my hobby into something that can earn me money.' Her smile became decidedly mischievous. 'And I have to admit it gives me the opportunity to get my revenge.'

'Revenge?' He could not imagine this open, straightforward woman ever doing anything as underhand as exacting revenge on anyone.

'Yes, in my first book I had a character called Baron, who is a pig. He gets his comeuppance from Lambsie, who is of course a little lamb Baron thinks is powerless and he can bully.'

James laughed at this ingenious form of revenge. 'I take it Baron the pig is based on Baron Hogmore and Lambsie is you, Miss Lambton.'

She bowed her head. 'I even gave Baron the same sanctimonious, pompous and, well, downright stupid qualities of Baron Hogmore.'

James laughed at this further audacity. 'I better make sure I don't cross you in case a toad called Earl appears in one of your books.'

'More likely a wolf,' she said, then colour exploded on her cheeks. 'Or maybe a mule,' she stumbled on.

'Given that you're being so stubborn about coming to Christmas dinner.'

His laughter subsided and he smiled at her. How long had it been since he had laughed? He could hardly remember. He ran a finger down his scar, certain that he had not done so since the accident.

She continued to smile back at him, her cheeks remaining that delightful shade of pink, as if she had just taken a brisk walk on a summer's day.

'Well, it looks like my mulish behaviour is going to be a moot point,' he said, looking out the windows, where the still-falling snow was lit by the candlelight spilling out from the windows. 'I doubt either of us will be going anywhere soon. I hope William won't be worried about you or attempt to send a carriage to find you in this weather.'

'No, he won't be worried.' She looked down at her hands, then back up at him. 'I have a confession to make.'

He raised one eyebrow in question.

'I took a carriage here, so William knows I arrived safely.' She lightly bit the edge of her lip. 'I was hoping it would start to rain and you would be obliged to bring me home in your carriage and we could encourage you to join us for carol singing.'

'So you are capable of subterfuge as well as revenge. Miss Lambton, you do surprise me,' he said, amused rather than offended.

'Oh, please, call me Alice. I think when you've pulled someone's plaits you can drop formality.'

'I don't believe I ever pulled your plaits,' James said, shocked that he would be accused of such a thing.

She rolled her eyes. 'On more than one occasion.'

'Then I apologise for my younger self and promise I will never do such a thing again.'

Her cheeks blushed a deeper shade of red. For a confident, independent woman she did do rather a lot of blushing.

'But as I said, I'm surprised you are capable of subterfuge, but like many ruses, I'm afraid that one failed. I won't be singing carols tonight.' *Or ever.* 'And nor will you. As this weather looks like it will not be abating it will be safest if you dine here this evening, and I believe you will also have to stay the night.'

He walked over to summon a servant. When the footman arrived he informed him there would be two for dinner and asked him to arrange for a bedchamber to be prepared for Miss Lambton. He then crossed the room to top up his glass, and once again tilted the decanter towards her. 'Would you like a drink?'

'Oh, I shouldn't, really.'

'Even though it's Christmas?' James could see no reason why the time of year should make any difference, but as she put such stock in the festive season he suspected she would see it as a time to indulge.

'Oh, all right, perhaps a small one.'

He smiled to himself as he poured, amused that his assumption had been right.

'How did you become the author of children's books?' he asked as he took his seat.

'I started drawing these funny little animals to amuse the local children, and they were so popular I decided I'd have nothing to lose if I sent it to a publisher. I did so and much to my amazement he published them.'

'Well done,' he said, raising his glass in a toast.

'And I'm making quite a nice income from them, proving that I don't need a husband and never did.'

'Good for you.'

Although he doubted the income from her books would be anything like the income a man like Baron Hogmore got from his land and various other interests, but presumably she was not the type of woman who needed entire wardrobes of gowns from French couturiers each season, or a flotilla of servants whose sole job was to make her look beautiful.

Unlike Clara.

Damn, why did he have to think of her again? She was now married to the Duke of Brimley. She was gone from his life and the sooner he banished her from his thoughts the better.

For a moment, James had almost looked happy, as if he was enjoying her company. He had even laughed, which had been such a wonderful sound, and then that darkness had descended, yet again.

And for a moment, Alice had almost forgotten she was in the company of a man who left her flustered and blushing, compelled to keep smiling as if her life depended on it. Almost.

Although she was hardly to blame. It was so hard to act naturally when in the company of such a man, but somehow that was exactly what she must do. She had to focus and not be distracted by his intense good looks, nor the effect his deep, resonant voice had on her, nor the disarming nature of his laughter.

Matchmakers did not get distracted. They did not blush, giggle or act like nincompoops. They were serious women with a serious job to do. And that was what she had to be. Serious. There was too much resting on her shoulders for her to behave otherwise: her friend's very happiness, and there was nothing more important than that.

She placed the untouched glass of brandy on a nearby table. If she wanted to keep her wits about her, and if she wanted to stop her cheeks from burning in such an unflattering manner, drinking brandy was the last thing she should be doing.

Not that it mattered whether the state of her cheeks was unflattering or not. She was not here to impress the earl, not that she could if she tried. If she couldn't impress an unattractive buffoon like Baron Hogmore she was never going to impress a man like James Marlowe. She shook her head lightly to drive out that thought. It mattered not whether she impressed him. It mattered even less if her cheeks burned as brightly as a winter's fire. That was not why she was here and the sooner she got him and Beatrice together so she could step back and let nature take its course, the better.

*Focus, Alice.*

She needed to forget all about the expectations she'd held when her father's uncle, the Earl of Hargrove, had announced he would pay for her Season and his wife would sponsor her coming-out in front of Queen Victoria.

At the age of twenty-three, it had become apparent she would not meet a husband in Ferndale, and the prospect of a Season had rekindled dreams of love, marriage, children and a home of her own. It hadn't taken long for Baron Hogmore and those other laughing men to make it clear such dreams were futile.

But none of that mattered now. Beatrice was facing the prospect of a miserable future, and it was within her power to save her. That was all she should be thinking of, not her dashed hopes, or the way harbouring such hopes had exposed her to ridicule.

'I daresay while you are in residence you will be wanting to meet as many of your tenants as possible and the people in the surrounding area,' she announced as cheerfully as possible. 'I believe that is what is expected of the earl.'

*Good move, Alice.*

It was a bit underhand, but if it took guilt to get him to attend social events where he could be in Beatrice's company, then it was all in a good cause.

He shrugged and Alice frowned. Why was everything he did so manly and so attractive? He was just shrugging one shoulder, for goodness' sake. It was a simple gesture, not one that should cause her heart to go all fluttery. But it was a gesture that drew her attention to how broad his shoulders were under his dark jacket, and that was the cause of her unfortunate reaction.

'I suppose I will have to at some point but I have no immediate plans to do so,' he said.

'But everyone is anxious to meet the new earl.' *And I'm anxious for you to meet Beatrice.*

'And they will, in due course.'

'Well, there's no better time than right now. Many people are taking a break from their labours to celebrate Christmas. It's the ideal time.'

'Hmm.'

She looked at the windows and frowned. 'It's a shame about the carol singing. You would have met so many people then.' She turned back to him and smiled. 'But there's still Christmas dinner at Rosetree Manor, and on Boxing Day we distribute presents to the poor and needy. That will be an excellent way to meet many of the less wealthy members of the community. And on New Year's Eve we have a ball in the village hall for the resident gentry. Then the local guilds have a special feast day. These are all good opportunities to meet up with the local people.' *And to spend time with Beatrice.*

He released a slow sigh, then took a sip of his brandy.

'Everyone is so looking forward to hearing all about your adventures abroad.'

'Really?' he said, drawing out this one word as his hand ran down the scar. 'They will all have to wait until I am good and ready to meet with them.' A snappish tone entered his voice as he placed his hand under his knee and lifted his leg as if it pained him.

The footman entered and announced dinner was served, much to Alice's relief. Mentioning America had put James on the defensive once again. That was not good. She only had two weeks to get him and Beatrice together, and that was only going to happen if she could prise him out of his house.

They moved through to the dining room. A cheerful fire was burning in the hearth, but apart from that, the room was just as bleak as the rest of the house.

'I see the servants haven't decorated this room either,' she said, stating the obvious. 'One could be forgiven for thinking it was not Christmas at all.'

'*I* don't seem to be able to forget it, whether I want to or not,' he said, and she frowned at his sarcasm.

'This room could look magnificent if it was decorated properly.' She gazed around at the ornate wood panelling on the walls, the gilded frames containing paintings of pastoral scenes and the highly polished mahogany sideboard and dining table.

It was certainly pleasant enough, especially with the fire crackling in the hearth and gaslights in the wall sconces sending flickering light dancing around the room. But it would be so much more festive if it was bursting with holly, ivy and an array of colourful baubles.

When Beatrice was finally in residence here at Thornwood Hall, Alice was sure she would make it look cheerful and inviting on Christmas Day, especially once she and James had filled the house with a brood of children.

A sudden stab of regret pierced her heart. She pushed it away with a smile. Alice had reconciled herself to the fact that she would never have children of her own, but being an unofficial aunt to James and Beatrice's children would be almost as good.

Wouldn't it? Yes, of course it would, especially as it was the only option available to her.

The footman served the first course. Vegetable consommé. No one but the most ungrateful guest would be disappointed with such nourishing food, but it was hardly festive. At Rosetree Manor they would have started off with some mulled wine around the fire, followed by a quick meal so they could get outside and join the rest of the choir and begin entertaining the villagers.

She looked at the dark windows, being pelted by snow which now contained sleet. 'I think you're right. There will be no carol singing tonight. I doubt if anyone will even want to venture out to the village hall on a night like this. The choir will be just as disappointed as the villagers.'

'Can I assume that you are an active part of village life?'

Alice gave a small laugh. 'Yes, I think you can safely assume that. I tend to be the one that organises things.' She shrugged. 'I suppose as an unmarried lady I have time and, well, as there is no Countess of Thornwood yet, and hasn't been for some time, the role she would take in the village has rather fallen to me.'

He raised his eyebrows, his spoon halfway to his mouth, presumably registering her word *yet*.

He claimed he had no wish to marry, but it *was* expected of an earl and she was going to try her hardest to make sure he fulfilled that expectation.

She waited for him to ask some more about the activities the countess would be expected to undertake. He didn't and they ate their soup in silence.

When finished, he signalled for Alfred to remove their soup dishes and serve the next course.

Once the salmon had been placed in front of her she took in a fortifying breath so she could broach the subject he was obviously wanting to avoid.

'I suspect the villagers will be expecting you to take a bride in the near future. They'll be hoping there is someone who can make sure the tenants' needs are being met, who can take charge of the women's charity and church groups, host social events, that sort of thing.'

He made no comment, just continued to eat his meal.

'I can't imagine you doing that along with all your other duties,' she said with a laugh and waited for him to agree.

'As you are already taking on that role, I believe there is no reason for anything to change.'

'Oh, not once you marry. Then it will be your wife's job. If I may be so bold—'

'I doubt I could ever stop you from being bold.'

She laughed as if it were a joke, although she was fairly certain it was not. 'If I may be so bold, may I suggest that there are many young women among the local gentry who I think would make admirable countesses.'

Those dark eyebrows didn't rise this time in question but drew together. In disapproval? It looked like she had in fact been a tad too bold.

'There are so many lovely young women in the county. Take my friend Beatrice, for example,' she rushed on before she completely lost her nerve. 'Well, she isn't really a local, but her aunt lives in the village and she is staying here for Christmas. You will meet her Aunt Sophia and Beatrice on Christmas Day, or Boxing Day, or the New Year's Eve Ball.'

He continued to say nothing, and his eyebrows remained knitted together.

'Beatrice is the daughter of the third son of Baron Chigwell, and her mother's family is connected to the Earl of Dunleigh. She hasn't had her coming-out yet, even though she's twenty and very responsible. Her aunt had plans to present her to Queen Victoria at the start of the next Season—that's if she's not married before then.'

She gave a little laugh but he made no reaction.

'She's so beautiful, graceful and charming, it's hard to believe we are such good friends.'

'You do yourself a disservice,' he said, missing the point of everything she had said. 'And I'm sure if your friend is as beautiful, graceful and charming as you say, she will have no trouble finding a suitable husband.'

He went back to eating his meal as if this had nothing to do with him.

'Yes, I'm sure she will,' Alice mumbled, trying to think of a way she could pique his interest in meeting her friend. 'Beatrice has been such a help with organising the village ball. One would think she was born to such a role.'

He continued eating as if he had not heard a word she had said.

'And her watercolours are simply divine and no one can produce a better embroidery sampler.' Alice cringed at finding herself listing the attributes that a desperate mama would use to entice a potential beau for her daughter.

James stopped eating and slowly placed his knife and fork on his plate. Then just as slowly looked over at her, still saying nothing.

She continued smiling. He continued to stare at her. Her smile became increasingly strained, then took on an unfortunate wobble.

'Miss Lambton,' he stated in a measured tone.

He had stopped using her given name. This did not bode well.

'If I am to marry, and that is an *if*, not a *when*, I am more than capable of selecting my own bride.'

Alice opened her mouth to speak, but no words came out.

'You may be adept at organising village balls and carol singing but that does not give you the right to try and organise my life.'

She closed her mouth. His unnerving stare and the biting nature of his words robbed her of speech. But this was no time to be timid. Beatrice's very happiness depended on Alice getting the two of them up the aisle. Beatrice was too lovely to be forced into a marriage with a man who repulsed her, who was older even than her own father and reputed to be a curmudgeon to boot.

Although, she had to admit, right now the earl was also displaying the behaviour of a curmudgeon, but no woman in her right mind would be repulsed by the Earl of Thornwood.

'I'm just saying—'

'Then don't.'

Alice frowned. Yes, definitely curmudgeonly behaviour.

He signalled Alfred to remove their plates.

'I don't wish to be rude, Miss Lambton.'

Alice was tempted to repeat what he'd just said to her. *Then don't.*

'But I do not want you or any other busybody attempting to marry me off, or interfering in my life in any way, shape or form.'

He stared at her, those dark brown eyes boring into her. If her task wasn't so important she was sure she would back down immediately. But it *was* important. Far too important to let her own discomfort get in the way.

'Do you understand?' he stated.

'Of course I understand. But there is no harm in you meeting the local young women.'

He sighed loudly as Alfred served the meat course. 'I believe it is time you changed the subject.'

Alice would leave it for now, as she could see that a tactical retreat was in order, but that did not mean she would be surrendering entirely. She had every intention of winning the battle and getting James and Beatrice up the wedding aisle.

## Chapter Four

James had been wrong about Miss Lambton. She was not quite as guileless as he had first thought.

While he was correct in his assumption she had no interest in becoming the next Countess of Thornwell, like all women, she had an ulterior motive, one that inevitably centred around the marriage mart.

He should have known that would be the true reason for this unexpected and unwanted visit. It had nothing to do with introducing him to the local community and everything to do with marrying him off to one of her friends.

He supposed he should be grateful. Miss Lambton had reminded him of why he wanted to remain in his home, away from Society, away even from what passed for Society in this isolated part of the world. He was an earl. He was wealthy. He was unmarried. That effectively meant he had a target painted on his back for every unmarried woman of his class and every mama in search of a husband for her daughter.

She had also reconfirmed his determination to not join her family for Christmas Day, even in the unlikely event the weather cleared. No doubt she had also invited her friend Beatrice, along with every unwed young lady from the surrounding counties, and he'd have to endure the tedium of young women attempting to flirt and flatter him all in a pointless attempt to convince him they were his ideal bride.

He did, however, have to give her some credit for taking this matchmaking action on behalf of her friend. Most unmarried young women were so hellbent on securing a good match for themselves, they had no time to think of anyone else.

Once again, Clara came unbidden into his mind. Miss Lambton had described her friend Beatrice as beautiful and charming, but in those areas he doubted anyone could surpass Clara, a young woman who had been the toast of New York Society.

Bitter bile rose up his throat at the memory of what he'd once had and had lost. When he had met Clara, no one had needed to convince him she was the one he wanted to marry. He'd been captivated the moment he'd laid eyes on her and could not imagine any woman ever again affecting him the way she had. It was as if she had cast a spell over him, and despite all that had happened since, despite his determination to forget her, he was still like a man possessed.

'Don't you agree?' Miss Lambton asked, breaking in on his reverie.

'Hmm,' he responded noncommittally, having not heard a word she had said.

'Excellent, it will be a wonderful opportunity to meet everyone in the village.'

He sighed loudly. He had agreed to nothing, but that did not stop her smiling expectantly at him.

'We've had such a lot of presents generously donated and it will give you a chance to meet some of your tenants and assess their needs.'

She was talking about distributing gifts on Boxing Day. He supposed that was not too onerous a task, and damn it all, she was right. Despite his desire for solitude, at some stage he did need to meet his tenants. Ensuring their welfare was among his duties as the new earl. And at least it was not carol singing.

'Was that something my brother partook in?' he asked as he signalled to the footman to remove their dishes and serve the cheese course.

'No, I'm afraid we saw little of your brother.'

*Perhaps he had been trying to avoid your matchmaking.*

'I believe your brother was more drawn to London than to the countryside and well, his duties were…'

She lifted one shoulder and it was easy to guess what she was not saying. He did not know the details of how his brother had lived, but from reading through the ledgers the estate manager had supplied him, it was apparent Giles took little interest in the estate. That was something James intended to change. Not just for the sake of everyone who depended on Thornwood being an economically viable concern but for the more selfish reasons of it providing him with an excellent excuse to remain removed from the Society he had come to despise and giving him something on which to focus his mind, a mind that wandered far too often and far too easily to Clara.

'You can rest assured, I intend to take my duties seriously,' he said.

'Oh, good,' she declared and he hoped she did not think that included marrying one of her friends.

'That is, I will be making sure the estate is well managed,' he clarified.

'And you will take part in the life of the village?' she said with a hopeful expression.

'Hmm' was once again the only comment he was prepared to make on that matter.

'Oh, good,' she repeated as if he had answered in the affirmative. 'Perhaps your brother was reluctant to do his duty because he did not have a wife at his side,' she added, causing James to inhale slowly and exhale loudly in annoyance.

'If he'd had the ideal countess, he might have entered into the life of the village,' she continued as if oblivious to his reaction.

'I seriously doubt that.'

Giles was rarely in Ferndale and the ledgers showed that apart from giving himself a generous allowance he took little to no interest in the welfare of the estate.

'Oh, I don't know. The right woman can make all the difference to a man.'

He glared at her. 'That is what you think, is it? You surprise me,' he said, his voice dripping with sarcasm.

'So I believe,' she said, either not picking up his displeasure with the direction in which she had once again steered the conversation, or wilfully ignoring it. 'If your brother had married, apart from providing the necessary heir, he would have been able to do all that was expected of the local earl.'

He speared a piece of Stilton and decided it was time to make his position very clear in words that could not be misinterpreted, misconstrued or ignored.

'Miss Lambton—'

'Alice.'

'Alice. I do intend to carry out my duties as earl, and if that includes taking part in some of the village activities, then yes, I shall do so, in my own good time. But as I have already been at pains to point out, I do not want you or anyone else trying to marry me off.'

He enunciated each word clearly and precisely, leaving no room for argument. 'Now I wish you to drop the subject,' he added, just in case it was not clear or precise enough.

She blushed a deep shade of scarlet, looked down and began moving cheese around her plate, but he did not care if he was embarrassing her or making her uncomfortable.

'Is that clear?'

'But—'

'I said, is that clear?' he repeated, somewhat louder.

'Yes, it's clear. I will not try and marry you off,' she replied, a certain petulance in her voice.

Good. Now the subject could finally be dropped, but if there was even a hint of her or anyone else in this forsaken part of the country trying to match him up with any unmarried women, they would soon find out, just as Miss Lambton had, that such behaviour would not be tolerated.

He couldn't possibly mean what he said. Of that Alice was certain. Of course he wanted to marry. He was so completely eligible, and he would realise that the moment he met Beatrice. And even if he was being a bit, well, tetchy about the subject, she *had* made progress. She'd managed to get him to tentatively agree to attend some of the local social events.

With the meal over they retired back to the drawing room for coffee and Alice decided not to let his attempt to undermine her put her off doing something which was in the best interests of her friend, and ultimately in the best interest of James, even though he didn't yet realise it.

It was unfortunate he hadn't made it to Christmas carols, and if he did not come to Christmas dinner tomorrow, she would most certainly get him out distributing presents on Boxing Day. All she had to do was make sure he was paired up with Beatrice. They would have a delightful time together wandering around pretty snow-lined country lanes, hopefully arm in arm, and he'd be able to see what a treasure she was.

Then she would have to make sure he came to the village ball, where he would dance the night away with her friend, and before the Christmas holidays were over he'd propose and everyone would be happy.

They would make such an attractive couple. She sighed lightly as she took her seat. Beatrice was such a lucky woman, or she would be once Alice had put them together and allowed their destiny to unfold.

James took the seat across from her beside the fire, picked up a ledger from the pile stacked on a nearby table and ran his eye down a list of figures. It was apparent all polite conversation was now at an end.

She hoped he did not behave like this when in Beatrice's company. It would be terrible if her friend dismissed him as a potential husband because of this tendency to be withdrawn.

Although given how handsome he was, he hardly

needed much of a personality. She stifled a small laugh. That was how men tended to think about young ladies when they were assessing those available during the Season. Looks always triumphed over personality and even the dullest of women would shine if she was deemed a beauty.

Her smile died. Unfortunately, or perhaps fortunately, when it came to both personality and looks she was decidedly lacking. But those days were over, thank goodness.

She no longer had to even think about whether a man found her attractive or not. Her gaze once again moved to James, frowning at his ledgers.

Yes, thank goodness for that. Being in the company of such a disarmingly good-looking man was certainly made easier by knowing he would never see her as anything other than his friend's little sister.

She looked around the room. As James had made it clear, conversation was at an end, she would have to find something else to do. She stood up and walked over to the paintings adorning the walls, their gilt frames glinting in the gas lamps. Her gaze moved to the multitude of porcelain figurines, vases and bowls decorating every surface.

She picked up a small piece of Dresden porcelain depicting a group of dancing cherubs and caught James watching her from across the room. She quickly put it back down. He probably thought she was about to wreak havoc and send his family's collection shattering to the ground in a thousand pieces, like the proverbial bull in a China shop.

She spotted a pile of books on a sideboard at the far side of the room and made her way to an area where she could cause little damage. Searching for something to keep her occupied, she scanned the leather-bound books and stifled a yawn at the boring titles. *Sheep farming in Northern England* and *Principles of Crop Rotation* were among the most interesting.

She reached the bottom of the pile and gave a yelp of delight. A battered copy of Jane Austen's *Emma* was buried under the dull tomes, like a hidden treasure.

That would do splendidly.

Alice had read it many times but could think of few things she'd enjoy more than once again disappearing into Miss Austen's romantic Regency world.

James looked up at her as she rushed back to her seat with renewed happiness.

'That was my mother's,' he said. 'It was one of her favourite books.' His voice held a degree of affection she had not heard before.

'Yes, it's one of my favourites as well.'

'I believe it's about a matchmaker who is taught the folly of her ways,' he added before going back to his own reading.

Alice scowled at the top of his head. He'd already

made his opinions on that matter very clear, and he was wrong. She was nothing like Emma Woodhouse. Miss Austen's heroine was trying to match completely incompatible people, whereas she was matching two people who were meant to be together.

Choosing not to counter his veiled criticism, she opened the book. It wasn't long before she was completely absorbed in the story and found herself laughing at the antics of the characters. Occasionally, she would look up and see him watching her, and it would become embarrassingly obvious she was laughing out loud.

'Sorry,' she said after a rather loud guffaw.

'Don't apologise,' he said. 'I remember when my mother used to read those books she too would laugh.'

She smiled at him, delighted she'd just had a glimpse of the young man she remembered. The one who was friends with William and was often seen smiling and laughing when he visited Rosetree Manor. She just had to find a way to make sure that man was present when he met Beatrice, so she was not confronted with the grumpy James who shut himself away with ledgers and brooding silences.

But until that time came, she would content herself with Emma's meddlesome behaviour and that of the wise if rather stern Mr Knightley.

## Chapter Five

James was reluctant to admit it, but it wasn't entirely unpleasant having company, even if it was uninvited company. Now that Alice had settled down and was reading a book and not trying to force him into attending dinner parties or regaling him with the virtues of her eligible friends, he had no objection to her staying.

He did, however, hope the snow would stop overnight and the roads would be clear when they woke. If she was forced to spend Christmas Day with him, he hated to think what her expectations would be.

A frightening image entered his mind of her forcing him to sing Christmas carols. He stifled a smile. He would not put that past her.

How she had managed to remain so relentlessly jolly he had no idea. Most women who had been all but humiliated during the Season and then forced to return home to take up the life of a spinster would be miserable at the very least, or even bitter.

He looked over at her as she laughed again at something she had read and had to wonder. Did she really find Baron Hogmore's offensive behaviour amusing or had she turned it into an entertaining story as a means to cover up her inner pain?

He could not imagine doing so himself, turning what had happened between him and Clara into a light-hearted anecdote for others' entertainment. So how did she do it? How did she continue to laugh and joke when her life had surely not turned out how she would have wished?

She looked up at him and smiled. He was staring at her, something he should not be doing.

He returned to his ledgers. It mattered not what Miss Lambton really thought of her situation as an unmarried woman. She was not his concern. All going well, tomorrow she would be on her way and he would rarely see her again. And hopefully, she would put aside all misguided attempts at finding him a wife.

Like her, he too would be settling into a single life. Although unlike her, that did not mean his life would be devoid of the company of the opposite sex. He just had no intention of marrying. He had attempted to go down that path once before and wasn't about to embark on it again.

He paused in his perusal of the accounts, his finger still on the list of figures.

It was difficult to believe that only a few months

ago he was preparing himself to make a proposal to the woman he was in love with.

If the accident hadn't happened…if the Duke of Brimley hadn't arrived in New York in search of a wealthy heiress to marry…if he hadn't descended from a man who considered himself worthy of a beautiful, vivacious woman's attention to a scarred cripple who could offer her nothing, would he now be entertaining his new bride?

Would they be spending Christmas together as man and wife?

He clenched his teeth together to suppress the angry growl threatening to escape.

But the Duke of Brimley *had* arrived in New York in search of a wealthy bride. James *had* been forced out of Society to convalesce from his injuries. And when he'd recovered he was not the man he had been. He was a man dealing with physical and emotional pain. He was a man no woman would want, especially one as full of life as Clara, a woman who was never destined to be a nursemaid.

That was the reality. That was why he was better off on his own, even if it did mean living in the desolate, echoing house in which he had grown up.

Alice laughed again. She looked up and smiled at him, their eyes meeting.

'I'm sorry you weren't able to join your friends in the choir tonight,' he said, suddenly aware that her being stuck with a man as miserable as him was probably far more frustrating than him being stuck with Alice Lambton.

'It can't be helped and, well, I've got no one to blame but myself. William warned me about setting out when the weather was about to turn, but I thought all that would happen would be some harmless rain would fall.'

'And if the bad weather doesn't clear you might be stuck here tomorrow as well, in this dull mausoleum without one single piece of holly or ivy in sight.'

She smiled as if he had made a joke. Of course she smiled. She always smiled.

'No one who is sitting beside a warm fire with a good book to read really has a right to complain. And as for bad weather, snow at Christmas time is never bad weather. And once it does clear it will be lovely to walk along the country paths with all the trees and plants draped in white or beside the river sparkling in the crisp sunlight. Don't you just love this time of year?

'Winter? No, not especially.'

He ran his hand along his scar and his knee gave a twinge. He could almost see the overturned carriage in the snowdrift and hear the children crying out for help. He doubted he would ever again see anything to love about winter.

'And as for being stuck here on Christmas Day,

again, I've no one to blame but myself and we'll just have to make the best of things. We have plenty of wood for the fire, plenty of food, books to read, everything we could possibly need.'

James was tempted to once again list all that she would be missing out on. Spending the day with her family and friends in a house that was presumably decorated within an inch of its life, talking, laughing, probably singing those infernal carols she was so fond of around the piano. But if he did inform her of all that she would be missing, he was sure she would have some jolly response that suggested everything was all as it should be and they should be grateful for what they did have.

This relentless joyfulness must be the result of growing up in a loving, happy family. As a child Rosetree Manor had provided him with a refuge from the loneliness of Thornwood Hall. It was rather ironic that it was now Thornwood Hall that was providing him with a much-needed refuge from the world.

'Although if I do have to stay here, I hate to think what Christmas Day will be like if it's all left up to William and Father.' She sent him a mock frown. 'Neither of them have ever taken on the role of host before. That's always been left to Mother and now me. I'm sure they'll make a mess of things.'

A twinge of guilt nipped at his conscience. William had tried to make conversation during their train journey, but James had been taciturn with his exuberant childhood friend. He'd been grateful it was an overnight train and he'd had the excuse of secluding himself in the sleeping car for much of the trip so he could avoid all unwanted discussions on his time in America.

'So how is William? How is his legal practice fairing?' These were questions he should have asked the man himself.

Alice closed her book around one finger to keep note of her place. 'He is doing splendidly, and loving every minute of his time in London, and his work with the firm of barristers.'

'Do you see much of him?'

'Not as much as I'd like. He spends Christmas up here and makes the occasional visit, but it is a long way to travel. I stayed with him during my short-lived Season.' She pulled a grimace that was intended to be comical. 'And I pop down to London occasionally to see my publisher. It's always a treat to stay with my big brother, even if his household is hopelessly disorganised.'

'It is heartening that the two of you have remained so close.'

Her smile turned into a frown. 'It's a shame you and your brother were never able to spend much time together and get to know each other.'

James shrugged. It was not something about which he gave much thought.

'It's also a shame he did not marry, or that your father did not remarry, just as my father is planning to do.'

'Who on earth would have the miserable old bast—' He paused, remembering who he was talking to. 'I'd certainly pity any woman who found herself lumbered with a cantankerous old blighter like my father.'

'Maybe the love of a good woman would have changed him.'

By God, she was relentlessly optimistic. 'She would have had to have been a miracle worker to change that man.'

'Well, maybe love can work miracles.'

An optimist and a romantic. The first he had no trouble believing; the second was a surprise, given her own experiences.

'Love,' he said with a snort of disbelief.

'How can you not believe in love?' she continued. 'My parents loved each other. Father is now in love with Widow Harcourt. That's why he's planning to marry again.'

James shook his head in disbelief, partly at her naivety and partly at the way she had once again brought the conversation back to what was her favourite topic. Marriage.

'I believe you'll find they are the exceptions. In the

world in which we live, love matches are rare indeed.'
He looked back down at the ledger, wanting to end
this conversation.

'Well, they shouldn't be the exception. They should
be the rule,' she stated emphatically.

He looked up at her. For once she was not smiling.

'I would have thought your experiences during the
Season would have crushed any romantic notions,' he
said, his voice harsher than he intended.

How could it not? She had been humiliated and
left to sit alone on the side of the dance floor, all because she did not meet the expectations of idiots like
Hogmore, while other, less intelligent and interesting
woman were swept up as marriage partners. That experience should surely make even the most ardent romantic cynical about love and marriage.

'It crushed my romantic notions about the Season,
but not about love,' she said quietly. 'Love and marriage are not something I expect for myself, but they
are definitely what I want for the people I care about.'

He shook his head slowly. He had to admit there
was something noble and remarkable about her optimism, and she was surely the most selfless woman
he had ever met.

His anger towards her regarding her unwanted
matchmaking dimmed somewhat. He still had no intention of meeting this Beatrice woman, or any of the
other local unmarried young women she intended to

thrust in his direction, but he could see her clumsy attempts at matchmaking were done with the best of intentions.

'I believe when it comes to love and marriage, you and I are never likely to agree,' he said, returning to his account books and signalling that was to be the end of the matter.

How on earth did he get to be so jaded? And more to the point, how was Alice going to change him from a man who sneered at the concept of love and marriage to one ready to embark on a courtship?

Alice looked down at the book in her hand. It was unlikely to offer any instruction, unless one was anxious to know how *not* to go about pairing your best friend with a suitable man.

Was she making the same mistake as Emma?

No, surely not. Emma Woodhouse was trying to improve her friend. Alice was not trying to improve anyone. Beatrice did not need improving. She was perfect as she was. Yes, being married to an earl would elevate her in Society, just as Emma hoped to elevate Harriet Smith, but that was not Alice's ultimate goal. Unlike Emma, all Alice cared about was her friend's happiness.

And there was no one else bidding for Beatrice's hand as there was for Harriet's. If there was a lovely Robert Martin on the scene, courting Beatrice the way the fictional Robert was courting Harriet, and if he was someone Beatrice's father would approve of, like a wealthy, titled man, then Alice would not have become involved at all.

With that settled she went back to reading with a renewed sense of satisfaction, confident that she was doing the right thing and would soon see her friend happily married.

Then she bit her lip as she attempted to picture this eventuality. It was hard to imagine her bright, bubbly, cheerful friend with this sullen, world-weary man.

Would such a marriage really make her friend happy? She sneaked a look at James. Would his undeniable good looks, his wealth and his title be enough?

She swallowed a sigh. This was all so difficult. It would be so much easier if he was still the young man she remembered. The one who had departed from England twelve years ago. That man would have been ideal for Beatrice.

Ideal for any woman who had a pulse.

She stifled a laugh at that thought. But pulse was right. Every time she looked at him she became agonisingly conscious of her own pulses beating in her body. If he had that effect on her, he was sure to have it on every woman he came into contact with.

That was something else she'd do well to remember. She had to work quickly to ensure he fell for Beatrice before some other ambitious woman swooped in and grabbed the prize.

In that regard, maybe his world-weariness and distaste for Society were of an advantage. While he remained isolated at Thornwood they had time on their side, hopefully enough time for him to fall in love with Beatrice, before other unmarried women got wind that there was a single earl on the market.

She looked over at the dark windows. But that was not going to happen when he was stuck here with her. She just had to hope that tonight the weather would clear and tomorrow the love story between Beatrice and James could commence.

Her gaze moved down from the window to the clock ticking on the mantel. It was well past her usual bedtime. This would never do. If it stopped snowing overnight then tomorrow was going to be a busy day. As soon as the roads were clear she would have to dash home, hopefully well before the guests were due to arrive. Neither William nor her father were likely to be aware of the necessary last-minute preparations, and even if they were, she could not envisage them taking on those tasks themselves.

'I believe I shall take myself off to bed,' she said, placing the book on a nearby table.

'Of course.' James stood, crossed the room and called for a servant.

When Mary arrived she said good night to James and followed the maid up the stairs to the bedchamber.

Despite living in the county all her life, she had rarely visited Thornwood Hall and had certainly never ventured upstairs.

As a child she had known it to be enormous, but had not been aware of just how grand it was. Her uncle had a large estate in Northumberland, but this house dwarfed it. She couldn't possibly count how many rooms it had and the place was a veritable labyrinth.

'I've put you in the room that used to be the Countess's, when there was a countess,' Mary said, opening the door to a spacious bedchamber dominated by a large four-poster bed.

'After his lordship's room it's the nicest in the house,' Mary said with some pride. 'When the weather's fine it's got ever such a lovely view of the gardens. You can see right down to the river.'

'Oh, yes, this is delightful, and you've made it so welcoming. Thank you, Mary.'

Gas lamps had been lit and a fire burned in the grate. The thick brocade curtains draping the windows blocked out the night and any pesky drafts that dared to try to enter.

A chaise longue stood under the window, allowing the lady of the house to sit and read or embroider while looking out over the estate, and a desk sat in the corner waiting for her to write letters and invitations.

The walls were adorned with silk paper, featuring spring flowers in pastel shades, giving the room a delightful feminine feel. Intricate carvings on the bedposts depicting flower motifs matched the wallpaper, and the bed was draped with cream silk fabric delicately embroidered with the same flowers.

A little shiver rippled through Alice. Would this be the bed James shared with his wife?

A blush burned on her cheeks at such shameful audacity. It was not her place to think of such things.

'I'm afraid we couldn't find a nightdress that would fit you, miss,' Mary said, thankfully pulling Alice's thoughts away from the inappropriate place to which they had strayed. 'The late Countess's clothes were cleared out long ago, and all the maids are, well, rather smaller than you.'

Alice did not doubt it. Most women were smaller than her. When it came to her height, *statuesque* was perhaps the kindest word anyone could use.

'That's all right, Mary. I'm more than happy to sleep in my chemise.'

Mary helped her out of her clothes then departed. Alice climbed into the bed and was delighted to discover the thoughtful Mary had run a warming pan over the sheets and they were deliciously toasty.

She snuggled down in the bed, certain that tomorrow the weather would be bright and clear and James would be unable to come up with any excuses to stop him from joining them for Christmas dinner. Then he would meet Beatrice, their courtship could begin in earnest and all would be right with the world.

A pesky stab of jealousy gripped her chest, one that she had no right to feel, so she pushed it away and drifted off to sleep.

## Chapter Six

Alice woke the next morning and immediately rushed to the window, threw back the drapes and stared out at the winter scene before her. Snow was still falling, the wind still blowing.

A delicious buoyancy bubbled up inside her as she looked out at the gardens below, at the trees, hedges and bushes draped in white and the statues staring out from beneath their snowy coats.

She should be disappointed. It meant a precious day would be wasted. A day in which Beatrice and James could spend hour after hour together, getting to know each other, discovering how right they were for each other.

But what she was feeling was suspiciously like relief and happiness.

She really was a bad, bad person. Yes, she was enjoying James's company. Yes, she loved having the exclusive attention of such a handsome and magnetic man, but that was so selfish of her. Shamefully selfish.

Frowning to herself, she called for Mary to bring hot water and a washbasin, and to help her dress for the day.

There was nothing to be done about the situation. Snow *was* still falling. The roads *would* be impassable. She was stuck here for another day. It was not her fault. She had no reason to feel guilty.

Hopefully, the snow would stop soon and they would make it back to Rosetree Manor for Boxing Day. Failing that, there would be the New Year's Ball, where Beatrice and James could dance the night away together. Failing that…

She released a despondent sigh. Failing that, all would be lost and her lovely, kind, caring friend who deserved so much happiness in her life would be married off to an old man she did not love.

With the importance of her task once more foremost in her mind she descended the stairs to join James for breakfast.

'Merry Christmas,' she trilled with as much festive spirit as she could muster in this dull, undecorated room.

'Yes, Merry Christmas,' he said, looking up from the papers he was reading. 'I hope you slept well.'

'Oh, yes, indeed.'

She placed a piece of toast on her plate and smothered it with butter and marmalade. Usually on Christmas Day she barely ate at breakfast time, saving herself for the feast to come, but she doubted James had gone to the trouble of organising anything special for the day.

She looked out the window. 'It doesn't look like we'll be able to get to Christmas dinner at Rosetree Manor.'

He looked in the direction of the window. 'No' was his simple reply.

'It looks like we'll be having Christmas dinner here. Has your cook prepared anything special?'

'I shouldn't think so. I have not instructed the servants to make any fuss.'

Fuss?

Fuss was what Christmas Day was all about and she was sure his cook would enjoy making all the seasonal delights as much as her own did.

'But don't worry. I have informed the servants you won't be returning home today so you will be fed.'

Alice gave a rather unfeminine snort of laughter. 'I'm sure I won't go hungry but, well, I'm also sure the servants would rather not treat today like it was just any other midwinter's day.'

'Hmm,' he responded as he continued to peruse the pressing documents which were demanding his immediate attention. It looked like conversation was off the menu today, along with roast turkey, plum pudding and mince pies.

Alice buttered another piece of toast, looked over at

the tureens lining the sideboard and wondered whether she should have something more substantial to get her through till luncheon.

She munched on her toast, while he continued to pay her no heed. If she didn't take action, the day would be as dismal as the weather, so once the sombre breakfast was over, she excused herself and headed down the backstairs towards the servants' quarters to have a word with his cook.

She opened the kitchen door and a different world greeted her. Warmth from the stove and the smell of cooking filled the air. Unlike the rest of the house, everywhere she looked she could see bright red holly, deep green ivy, wreaths of dried flowers, strings of paper chains and in the corner sat a large Christmas tree decorated with delightful handmade baubles and sparkling with lit candles.

Alice clapped her hands together in delight, pleased to see their master's gloominess had not stopped the servants from celebrating this joyous day.

'This is wonderful,' she declared, looking around at the colourful cacophony.

'Miss Alice,' Cook said, brushing her hands on her apron as she rushed across the kitchen. 'His lordship said not to bother with a Christmas dinner, but well, I didn't think that right so we'll be serving roast turkey with all the trimmings.'

'Excellent,' Alice declared. 'And I just love the way

you've decorated this room. It quite puts my efforts at Rosetree Manor to shame.'

'Oh, that's Mary,' Cook said, looking over at the little maid, who was arranging a pile of mince pies on a plate and decorating them with sprigs of holly. She looked up and smiled at Alice, then went back to her work.

'She's got such an artistic touch,' Cook continued with pride.

'It's a shame James didn't get her to decorate the rest of the house. It does look a bit, well, un-Christmassy,' Alice said.

'Mmm,' Cook replied diplomatically. 'And it's such a shame you can't spend Christmas Day with your family, Miss Alice.'

'Oh well, never mind, but what of your families? Will you get to spend time with them?'

'Well, we are family now, and we're all rather looking forward to having Christmas dinner together,' Cook said, smiling at the other busy staff. 'And tomorrow most of us have the day off, so those that have got family nearby will be spending the day with them.'

'Let's just hope it stops snowing and we can all get home to our families.'

'Jethro says the snow won't last much later than midday and they should be able to clear the roads first thing in the morning.'

They both looked towards the gamekeeper, who was

pretending to pinch mince pies, while Mary playfully swatted him with her tea towel.

Jethro looked up at the mention of his name. 'Aye, I'll organise some men at first light. They'll all be keen to get the roads clear so they can visit their kin.'

'That's very good of you.'

Jethro nodded and went back to flirting with a blushing Mary.

Reluctant to return upstairs and sit in silence while James read his oh-so-important documents, Alice took a seat at the table and asked each servant about their family, many of whom had lived in the area for as long as Alice's family.

It was so good to be able to catch up on all the gossip, who was courting whom, which neighbours had fallen out with each other and what everyone's opinion was on the resulting feud.

She was laughing at a particularly funny story Alfred was telling about his brother's misadventures on his first day as a baker's apprentice, where he'd mistaken salt for sugar, when the room fell silent.

She looked over her shoulder and saw James standing in the doorway.

'I wondered where you had gone,' he said. 'For a moment I had thought you might have tried to walk back home.'

'Even I'm not that foolish,' she said with a little

laugh, trying to break the sudden tension. 'No, I was just catching up on all the local news.'

'Dinner will be served presently, my lord,' Cook said in a serious tone, turning back to the stove.

'Good, good,' James replied, looking uncharacteristically awkward.

'I suppose I should leave you all to your work.' Alice was somewhat reluctant to leave a room full of Christmas cheer but felt the need to take James away from this festive environment where he looked so out of place.

She joined him at the doorway and turned back to Cook. 'Please, make sure you enjoy your own Christmas dinner and don't worry too much about us.'

'Yes, miss,' Cook said, while everyone went about their tasks, the happy mood having evaporated. Even the gamekeeper was trying to look as if he was busy working, and not just here to enjoy the company of the other servants.

'I'm sure his lordship won't object if you open a few of his bottles of wine to go with your dinner,' she added. Everyone stopped and stared at her, then looked towards James.

'That will be all right, won't it?' she said, doubting he would be able to object even if he wanted to. 'After all, it is Christmas Day so they should be making it rather special and I'm sure you can spare a few bottles of your finest wine.'

'Yes, of course.' He nodded to the butler, who politely bowed, while trying to suppress a smile, something the other staff were no longer able to do, especially the gamekeeper, who was positively beaming.

'Oh, look,' the little chambermaid squealed. 'They're standing under the mistletoe. You have to kiss. It's tradition.'

Alice looked up at the bushy green plant hanging discreetly from the lintel, its white berries seemingly twinkling mischievously. Her gaze returned to the servants, who were staring back at them with gleeful expressions.

'I don't think— No,' she garbled, looking up at James, her cheeks burning with mortification. 'You don't have to just because—' She pointed towards the smiling maid. 'We should just—'

Before Alice could finish his lips were on hers.

James had no choice. He did not wish to kiss Miss Lambton, but refusing to do so would humiliate her in front of the servants. He would never be so unkind to any woman, especially one he was coming to respect and admire.

A quick peck on the lips would suffice. It would keep everyone happy, honour tradition and spare Miss Lambton any reminder of the insults she had already endured at the hands of callous and thoughtless men.

Just a quick peck.

That was what it was supposed to be.

And that was exactly what it would have been if the touch of her lips had not been so soft under his. The kiss might have ended immediately, if he had not been captivated by her feminine essence.

Was there anything more alluring than the scent of a woman? Like freshly picked spring flowers mixed with exotic spices that promised so much.

Instead, his arms wrapped around her. His cane clattered to the ground as he pulled her in closer, her body against his, her soft curves moulding into his body as if this was where she was meant to be.

This kiss had gone on longer than it should. He knew it had. He had to let her go, but he did not want to release her lips. He wanted to deepen the kiss, taste her fully, feel her breasts against his chest, her thighs pressed into his.

As if from a distance he heard cheering, whooping and clapping, breaking through his hazy mind like the wail of an alarm bell.

He released Miss Lambton and quickly stepped back. Her expression made it clear she too had reacted with more passion than she knew to be appropriate, and she too was now equally uncomfortable that they had shared such a foolish, unexpected embrace.

What on earth had just happened? James had to ask himself as he caught his breath. He was not attracted to Miss Lambton. Was he? Yes, her independent spirit was admirable and her good-natured approach to life was commendable, but she was simply not his type.

Clara was his type. Petite, pretty, flirtatious blondes were his type. Weren't they? And even if Miss Lambton was his type, which she wasn't, nothing could come of this. Men like him did not kiss women like her, unless there had been a marriage proposal.

Clara was the only woman he had wanted to marry. No other woman, and that included Miss Lambton.

He just had to be grateful that Christmas, under the mistletoe, was the only time such exchanges could take place without inviting dire consequences.

'I think we should leave the servants to their work,' he said, annoyed that his voice had taken on a ridiculous husky note.

'Oh, yes, of course,' a flustered Miss Lambton said, then she all but ran out of the servants' quarters and up the backstairs.

James reached down and retrieved his cane then followed on behind, unsure how they were to behave towards each other after such a kiss. Should he tell her it had been some time since he'd had a woman in his arms and he had perhaps overreacted? That would be far too insulting, and he wasn't entirely sure if that was correct.

It was correct he had not had a woman in his arms for some time, not since Clara, not since before the accident. But he was not so desperate that he would react in such a way to the kiss of any woman. He had en-joyed kissing Miss Lambton, had wanted to do much more than kiss her. God only knew why.

But whatever the reason, he should have done no more than what he had intended, given her a quick peck on the lips. That was what she would have ex-pected as well. She had not given him permission to take her in what was dangerously close to a passion-ate embrace.

Somehow, he had to make this right.

'I'm sorry about that,' he said as soon as they en-tered the drawing room. 'We had no choice really.'

'That's quite all right,' she responded in a breath-less rush. 'Tradition and all that. They would have thought we were right stick-in-the-muds if we hadn't obliged them.'

She quickly sat down, picked up her book, put it down again, moved it to one side of the small table, then back again.

'Cook said she's prepared a traditional Christmas dinner after all,' she said, her words tumbling over each other, while she once again picked up the book and put it back down again. 'It's awfully nice of her, isn't it?'

'Indeed,' James said ineffectively. He still hadn't made it right but was at a lost as to how to do so. He hated seeing her so uncomfortable. 'I didn't mean to—'

'Think nothing of it. Let's just forget all about it, shall we? Yes, let's do that.'

She picked up the book again, looked at the cover, then replaced it on the table.

Perhaps she was right. To discuss what had just happened might make things even worse.

'Hopefully, Cook preparing a special meal will go some way towards you having to spend Christmas Day away from your friends and family,' he said, desperate to say something, anything, to dispel the strain between them.

'Hmm, yes, probably,' she said, once again picking up her book.

'I should not have been so stubborn,' he conceded. 'I should have accepted your kind invitation and returned with you to Rosetree Manor last night.' *If I had, we would not be sitting here feeling so uncomfortable in each other's presence and trying to come to terms with what had just happened.*

'Oh, no, that's all right,' she said, still staring at her book.

'I promise that if the weather clears, I will join you tomorrow for the distribution of the presents.'

She looked over at him and beamed that now-familiar smile as if he had bestowed on her a great gift. 'That would be wonderful.'

Guilt gripped him with its nasty pincers. It was no

gift. All he was doing was trying to make amends for his behaviour.

'It's nothing,' he said, which was the truth. Sooner or later he would have to take on the role that was expected of him as the new earl. He'd been hoping to avoid those responsibilities for a while longer so he could remain hidden away and recovering from Clara's rejection. But it was the least he could do for Miss Lambton after what he had just done.

*Clara.*

While he was kissing Alice there had been no thoughts of Clara. She was usually somewhere in his mind at all times, either at the forefront or buried at the back, waiting to subject him to another sharp twist of his heart. But he had not thought of her when Alice was in his arms.

Curious.

Was kissing Alice the way to cure himself of Clara's hold on him?

He stifled a mirthless laugh. Of course there would be no repeat of that kiss.

The footman entered and announced that dinner was served.

Did James catch a smirk on the man's face? If he had, it died the moment he saw James's scowl and returned to the standard impassive look of a servant.

He took Alice's arm, as protocol demanded, and they walked down to the dining room. They were barely touching each other, but that did not stop his body from remembering what it was like to hold her curvaceous body.

This was ridiculous. He was not attracted to her, he repeated to himself.

As he pulled out her seat, he made a point of holding his breath, lest he inhale that intoxicating feminine scent and his admonitions were forgotten.

He signalled for the footman to serve the first course and fought to come up with a polite topic of conversation so they could put the unfortunate incident in the kitchen behind them.

'Oh, chestnut soup, lovely,' she said.

He smiled, suspecting she would have declared anything she was served to be lovely. She was possibly the most affable soul he had ever met, along with being the least affected or snobbish.

While the Lambtons were not wealthy by the standards of Clara's family, or indeed now himself, they were certainly well-to-do, but she had none of the self-important affectations one would expect from someone of her class.

She even seemed completely at home in the servants' quarters and appeared to know all their names, something he certainly did not, and suspected neither his brother nor his father had ever bothered to learn.

That, he was loath to admit, was something that always irked him about Clara. During his time in

America he had mixed with a wide array of people of different classes and had come to see that integrity, intelligence and dignity could be found at all levels of society, along with ruthlessness, pride and entitlement, the latter being found more commonly in members of his own class.

He was sure Alice would have been completely at ease in many of the less refined places he had visited in America, just as she was in the servants' quarters.

She had asked him about his travels and he had cut her off; perhaps he should not have been so dismissive.

'The last time I had chestnut soup I was working in Boston,' he said.

She put down her spoon and looked at him with wide-eyed curiosity. 'Boston? Marvellous, what was it like?'

'It's…' He thought for a moment as to the best way to sum up that city full of contradictions. 'It's dynamic. On the one hand it has wealthy families who have lived in the area for generations and are just as obsessed by social status as some of England's families.'

'Surely not?' she said with a comical frown.

'Maybe even more so, if that is possible. It's also full of immigrants from all over the world, bringing in their culture and way of life. And it's a bustling hub for industry.'

'A bit like London then?'

'Yes, and no. It's hard to explain. Maybe it's because there seem to be more possibilities in America, even for people from the lowliest of backgrounds.'

After all, Clara's father had started as a lowly clerk and was now one of the richest men in America.

'So what were you doing in Boston? You said you were working there when you last ate chestnut soup.'

'I was working for Randolph Waverly, the railway magnate, as a sort of liaison with his European and English investors.'

James paused before he took another sip of his soup. That had been where he met Clara, and he had been smitten from the moment he had laid eyes on her, had even, in an overly poetical manner, deemed her the most beautiful woman in creation.

He placed the soup spoon in the bowl.

'That must have been so exciting?' Alice said. 'Seeing new sights, meeting different people.'

He looked across the table at her. She was staring back at him with such an interested expression. 'Is that what you'd like to do? See new sights, meet different people?'

She shrugged. 'There's no point yearning for things that you can't have, but I love hearing about other people's adventures out in the world.'

'Hmm,' he said and went back to eating his soup. In that too, she could not be more different from Clara. Clara was as ambitious as her father. If she yearned for something, she would set her mind to it and get it, whether it was the man she wanted, the life she wanted or the adventures and excitement she craved. That vibrancy and thirst for life, along with her beauty, was what first attracted him, and after the accident, was what he knew he would only destroy if they remained together.

He gave a mirthless laugh. Not that he was doing comparisons, but he could never imagine Clara settling for the quiet life of a single lady in a remote part of England.

The soup course over, he rang for the footman, who entered, minus the smirk, and removed their dishes, while another served the roast turkey and vegetables.

He waited for Alice's reaction.

'Oh, lovely, Cook has even made sage-and-onion stuffing, my favourite.'

Once again he smiled to himself, suspecting no matter what Cook had made it would be her favourite.

'So where else did you travel in America?' she asked.

'Too many places to mention. Randolph Waverly's railways stretch from one coast to the other, so I traversed the country several times, from Boston and New York in the east, to San Francisco in the west, and everywhere in between, stopping off at countless frontier towns that were, to put it politely, a bit rough and ready.'

Her eyes grew wide in amazement. 'How wonderful. No wonder you're a bit—' she made a mock frown '—disappointed about returning to this quiet little corner of the world.'

'Hmm,' James answered. He'd had no choice but to return when his brother died so suddenly, and while he would never have wished his brother's death, it had come at a time when he had needed an escape.

'You must have met some fascinating people.'

'People are the same everywhere,' he responded. 'Some are good, some are bad.' *And some rip your heart out of your chest.*

'Yes, I suppose so.'

'So tell me about your life here in Ferndale,' he said, having talked more about his American travels than he had since his arrival back in England, and not wanting to go into any more details.

'I wouldn't want to bore you or cause you to miss the excitement of America.'

'There is no danger of that.' Anything that drew his thoughts away from his time in America would be welcome, and he had to admit, he was coming to find Miss Lambton a not too disagreeable distraction.

Throughout the rest of the meal, she entertained him with tales of the goings-on in the village and surrounding areas, much of which he suspected she had gleaned from his servants during her time in the kitchen.

'I can see my tenants are a lively lot,' he said as the footman removed their dishes while another footman served the pudding.

'Oh, plum pudding, my favourite,' she declared, as the footman poured the brandy butter.

She took a mouthful, closed her eyes and sighed with bliss. An image of how she had sighed when he kissed her flashed back into his mind.

Her eyes sprung open, and she paused in her eating, suddenly looking uncomfortable. Was she too remembering that unfortunate kiss?

He needed to tell her another story, perhaps one involving the last time he'd had plum pudding, but as he stared across the table at her, nothing would come to mind. All he could think of was the one thing he most certainly did not want to think about. That kiss.

## Chapter Seven

Think about Beatrice. Think only of Beatrice, Alice reproached herself.

*Do not think of that kiss.*

She cursed herself under her breath. Surely, any idiot knew that if you didn't want to think about something, the worst thing you could do was tell yourself not to think about it.

Now all she could think about was that kiss, the feel of his lips on hers, his arms encircling her, his chest so close to her that the temptation to lean forward and feel his hard body had been all but impossible to resist.

Her body tingled as if she was still in his arms. She could almost taste him on her lips, and his masculine scent—sandalwood and leather, with a hint of his fresh citrus cologne—filled her senses.

She sighed again, then blushed even more furiously.

*Stop sighing. Do not think of that kiss. Think only of Beatrice.*

She ate another spoonful of the delicious plum pudding. She really had to be the worst of all possible friends. Beatrice was facing a life of misery. Alice had the chance to save her, and all she was thinking of was how much she wanted to be back in James's arms. That should never have happened in the first place and would not have happened if it wasn't for that little chamber maid and that terrible piece of mistletoe.

But one thing was certain; it would not be happening again. Unless of course they accidentally found themselves under a piece of mistletoe. She'd have to be on the lookout for mistletoe for the rest of the Christmas season and if she spotted those treacherous green leaves and deceptively innocent berries, she would make sure she gave them a very wide berth.

'You must be looking forward to delivering those gifts on Boxing Day,' he said, rubbing the side of his neck and not looking in her direction.

He appeared as awkward as she felt, but she was grateful to now have something else to focus on other than that kiss, mistletoe and future evasive actions.

'I'm sure everyone we deliver presents to tomorrow will be delighted to meet the new earl,' she said. 'You'll be able to meet all the people I've told you about today.'

*And my friend Beatrice*, she added to herself. Then this torment would be over. She could step back and watch James fall hopelessly in love with her beautiful, charming friend. Then their kiss would become a faint and distant memory.

Although, it had probably already faded from James's memory, she thought, a sudden pang twisting her heart.

'If I'd known about this tradition I would have become more involved,' he said.

*More involved?* Alice's breath caught on a gasp. *His kiss would have been more 'involved' if he'd known about the mistletoe tradition? And what would that entail?*

'I would have contributed to the presents,' he added. 'I believe that is one of my duties as the new earl.'

Alice released her breath as colour tinged her cheeks. *He's talking about the Boxing Day gift-giving tradition, you fool. He's forgotten all about mistletoe and kisses.*

'We use money raised at the church and people donate goods,' she said, willing her cheeks to settle down.

She could add that neither his brother nor his father had ever donated a single present, so the local gentry had been undertaking this task for many years.

'I think people will be just pleased to meet the new earl and to know he's going to take part in the local community. I'm also so pleased you agreed to attend the New Year's Ball.'

Alice was uncertain if he had agreed to attend the ball, and his raised eyebrows suggested otherwise, but he'd already missed Christmas Day. She could not let him miss spending that precious time with her friend in a setting where they could dance, laugh, flirt and fall in love.

They were among the activities Alice had never had the opportunity to indulge in when she'd been sitting beside the potted ferns at every ball she had attended, but she was certain Beatrice would have more success. After all, her friend was exactly the type of woman she was sure would appeal to a man like James.

To be certain that they did fall in love, perhaps she should hang some mistletoe at the ball and engineer a way of getting James and Beatrice to stand under it.

The gripping of her heart returned, tighter and with greater intensity.

She gasped in a quick breath, reached for her water glass and with shaking hands took a sip.

The thought of James with another woman, even her dear friend Beatrice, should not be causing these ridiculous stabs of jealousy to prick her heart, if for no other reason than it was absurd to imagine a man like James Marlowe, the Earl of Thornwood, would ever want to kiss a wallflower like her, unless he was coerced into doing so.

*For goodness' sake, you were spurned by a man like Baron Hogmore.*

Yes, that kiss had affected her more strongly than she would have thought possible, but she had to get over it. She had to forget all about it, not just because of Beatrice, but for the sake of her sanity.

She forced herself to smile. 'I'm sure our humble little ball won't be a glittering occasion, not like the ones in New York. I've read all about that grand costume ball Mrs Vanderbilt hosted. Fancy inviting one thousand people to your ball! I found the London Society balls of a hundred or so overwhelming enough.'

She shook her head in disbelief, pleased she'd found a diverting topic that had nothing to do with mistletoe or kisses. 'And I heard she spent fifty thousand pounds. Why, you could buy a large English estate for that amount of money.'

'Hmm,' James said, as if not impressed in the slightest by this extravagance. 'Or do a lot to ease the staggering level of poverty in New York. But Mrs Vanderbilt's ball occurred before I arrived in New York.'

He pushed away his untouched plum pudding. 'Mrs Vanderbilt was trying to establish herself in New York Society and saw spending extravagantly as a good way to do that. I believe she is also determined to marry her daughter off to a titled man.'

'You better watch out,' she said at an attempt at humour.

An attempt that fell flat as he all but glared at her across the table. But his story was a timely reminder that she needed to work quickly before some American beauty got wind of the fact there was a wealthy, unmarried earl up in Cumbria who was ripe for the picking.

She grimaced, looked down at her napkin and adjusted it on her lap, aware she was doing exactly that. But surely she had nothing to feel guilty about. She was doing it for the most honourable of reasons, not simply to increase anyone's social status, but to save a friend.

'So, if you didn't go to the famous Vanderbilt ball, did you go to any other glittering affairs?'

'As I said, I worked for Randolph Waverly. He had gone from being a clerk in a shipping company to owning railways throughout America. His wife was determined to show off the family's wealth and joined the battle to become the dominant force in New York Society. So yes, I attended quite a few balls that his wife hosted.'

This was all said with a decided lack of enthusiasm.

'You make it sound more like you were being forced to go into war rather than attend a joyful celebration.'

'Because that is exactly what it is. Behind the glittering decor of the ballroom, a war was being waged, every bit as fierce as their ruthless husbands' business rivalry.'

She frowned. 'It sounds even worse than those balls I had to attend.'

'It seems neither of us were made for that particular battle.'

She gave a little laugh. 'But I can assure you, we will not be spending fifty thousand pounds hosting our little ball in the village hall.'

'I'm very pleased to hear that,' he said with a slight smile.

'And I can guarantee there will be no wars, no battles and no rivalries.'

'A bold claim,' he said, raising his eyebrows in disbelief.

'Oh, all right, there is usually a bit of rivalry between Mrs Stratford, the wife of the local Member of Parliament, and Mrs Crawford, the wife of the local Justice of the Peace, over whose dress is the most elegant. And last year during the harvest festival celebration, Squire Ashcombe lost the largest-pumpkin competition to one of the tenant farmers, Mr Brown. That caused some consternation and accusations of cheating, something about the use of forbidden fertilisers. But apart from that, they're fairly tame affairs.'

'I'll keep those rivalries in mind when I meet them.'

'Good. Just remember to compliment both Mrs Stratford and Mrs Crawford on their appearance, but not in each other's hearing.'

'And don't mention pumpkins to Squire Ashcombe.' She laughed. 'Exactly.'

A glorious smile transformed his face, crinkled the

edges of his eyes and exposed those perfect white teeth. Was everything about him perfect? Alice wondered. She suspected it was.

*Think of Beatrice*, a small voice at the back of her mind fought to be heard as she continued to smile back at him.

Alice Lambton was not his type—of that he was certain—but he would admit she had a delightful smile, which made it all but impossible to not smile back at her.

And why had he ever thought her eyes were just plain grey? They contained an array of colours from soft grey to light blue, which sparkled and danced when she laughed, something she did often and something which was becoming increasingly welcome.

He signalled to the footman to remove their pudding plates. 'Please serve coffee in the drawing room.' He was sure Alice would remember the man's name but for the life of him he could not recall what it was.

James stood and pulled out her chair. As he leaned over her, he once again inhaled her feminine scent. Spring flowers, it was so appropriate.

'You'll have to be my diplomatic adviser when I meet the local gentry,' he said, offering her his arm, and leading her back down the hallway towards the drawing room.

'Oh, if you've survived the cut-throat world of

New York Society, I'm sure you'll get the hang of things quickly and will soon be dancing with all the local belles of the ball,' she said, that smile wavering slightly.

James's smile also wavered, not wanting to think about those New York balls or the most successful of those beautiful belles.

They entered the drawing room, and she took a wing-back seat beside the fire.

'I take it you're going to miss the New York Social Season as much as I miss the London Social Season,' she said.

'Indeed,' he replied, his knee giving a slight twinge as he took the facing chair.

'Can I assume you would have returned to England even if you hadn't inherited the earldom?'

James shrugged, uncertain of the answer. 'Perhaps. When I got the message my brother was ill I would have returned immediately, but I was bedridden myself at the time. By the time I was fit to travel, I'm afraid my brother had passed away.'

'That's terrible,' she looked down at her lap. 'Why were you bedridden?' she asked quietly.

'I had an accident.' That would hardly be news to her. She could not have missed that he walked with a limp and his face was scarred.

'What sort of accident?'

He paused, unsure if he wanted to discuss the details.

'If it is something you would rather not talk about then please forgive my impertinence in asking.' She sent him an apologetic smile.

'No, it's no secret what happened. I believe it was even covered in the local newspaper.' He gave a self-deprecating laugh that such an everyday event would draw the interest of any journalist. 'I was walking along Broadway, a wide road that runs through the heart of New York.'

'Like Regent Street?'

'Yes, but perhaps even busier.'

He looked into the fire and he was transported back to that bustling street last winter, and the sudden unexpected change in the weather that had taken everyone by surprise. His mind conjured up the carriages and horses leaving tracks in the snow, the clattering of hooves and sound of streetcars muffled slightly by falling snow.

But even the sudden snowfall couldn't dampen the calls of street vendors hawking mugs of spiced cider and roasted chestnuts, nor the spirited voices of the newspaper boys on every corner, bellowing out the headlines from the rival publications.

'I saw a driver lose control of his carriage.'

The stamping of horse's hooves, their loud, panicked whinnying and the driver's desperate shouts pushed out all other memories.

'The driver tried to gain control, but the horses were terrified and heading towards a family crossing the street. I had no choice but to race out and attempt to grab the horses' harnesses. It diverted them long enough so they didn't run over the family, but it was a foolhardy move, as I was caught by the carriage wheel, and I believe a horse trampled on my knee.'

He looked up from the fire to see her staring at him wide-eyed, her hand covering her mouth.

'And the family?' she asked quietly.

'They were all safe. The mother recounted the event to a journalist, who wrote it up as a heroic event. Apparently, I had a moment of fame.' A bitter laugh escaped. 'Although it was lost on me as I was laid up in hospital.'

She continued staring at him with those worried grey eyes.

'It was while I was convalescing at home that I received notice my brother was dying, but I was in no fit state to travel.'

He had told that story to no one and wasn't sure why he had shared it with Alice. Perhaps it was because unlike most people she had not asked about why he walked with a cane or what had been the cause of his scar. Nor did they appear to draw her attention, as they did with most people he met.

But that was all he would be telling her about that unfortunate accident.

He would not be telling her he had been walking down Broadway towards Tiffany's to buy Clara an engagement ring. Nor would he be discussing the discomfort they both felt when Clara finally visited him on his return from hospital. It was obvious Clara was far too vivacious to be tending an invalid and doing so would just crush her spirit.

And nor did he make an agreeable patient. He'd been in pain, was incapable of doing even the most basic functions for himself and hated being so dependent on others. He was suffering and unfortunately made everyone around him suffer. It did not take long before it became apparent that while they were perfect for each other in the ballroom they were far from perfect together in the sickroom.

So he'd done the decent thing, as it were, told her he did not want to see her again and gave her the freedom to once again enjoy her life. She took him at his word, and by the time he had recovered enough to leave his sick bed, after many long, agonising months, she was engaged to the Duke of Brimley, a match James was sure would please Clara's father much more than an engagement to the second son of an earl, particularly one who was now crippled.

'As soon as I was able, I booked a steamer bound

for England,' he said instead. 'But unfortunately, my brother died while I was crossing the Atlantic.'

'I'm sorry,' she repeated. 'It must have been such a shock, not just that your brother died so unexpectedly, but also that you were now an earl and had to take on the responsibilities of the estate.'

'Hmm, it is not what I expected from my life.'

If events had happened differently… But there was no point thinking of that now.

'All in all it was a terrible ordeal for you to go through,' she said with compassion.

He knew she was talking about the accident and his brother's death, both of which were indeed ordeals, but James would be lying if he did not admit that the greatest suffering was caused by losing Clara.

He had momentarily thought he could experience the happiness and contentment that others seemed to achieve so easily. Then it had been snatched away from him, and he had been reminded that such things were not for him.

Men like him, born into a family like the Marlowes, might chase after happiness, but never seem to capture it. He suspected his brother's indulgent lifestyle in London was an attempt to grasp that illusive emotion, and he also suspected the man had as much success in that area as James.

'It is such a pity you were not able to see your brother one last time before he passed away.'

'Yes, I do regret that, even though we hardly knew each other.'

'No, but family is important.'

'Is it?' James frowned at her. 'With my brother's death I now have no family left.'

It was a strange thought, to be all alone in the world, but then, hadn't he always been alone, even when he did have a family?

She made a tentative smile. 'Then perhaps you need to marry, have children and start a family of your own.'

He suppressed a groan. He had all but forgotten her matchmaking plans, but it seemed she had not. She still had ambitions to foist her friend on him, but she would soon discover he had no intentions of ever travelling down the treacherous road of love ever again.

## Chapter Eight

James's reaction to her suggestion he marry and have children was somewhat underwhelming, to say the least. Anyone would think she had suggested he should jump in the freezing-cold sea and swim to France.

It was marriage she was suggesting, for goodness' sake. Children. It was what everyone wanted. Well, everyone other than her, but that was a choice she had been denied. But why James should be so adverse she could not understand. He was eligible and an heir. It was expected of him.

She would not be put off by his stubborn refusal to agree with her sensible suggestion that he find a wife. Nor would she be affected by the evident displeasure in his expression.

She would ignore them just as she had successfully ignored her reaction to that kiss.

Well, no. She would do a much better job than she'd done regarding that kiss.

The footman entered, bearing a coffee pot and a plate of mince pies.

'Miss Lambton?' he asked, the coffee pot hovering over an empty cup.

'Thank you, Alfred,' she said, which elicited an inexplicable huff of laughter from James.

'And please, tell Cook everything was absolutely delicious. She did a marvellous job, particularly as she had so little time for preparation.'

'I will, miss,' he said handing her a cup.

'I hope you were able to enjoy a Christmas dinner as well,' she enquired as he placed a full cup on the table beside James.

'Yes, miss.'

'And have had a glass or two of wine.'

Alfred smiled. 'Not yet, miss, but I believe some has been saved for me for when I finish serving, and it was most appreciated by the staff, my lord.'

'Which bottle did the butler choose?' James asked.

'I believe it was a Château Rothschild.'

James stared at the footman, seemingly speechless. 'I suppose you did say the finest bottle of wine,' he said to Alice. 'It looks like the butler took you at your word.'

'Is that an expensive bottle of wine?'

'You could say that.' James nodded to the footman. 'That will be all for this evening, Alfred. I believe there is a glass or two of wine waiting for you downstairs.'

'Thank you, my lord, miss.' Alfred bowed. 'And Merry Christmas.'

'Merry Christmas,' they both chorused back.

'Those bottles of wine have been sitting in the cellar since my father's time,' James said when Alfred closed the door behind him, a smile curling the edges of his lips. 'Apparently, he bought them when Giles was first born so they could be opened when his eldest son married. I suppose it's better the servants drink them than they go to waste.'

Alice could mention they could be drunk at *his* wedding, but suspected further mention of his hoped-for marriage would not be appreciated. Instead, she smiled, pleased he could see the humour in the situation, and pleased there had been some softening to that gloomy man who had reluctantly greeted her when she first arrived.

That man had seemed incapable of smiling at anything, and she doubted he would have seen the humour in his servants drinking his expensive wine.

Perhaps it wasn't such a shame after all that he had missed spending Christmas Day with Beatrice. If Beatrice had met him at his grumpiest, her friend might not have seen what a suitable husband he would make.

She would, however, have noticed his good looks; how could any woman not? And there was, of course, his title and wealth, both of which would make him eminently attractive to any young woman in search of a husband. But Beatrice deserved more than that. She deserved a man who would make her laugh, who would provide good company, who would bring warmth and joy into her life.

Maybe Alice needed to spend Boxing Day with him as well, just to remove all traces of the irascible James. She lowered her coffee cup, shame once again washing through her.

She knew the real reason her thoughts had strayed in that direction. She wanted to keep him to herself for as long as possible. That was not right. How could she even consider such a thing? Beatrice would be returning home in less than two weeks. Time was of the essence, and one whole day had already been wasted.

She looked over at the clock ticking on the mantelpiece. It was just gone four o'clock. At this time of year, with the days so short, night was already starting to fall.

Even though the snow had stopped falling, the roads would not be cleared until the morning. She would have to stay at Thornwood Hall one more night.

She reached out and placed a mince pie on her plate. There was nothing she could do regarding her matchmaking plans for the time being, so at least for tonight she might as well enjoy his company, and Cook's delicious baking.

She looked over at him. He was watching her with a thoughtful expression.

'What?' she asked, knowing something was on his mind.

'Thank you.'

She tilted her head, wondering what on earth she had done that required his thanks.

'You were right when you said it would be miserable to spend Christmas Day on my own. Thank you for your company.'

Alice felt decidedly pleased with herself.

'Does that mean next year I'll be able to coerce you into joining us for carol singing?'

He laughed, a lovely, deep, resonant laugh that caused her heart to swell. 'No, I can't see that happening.'

Alice smiled back at him. She had to admit she too had trouble seeing him standing with a candle and songbook, belting out 'While Shepherds Watched Their Flocks' for the entertainment of the villagers.

'But next year I might just agree to spend Christmas Day at Rosetree Manor, if the invitation still stands.'

'It's an open invitation. You are welcome anytime, just as you were when you were a child.'

'Thank you.'

She sighed and settled back into the comforting softness of the armchair. It was a small victory but a decisive one.

'That sounded like the sigh of contentment that follows a good meal,' he said.

'Yes, I must admit I feel decidedly relaxed. This Christmas has been different from any other I've celebrated, probably since I was a child. Usually by this time in the evening I'm completely exhausted, having spent all day entertaining guests and making sure everyone's needs are catered for.'

'And what of your needs?'

She frowned at him, unsure what he meant.

'While you are spending all your time thinking of others, when do you have a chance to think of what you want or need?'

Her frown deepened. Again she was unsure what he meant. 'I suppose making sure everyone else is happy brings *me* happiness.'

His eyebrows rose as if he did not believe her. 'On Christmas Eve you organise that carol singing. Christmas Day you entertain all and sundry, and even try to gather up a stray earl or two. Then on Boxing Day it's organising gifts for the local needy. New Year's Eve it's the ball. Do you ever give a moment just for Alice Lambton?'

'I enjoy it,' she said, surprised that anyone should ever question such a thing. 'It makes me happy.'

'Happy?' He frowned as if that was an unfamiliar concept.

'Yes, happy. Surely you know what that is?'

He gave a wry smile. 'I sometimes wonder if that really exists, or whether people pretend they are happy so as not to worry others.'

Alice bristled at his accusation, which she could not help but take personally. And it was not true. She did not pretend to be happy when she wasn't.

Did she? No. Of course not. She *did* enjoy helping others. She loved being busy. And yes, sometimes she smiled even when she wasn't exactly full of joy, such as when she was humiliated in the middle of a ballroom by an odious baron, but that was no crime. And yes, sometimes she stayed busy so she didn't have to think about how her life might have been if she'd had a successful Season, but again, there was nothing wrong with that.

'Well, it's better than indulging in self-pity,' she said defensively.

He gave a short, joyless laugh, and lifted his injured knee, which was presumably hurting him.

'Oh, I'm so sorry. I didn't mean that you... Well, I mean, you have lots of reasons to feel sorry for yourself. You had that accident, and your brother died and, well, you didn't want to have to be an earl or return from America. If all that had happened to me I'm sure I'd feel sorry for myself as well. Not that you...'

She stopped talking, knowing that with every extra word she dug herself into a deeper hole.

He continued to watch her, his raised eyebrows causing her to blush at her clumsy ramblings.

Then a smile curled the edges of his lips and she released her held breath. She had not offended him with her blathering.

'Even if you were reduced to being a scarred cripple, I doubt you would sink into self-pity,' he said. 'You would just keep smiling and put all your energies into making others happy. I am sorry for criticising you, and for my sombre mood.'

'Oh, you're not a—' She stopped. How could she say that even with his disability, and his scar, he was still the most handsome, most irresistible man she'd ever had the fortune, or should that be misfortune, to lay eyes on? To even try would be most inappropriate.

But she wanted to say something, anything, so they could go back to that comfortable state they were in just a few moments ago, but no soothing words would come.

'You probably won't believe this, but for a time when I was in New York I actually thought *I* was a happy man.' He gave another laugh that lacked humour. 'I had fallen in love,' he added so quietly she was unsure if she had heard correctly.

'In love with the most beautiful woman in New York and hoping to be married,' he continued as if to himself.

A sudden, gnawing tightness gripped Alice's chest.

Despite being all but breathless she forced herself to ask a question she both wanted and did not want answered.

'What happened?' she gasped out.

'Reality happened. She got a better offer.' He crossed the room, picked up the brandy carafe and tilted it in her direction in question.

She shook her head. He poured one for himself and returned to his seat.

'I'm so sorry,' she said, unsure if that was true. If he had found love and happiness in New York, they would not be sitting here together now. He would not be an eligible earl.

'Nothing to be sorry for. That is life.'

'It doesn't have to be like that.'

He laughed, but it was a hollow sound. 'You would say that, preferring to see the bright side of everything, but I'm afraid I've seen more of the world than you, and know how harsh reality can be.'

Alice wanted to tell him he was wrong, but all she could focus on was that he had been in love, with the most beautiful woman in New York—that and the dull, constricting sensation that had settled in the middle of her chest.

James took a much-needed sip of his brandy. He had done it again, revealed more of himself to her than he intended.

'I'm sorry. I've rather ruined the festive mood, haven't I?'

'Not at all,' she murmured and attempted to smile.

He was unsure why he had mentioned Clara. Had he wanted to convince Alice that he wasn't always such a misery? Had sitting companionably with her after dinner reminded him of what he had lost, what he might have had if he had married Clara?

Or did he want to let her know that he had once pursued the happiness she believed he could find through love and marriage, and it had all turned to dust?

Did he have to remind himself that such possibilities were not for men like him? That if he chased love and happiness it would only be snatched away from him, yet again, so it was much better not to enter the chase.

She rose from her chair and crossed the room to retrieve her book. His gaze followed her. Last night he had noticed the way she moved, with such effortless poise. Willowy—that was the word that had occurred to him. Tall, slender and graceful, like a willow tree moving gently in the wind.

And that grace and poise were accentuated because it was unaffected. Clara also possessed those qualities, but it was obvious she was constantly aware of them, just as she was aware of the effect she had on the men who could never take their eyes off her, including him.

Alice looked down at her book and smiled. It was

such a delighted expression, and he couldn't help but smile back.

A woman like her *should* be married and filling her house with noisy children. Her mother had made Rosetree Manor a happy home for her own children and a retreat for many of the children in the village, including him. He suspected Alice would do the same if given the chance. But fools like Hogmore would never see that. They wanted women who conformed to what was fashionably beautiful, woman who would make them the envy of their friends.

Women like Clara.

This thought hit him like a physical force. He looked down and swirled the brandy around in his glass. Was that why he thought himself so in love with Clara, because she was beautiful and he knew other men wanted what he had?

Was he really that superficial? No, he could not be. Clara had many other lovable qualities. She was intelligent, lively and magnetic and he had never met anyone like her. Of course he was captivated by her beauty, and yes, he did have to admit having such a woman on his arm and being the envy of all other men did feed his masculine pride. But it was more than that.

The rustle of fabric broke through his thoughts, and he looked up to see Alice taking her seat. One thing the two women did have in common: they both took pleasure in what life had to offer, although in Clara's case that involved dancing, laughing and the excitement of the social whirl, whereas Alice found it in quiet pursuits and the care of others, and he certainly had no right to judge her for that.

He smiled at her, hoping she would forgive him for his previous bad behaviour. Who cared if, as he suspected, she used helping others as a way to cover any feelings of sadness? There were worse ways of behaving, such as indulging in self-pity, as she had pointed out.

'Back to reading about your beloved matchmaker?' he asked with as much levity as he could muster.

'Yes, I'm at a really good part now,' she said with a delightful, forgiving smile. 'Mr Elton has just proposed to Emma. I know how it ends but it's still a shame I won't be able to finish it before I return home.'

'Then you must have it. Take it with you when you leave.'

'Oh, no, I couldn't. It belonged to your mother.'

'I'm sure she would want you to have it.'

'I couldn't.' She looked at him in shock as if he was offering her the crown jewels.

'You can and you will. I insist. It will be my Christmas present to you.'

'But I haven't got you a Christmas present.'

'You gave me your company on what would have

been a cold and miserable Christmas Day. That is your gift to me.'

She smiled once again. A lovely smile that made her face glow and her eyes shine with pleasure. 'Thank you.'

James felt absurdly pleased with himself. He had merely given her an old, tattered book that no one had looked at since his mother's passing, but he felt as if he was being the most magnanimous of men.

She went back to reading and he knew he could not spend the rest of the night watching her as she contentedly buried herself in her book, so he reached over and picked up the account books he had intended to study.

Soon he too was immersed, not in Regency England, but in debit and credit and the somewhat less than fascinating subject of double-entry bookkeeping.

'What is the problem?' Alice's voice broke in on his musing.

He looked up and frowned at her. 'Problem?'

'You've been sighing for the last half hour. Now you're making huffing and puffing noises.'

James was unaware he had been doing any such thing. But if he had it would not surprise him.

'These accounts are a revelation. My brother invested nothing in the estate in the entire time he possessed the title. Not a penny has been spent on new machinery for the farms. He's collecting rents from the tenants but I see no expenditure for repairs or improvements to their homes. Although there are rather large expenditures for entertainment and the upkeep of the London town house.'

He shook his head in disbelief and sighed, just as she had said he was doing. 'If Giles had continued on this way, eventually he would have run the estate into the ground.'

'Just as so many members of the aristocracy have done. They think that because their estates have been producing wealth for centuries they will continue to do so, but the world is changing.'

'It is, and this estate is going to have to change with it.'

'Good for you. I've often thought it a misguided system for the eldest son to always inherit the estate. It would be much better if it went to the one who was best able to manage it efficiently and wisely.' She sent him a teasing smile. 'And sometimes that might even be one of the daughters.'

'I suspect *you* would be able to run an estate efficiently and wisely.'

'I'm not sure if I could, but I suspect I'd thoroughly enjoy trying.'

He laughed. 'I believe you would.'

With that she returned to her book, and he returned to the shocking state of the ledgers.

A knock on the door drew their attention and the gamekeeper entered, his florid face suggesting he'd had ample servings of Christmas dinner and more than a glass or two of the Château Rothschild.

'I thought you'd like to know the snow stopped a few hours ago, my lord, and the sky has cleared,' Jethro said with a somewhat clumsy bow. 'I'll organise for the men to be ready at first light to clear the road so Miss Lambton should be able to get back to her family tomorrow.'

'Thank you,' James said and the man departed.

'That's good news,' he said to Alice.

'Yes, it is.'

Did he hear a hint of disappointment in her voice, and was that what he too was feeling? No, of course not. Once she was gone life would get back to normal. Whatever normal now meant.

'You'll be able to help deliver the Boxing Day presents,' she added.

James waited for that sense of exasperation to descend on him at the thought of having to spend time in the company of others, of having to pretend enjoyment as he distributed gifts like a begrudging Father Christmas. Strangely it did not come, so he nodded his agreement and went back to his ledgers, until it was time to retire for the night.

## *Chapter Nine*

Alice woke the next morning with a sense that real life was about to begin after her dreamlike interlude. The snow had stopped. Mary had informed her the men had declared the road safe, and there was no reason for her to remain a minute longer at Thornwood Hall.

Today was the day she hoped the true romance would begin. James and Beatrice would meet. They would fall in love, marry, have children and spend their lives together. And they would both have Alice to thank for their happiness.

As they drove home to Rosetree Manor, Alice could hardly sit still on the carriage bench, so many emotions were spinning around inside her. Nervousness, excitement, anticipation and several she would prefer not to name as they felt decidedly like emotions a caring friend would not feel in these circumstances.

Just as Jethro promised, the men had been out shovelling snow off the roads at first light, but the carriage still moved at a slow pace along roads that had become somewhat boggy, but at least they were passable and she would not have to waste another day at Thornwood Hall.

Not that she'd ever really class the time they spent together as a waste. In fact, she suspected she was going to treasure memories of this Christmas Day for a very long time.

She looked across the carriage at James, who was sitting opposite her, staring out the window. She followed his gaze towards the pristine white snow covering the fields and glinting like diamonds in the sunlight. It was an idyllic winter scene and would provide a glorious backdrop as Beatrice and James strolled around the countryside together, distributing gifts and getting to know each other.

Her smile became strained as that image grew in her mind, of the two of them exchanging endearments, even kisses. But surely that was what she hoped for. For her to want otherwise would be unforgivable.

The carriage drew up in front of her home, and James helped her down. She held his hand for perhaps longer than she should, aware that this might be the last time they would be alone in each other's company.

Was he feeling the same way? Of course he was not. She was being delusional.

She dropped his hand, turned and saw William racing down the front steps. He was smiling fit to burst as he all but ran down the flagstone path. Anyone would think she had been absent for months instead of two nights.

'Alice, James,' he called out as he reached them. 'I am so pleased you managed to make it. I was just wondering whether I should venture over to Thornwood Hall and rescue my sister.'

'I hope you weren't worried,' James said. 'I thought it best that Miss Lambton remain at Thornwood Hall until the snow stopped.'

'When it started to snow I confess I was a bit worried. I feared Alice would be so fretful about her guests she would throw all caution to the wind and try and make it home for Christmas Day. The only thing that stopped me from heading out into the storm to find her was I was certain you would be sensible and would not let her leave.'

Alice frowned at her brother's unfair assessment of her character.

'Thank you for keeping my sister safe,' William said, slapping James on the back.

Alice suspected if she was not a woman who had been classified as an unmarriageable spinster, her brother would show some concern about her spending the night alone with a man, but instead of insulted, she chose to feel relieved that no one was worried about her honour.

'So how was Christmas Day?' she asked as William

escorted them up the path, through the brick portico and into the entrance hall.

'It was splendid. Beatrice and her aunt arrived early and Beatrice took over all the hostess duties. All I had to do was make sure everyone's glass was topped up. A task I believe I performed admirably, if I do say so myself.'

Alice looked at James to see if he had registered that Beatrice was someone who could step into the fray when needed and would be more than capable of acting as a hostess for any parties they held at Thornwood Hall.

He appeared not to notice.

'It hasn't changed a bit,' he said, his gaze moving up to the high ceiling with the dark brown exposed wooden beams, then down to the panelled walls and to the carved wooden furniture.

He was right; little in the house had altered since he last visited, and much of it, including this entranceway, was exactly as it had been when the manor house was first built in the sixteenth century.

He crossed the tiled floor to the tarnished knight who stood in the corner, draped in wreaths of ivy.

'Remember when we tried to climb into this suit of armour?' he said to William.

William laughed. 'Yes, we planned to stage a battle but couldn't get the bits apart and ended up sending it clattering to the floor, bringing the entire house-hold running.'

'Then we tried to hide behind the tapestry,' James said, joining the laughter and pointing to a large, faded tapestry that depicted some battle scene or other that one of the Lambton ancestors had been involved in. 'How we ever thought we would get away with it, when our feet were so obviously sticking out the bot-tom.'

'We panicked, I suppose,' William said.

'We wanted to be knights and ended up as just a couple of mischievous children.'

'So did you arrange for Beatrice to join us today?' Alice asked, breaking in on their childhood remem-brances.

'No, I'm afraid not,' William said as he indicated for James to move through to the drawing room. 'Her aunt had, shall we say, a bit too much of the port yes-terday and has taken to her bed at home. Beatrice has chosen to stay with her.'

'Oh, William, how could you?' She scowled at her brother behind James's back.

'How could I what?' he asked as the three took their seats in the drawing room.

'Well, you should have made sure the aunt did not drink more port than was good for her.'

'I was hardly going to reprimand an elderly woman or warn her about overindulgence.'

'No, but you could have signalled to the footman to stop refilling her glass.'

'No harm done and she seemed to enjoy herself.'

That was hardly the point. If Beatrice did not join them, another day would be wasted.

'All in all I think it was a memorable Christmas,' William said and actually sniggered. 'Beatrice's aunt and an equally tipsy Widow Harcourt performed an interesting rendition of "Jingle Bells", which I suspect I'll never forget. They even tried to dance along to it. Priceless.'

She looked over at James, hoping he would not think Beatrice's aunt was prone to such behaviour and would be an embarrassment when she joined his family, but he had picked up a copy of her first book and was slowly flicking through the pages.

Thank goodness he was distracted.

'And how did father take all this revelry?' she asked quietly.

'Oh, he enjoyed every minute of it, and the more port that was consumed the more friendly he and Widow Harcourt became, if you get my meaning.'

Unfortunately, Alice did get this meaning, and she was rather pleased she had not been present to witness it.

'That's where father is now,' William continued. 'Making sure Widow Harcourt did not come down with the same affliction as Beatrice's aunt, although

he looked a bit the worse for wear himself, I must say.'
William laughed as if this was all a source of great
amusement, then turned his attention to James.

'So my sister has roped you into helping in one of
her worthy causes, has she?'

She sent her brother another look of disapproval.
Yes, she had *roped him in*, but only because it would
have provided the ideal opportunity to put James and
Beatrice together. An opportunity that William had
ruined by serving too much port to her aunt, just as
surely as he had ruined the chance of putting them
together on Christmas Day. Not that she could blame
him for the weather, but if he could have been more
insistent in his invitation to James when they'd travelled up to Ferndale by train, she wouldn't have been
forced to go over to Thornwood Hall herself.

Then she would not have had to stay the night,
would not have kissed James under the mistletoe
and would not have had to grapple with an array of
perplexing emotions. Everything would be straightforward and by now James and Beatrice would be
courting and all would be as it should be.

Once again she looked at her brother in disapproval,
causing him to send her a blank glare, as if he had no
idea why she was frowning at him.

He really was impossible.

'There's rather a lot of them,' James added, looking at the Christmas tree in the corner surrounded by

piles of brightly wrapped gifts. 'Are we going to have to deliver them all today? Before nightfall?'

'Oh, don't worry about that,' William said with a sly laugh. 'You'll be helped by most of the ladies in the parish.'

As if on cue, the sound of many boots marching up the front path was heard, followed by a loud knocking on the door.

'That will be them,' William said. 'I'd advise you to hide behind the tapestry, but as it didn't work when we were children it's unlikely to work now.'

Her brother was still laughing when the door burst opened and the women from the Ladies Benevolent Society, wrapped up in warm cloaks, scarves and hats, bustled in before the footman had a chance to announce their arrival.

Loud female voices immediately filled the room in a cheerful, overlapping chorus of greetings to Alice and William.

William introduced James but said nothing about him being the new earl. The women all nodded their greetings, and expressed their admiration at his community spirit when William informed them James would also be distributing gifts.

Greetings out of the way, the women swooped on the parcels and piled them up into each other's arms, with much discussion about who was to do what, when and how.

Then, like a sudden whirlwind that quickly passes through, stirring up everything in its path, they left, leaving a quiet drawing room in their wake.

William was still smiling as if they had just laid on some entertainment for his amusement.

'You got off very lightly, my friend, very lightly indeed,' he said to James. 'If I'd told them they were in the presence of the new Earl of Thornwood then their reaction really would have sent you scuttling for sanctuary behind the tapestry.'

Alice shook her head at her brother's irreverence. Was there nothing he took seriously?

'But judging by their expressions when I said you planned to help out, I suspect gossip about you and Alice will have spread far and wide by the end of today.'

'Gossip you could have nipped in the bud,' Alice said with more sharpness than intended. 'You should have informed them that James is the new earl and all he's doing is taking this opportunity to meet some of the locals.'

William held his hands up in mock surrender. 'I was just protecting my friend.'

*But not caring a fig about my feelings*, Alice could have added.

'At least the pile has diminished to something more manageable,' James said, thankfully changing the subject.

William stood up and stretched. 'While you're out

distributing the gifts I might pop round to see Beatrice and her aunt, and apologise for allowing Lady Chigwell to overindulge last night.'

'You won't say that, will you? Alice said, aghast. 'It will embarrass both Beatrice and her aunt.'

'Give me credit for some sense, Ali,' he said with a laugh that imbued her with no confidence whatsoever. If he had a modicum of sense he would have worked in with her plans and James would now be spending the day with her friend Beatrice.

'I suppose we should make a start,' she said, standing up and crossing to the Christmas tree.

She picked up the pile of gifts and placed them into James's outstretched arms.

With that done, they left the house, climbed back into the carriage and drove towards the homes where Alice was certain the children were waiting for their arrival as anxiously as if they were Father Christmas.

As they drove through the countryside towards where the tenant farmers lived, James marvelled at how, with the sun out, the day could not be more different from the storm that had kept him and Alice trapped at Thornwood Hall.

He looked out at the snow that stretched across the fields in a smooth blanket. It reminded him of that Christmas carol they had sung at church.

'Good King Wenscelas'—that was it. Just as that

thought occurred to him, Alice started humming the same carol.

He turned on the bench and stared at her.

'What?' she asked.

'I was thinking of that carol just as you started to hum it.'

'Well, it's not that surprising. It is Boxing Day, which is the Feast of Stephen, and the snow is lying round about—'

'"Deep and crisp and even",' they said together and smiled.

'I'll make a carol singer of you yet,' she said.

James could almost imagine that happening. When he'd arrived by train just two days ago, he never thought he'd be driving through the snow about to distribute Christmas presents like the jolly old Saint Nick himself.

The carriage came to a halt at the edge of a settlement and James helped Alice down. He looked at the line of ramshackle stone homes. Signs of his brother's neglect were evident everywhere. Houses had been repaired in a makeshift manner, with what appeared to be salvaged material, and some were so dilapidated they had been abandoned entirely.

Shame consumed him, but he was pleased he had agreed to join Alice on this excursion. It was one thing to read about his brother's lack of expenditure in the ledgers, quite another to see for himself the effects of that negligence and to witness how his tenants were expected to live.

Alice removed two presents from the pile in the carriage, then led him up a pathway and knocked on the door. The sound of countless little feet could be heard running towards them.

A little girl pulled open the door, surrounded by a swirl of smaller children in somewhat shabby dress.

'Hello, Mattie,' Alice said. 'Hello, everyone.'

'Hello, Miss Lambton,' the children all chorused together. Their eyes then swivelled to James. The welcoming smiles faded. They instantly became shy and several thumbs immediately went into mouths.

'This is my friend James,' she said.

He raised his eyebrows.

'All right, perhaps William was correct,' she whispered. 'We can do the proper introductions at another time,' she said quietly.

'Doesn't that rather defeat the purpose of my visit,' he whispered back as the children watched them. Hadn't she insisted he come because it would be a good opportunity to be introduced to his tenants?

'Well, I don't want to ruin the children's day. If I tell them who you are it will only make them uncomfortable and think they have to be on their best behaviour.'

They entered the humble cottage to discover even more children were waiting for them, along with their mother and a pot of tea.

'A nice cup of tea. Lovely,' Alice said as she settled herself at the scrubbed wooden table.

As discreetly as possible, lest the woman think him judging her home, he took a look around. The room was surprisingly clean, given the number of children, but he could see they were hopelessly overcrowded.

A cast iron coal range was barely keeping the small room warm, and it appeared the family did all its living in this cramped space. A narrow wooden stairway led up to a loft, where he presumed they all slept.

This really would not do, and it would be his first task to ensure that the living conditions of his tenants were drastically improved.

'James, give the large present to Maddie so she can distribute the treats to the younger ones,' Alice commanded.

Maddie solemnly took the gift from James, unwrapped it and passed out a treat to each child, making sure none got more than the other. The children immediately stuffed chocolate into their eager mouths.

'And this is for you, Maddie. Your teacher told me what an excellent reader you are, so you will be able to read it to the other children.'

'Oh, thank you, miss,' the girl said. Before she'd even opened the present, the children had all gathered around her and were looking up at their sister in expectation.

'You are so kind, Miss Alice,' the mother said as she

poured the cups of tea from a large, chipped enamel teapot. 'They did so love that last book you gave them. We never heard the end of what Little Lambsie was getting up to, and how she managed to put that uppity Baron in his place.'

James and Alice exchanged smiles. He could understand why the children would be so thrilled with their gift. When she'd talked of drawing farm animals he'd imagined rough sketches, but her illustrations were works of art in their own right, and he was sure the pictures delighted the children as much as the sweet, funny stories.

'So you'd be a friend of Mr Lambton, would you?' the mother said, handing James a cup. 'Up from London for Christmas, are you?'

'Actually,' Alice answered for him, leaning forward and talking quietly so the children wouldn't hear, 'James is the new Earl of Thornwood. We thought today would be a good opportunity for him to meet his tenants. Mrs Barnes's family have lived in this area longer even than the Lambtons or Marlowes,' she added, looking at James.

Mrs Barnes all but jumped to her feet, her cheeks red, and bobbed a curtsey. 'Begging your pardon, my lord.'

James also stood and gestured towards her seat. 'Please, sit down. This is just an informal visit. It's also a good chance for me to inspect the cottages and I can see they need a lot of work.'

'I do what I can, but as a widow, well…' She came to a halt. 'And everyone in the village is ever so helpful, and the estate manager does what he can, but…'

*But without funds being made available he is limited in what he can achieve*, James could have finished for her. 'Well, rest assured, my first task will be to make sure all the homes are repaired.'

'Thank you, my lord,' Mrs Barnes said with another curtsey before taking her seat.

They drank their tea as Alice asked about the family, questions Mrs Barnes answered politely, with glances towards James which were just as shy as the children's had been.

When they'd finished, they said their goodbyes and Mrs Barnes offered another embarrassed curtsey, while the children broke from their story to chorus out their thanks once again.

They made their way to cottage after cottage, and the entire procedure was repeated, including the offer of a cup of tea, so that by the time they had distributed all the gifts and were travelling back to Rosetree Manor James felt like he was floating on a sea of tea.

The carriage came to a halt in front of her home and he escorted her up the path.

'Won't you come in?' she said. 'I could offer you a nice cup of tea.'

He groaned, causing her to laugh.

'No, I will leave you to spend some precious time with William, but thank you for today, Alice,' he said. 'You were right. It was essential that I meet my tenants and I can see I have a lot of work to do.'

She continued to smile at him. 'But you will be attending the New Year ball, won't you?'

James cringed inwardly. It was one thing to meet his tenants, another to have to attend a social event and make small talk all evening with the local gentry, all trying to curry favour with the new earl, or worse, thrusting their marriageable daughters in his direction.

Suddenly retreating to Thornwood Hall once again appealed.

'You promised,' she stated emphatically, and he was unsure if he had done so.

'You've admitted I was right about visiting the tenants, and I'm sure you'll find I'm right about it being a good idea for you to attend the ball.'

'Has anyone ever told you you're rather bossy?'

She laughed as if he was joking. 'Yes, William does all the time. So I take it that is a yes and we will see you on New Year's Eve.'

'It looks like I have been given no choice,' he said with a bow of his head before departing.

## Chapter Ten

Alice walked down the hallway feeling rather pleased with herself. While today was yet another setback in her plan, it had all been rather fun, and James had agreed to attend the New Year's Ball. So at least she had another chance to introduce him to Beatrice.

She entered the drawing room, came to an immediate halt and stared aghast at the sight before her. William and Beatrice were taking tea.

How could her feather-brained brother be so, well, feather-brained?

He must have heard James's carriage arrive. If he'd used that underworked brain of his he would have rushed out and insisted James join them. Now yet another opportunity to get James and Beatrice together had been missed. All because of him.

William and Beatrice smiled at her, and a terrible thought occurred to Alice. Was her brother showing an interest in her pretty friend? That would never do. Beatrice most certainly did not need the distraction of a pointless flirtation and her brother should know better than to waste precious time on a meaningless diversion. While Beatrice's father was certain to put aside his marriage plans for his daughter if she was being courted by a wealthy earl, he was unlikely to do so for a barrister with a modest income and no more property than a town house in London.

The moment Beatrice left she would give her brother a stern talking-to. Although she suspected no matter how stern she was, the numbskull was unlikely to ever realise how imperative it was to find Beatrice a more suitable husband than the terrible man her father expected her to marry.

Sending a frown in her brother's direction, she crossed the room and kissed her friend on the cheek.

'I hope your aunt is on the mend.' Alice asked as she took her seat and waved her hand in front of her face to turn down the maid's offer of a cup of tea.

'Oh, yes, she's much improved. She said it was probably just a touch of the vapours.'

William laughed and Alice frowned at him, although Beatrice did not appear put out by her brother's irreverence.

'So how was your Christmas Day?' Beatrice asked.

'It was…not how I expected to spend the day,' Alice responded, unsure how she was to answer that simple question.

Beatrice tilted her head, indicating she wanted to

hear more, but what could Alice say? She couldn't say she enjoyed every moment she spent in the company of the man she hoped would soon be Beatrice's husband. She could not mention that kissing him had been sublime, that it had affected her both physically and emotionally, so much so that she was trying to erase all memory lest it undermine her determination to marry James to her friend.

No, she could not say any of that, so she kept silent.

'Alice had hoped to drag James back with her so he could spend Christmas Day with us,' William said.

Alice frowned at her brother. None of this was a source of amusement.

'Instead you spent it alone with the Earl,' Beatrice added, her face expectant as if she was looking forward to some entertaining gossip.

'I had no choice,' Alice blurted out, becoming increasingly uncomfortable as if she was facing an inquisition. 'There was a snowstorm. The roads were blocked. It would have been dangerous to attempt to come home. There might have been an accident.' These words tumbled out of her, as if she was justifying something that needed no justification.

Beatrice and William exchanged looks, the meaning of which she had no idea.

'So what did you do?' Beatrice asked.

'Nothing,' Alice insisted, her cheeks burning.

William and Beatrice continued to stare at her with

matching looks of curiosity, making it clear they expected more.

'Just the usual,' Alice said abruptly. 'We ate Christmas dinner. That's all.'

The heat on her cheeks intensified, and drat it all, she knew the reason why.

That kiss.

Not that she had anything to be embarrassed about. Not really. Lots of people kissed under the mistletoe at Christmas time.

'Did you and your aunt enjoy your Christmas Day?' she asked, hoping to turn the conversation away from herself, James and anything they may or may not have got up to.

'My aunt certainly did,' Beatrice said, exchanging a smile with William. 'I've never heard her sing with such gusto.'

'And she simply threw herself into the parlour games,' William added, which caused Beatrice to giggle.

'Parlour games?' Alice asked. No parlour games had been planned for the day.

'Yes, we played blind man's buff and musical chairs,' Beatrice said.

'And sardines,' William added, still laughing. 'The Vicar was most surprised and I think rather delighted to be squashed inside a wardrobe with Lady Chigwell.'

'I think they were somewhat disappointed when

we finally found them,' Beatrice added, joining in on the laughter.

While she was having a relatively restrained Christmas with James, it looked like they were having a riotous time. Perhaps she should have put William in charge of the entertainment. He might have been able to engineer Beatrice and James being squashed together in a wardrobe. That might be even more effective than James kissing her under the mistletoe.

That annoying gripping sensation in her chest returned, the one that felt decidedly like jealousy. But she would not be jealous, could not be jealous, and even if the green-eyed monster was trying to sink its fangs into her, she had to fight him off. This was not about her happiness. It was about Beatrice's. And even if she *was* becoming attracted to James—and what woman would not be?—it wasn't as if he would ever be attracted to someone like her.

Whereas her pretty, charming friend would be more than capable of attracting his attention.

She watched as Beatrice and William continued to laugh about the antics of the Vicar and her aunt. Her friend looked so pretty today, with her cheeks flushed from laughing and her eyes shining. These were exactly the right qualities to attract a man like James.

'So, no parlour games up at Thornwood Hall?' William said, turning his attention back to Alice. 'I thought that might be why you were blushing.'

Alice stared at her brother in disbelief. Most of the time he was oblivious to all that was going on around him. Why did he have to choose this particular time to suddenly become so observant?

'No, no parlour games,' she said, signalling to the maid she did want some tea after all, hoping it would provide a suitable distraction from her discomfort.

'Somehow I can't see James playing blind man's buff,' William added.

'Well, perhaps he is a bit serious, but he's got a lot of weight on his shoulders,' she said, feeling inexplicably defensive. 'Why, even today he was making notes of all the improvements he intends to do to the tenants' houses. I can see he is going to be an admirable earl and an asset to the community.'

William and Beatrice continued to stare at her, still with those matching expressions of curiosity.

Why they should be looking at her like that she had no idea. Everything she had said was true. And surely William should be mentioning all James's good qualities to increase Beatrice's interest, not focusing on his serious nature, which was not a fault at all.

'Did he explain how he got that limp and the scar?' William asked.

'The earl has a limp and a scar?' Beatrice repeated, tilting her head.

'He manages admirably with a walking stick, and

the scar hardly detracts from his good looks at all. In fact, I think it gives him a distinguished air,' she said.

'So did he tell you how he came by this distinguished scar and admirable injury?' William asked in a teasing voice. Although what he was teasing her about, she had no idea.

'I believe if James wants to share that with you, it is up to him,' she said, not wanting to gossip about something so personal and private.

'Quite right,' William said, turning back to Beatrice and their discussion about the antics that had occurred on Christmas Day.

Alice picked up her cup, put it to her lips, frowned, then replaced it in the saucer and tried to laugh along with her brother and friend.


The carriage pulled up in front of the house, and James entered Thornwood Hall. He stood in the echoing entranceway and the emptiness pressed down on him like a physical force.

This was what he wanted, wasn't it? Solitude. A place of retreat away from the demands and expectations of Society. Of course it was. And the silence would enable him to focus on the work ahead of him.

He handed his coat, hat and gloves to the waiting footman and told the man to summon the estate manager to his study.

'No, wait,' he called out to the man's retreating

back. 'It's Boxing Day. Let him continue to have the day off. I'll contact him tomorrow.'

'Very good, my lord,' the footman said. 'Shall I ask the maid to serve tea in the drawing room?'

James let out a low laugh, which caused the footman's eyebrows to raise slightly. 'No, I don't need any tea and tell Cook that sandwiches will do for my evening meal.'

'Very good, my lord.'

'And take the rest of the night off, and pass that on to any other servants still working.'

The footman bowed and departed.

James retreated into the drawing room. He would spend the evening compiling the list of repairs that needed to be made immediately to ensure the cottages were protected from the elements. Once the weather became more favourable, then a larger programme of improvements could be undertaken.

He also needed to discuss with the estate manager the equipment that could be bought to make farming practices more efficient. The ledgers showed clearly that neither his father nor his brother had bothered to invest in all the advances that were transforming farming. Anyone would think the steam age had never happened.

As Alice said, it was no wonder so many of the aristocracy were falling into poverty. Aristocrats like the Duke of Brimley. That was why they had to marry wealthy American heiresses to secure their financial future.

No doubt Clara's substantial dowry would be used to finance their lavish lifestyle rather than invested in the Duke's estate, and the problems of insolvency would merely be transferred down to the next generation. A generation that would have to repeat the process of searching the world for the daughters of wealthy self-made men who wanted to elevate their family's status through acquiring a title.

He huffed out his distain at this short-sighted thinking. That would not be his fate. He would not pass on a debt-ridden estate to his children.

James looked up from the documents spread around the table and stared out at the empty room in shock as if he'd uttered those words out loud.

His children? He had no intention of having children. To do so would require him to marry. That too would not be happening. He had wanted to marry Clara. He would not be stepping onto that perilous path again.

He looked back down at the lists and another astounding thought hit him. This was the first time Clara had entered his mind today.

Usually he was constantly aware that she was no longer in his life, and equally aware of the ache that had lodged itself permanently in his heart. He waited for that ache to return. It didn't. Instead, his thoughts turned to Alice, of her laughing, of her chatting to his servants and tenants as if they were old friends, of her surrounded by children who were so happy to see her again.

He had to admit, even if she was not his type, she was a remarkable woman. It was such a shame she had resigned herself to a life as a spinster. She would make a wonderful mother.

That arrogant lout Hogmore had a lot to answer for.

How could he possibly speak to any woman the way he had spoken to Alice, and in particular a woman who was in every way that buffoon's superior? The next time he had the misfortune to cross paths with Hogmore he would give him a piece of his mind.

He laughed to himself. Although Alice had already done that and it was clear she did not need any man fighting her battles for her.

But she deserved a man of a much higher calibre than Hogmore. Memories of that kiss entered his mind. In that fleeting moment he had glimpsed the passionate woman waiting to be set free. Even though it would never be him, he had to envy any man who could ignite that fire and make her burn with shared intensity.

He shook his head and looked back down at the papers scattered in front of him. What on earth was he doing? He should not even be thinking of Alice Lambton in that way. She was not for him, never would be, and was certainly not the sort of woman one toyed with.

She had chosen to be an unmarried woman, to dedicate herself to looking after her family and the wider community. She was an admirable spinster. That was all. And that was something he needed to remember at all times.

## Chapter Eleven

The evening of the New Year's Eve Ball finally arrived. The last week had dragged interminably, even though Alice had been busy with preparations for the ball, along with the other women in the village.

Now it was here and finally James and Beatrice would get to meet, provided William did nothing to thwart her plans yet again.

During the week she had tried to come up with a good reason why she and Beatrice could visit Thornwood Hall, but none presented itself, particularly as the weather did not cooperate. They could not use the excuse of being out for a walk when storm clouds were constantly looming overhead. And when the clouds weren't looming in a threatening manner, they were sending down sheets of rain, making walking an impossibility.

She had suggested on several occasions that Alice, William and Beatrice take a carriage ride over to visit James, but William was less than agreeable about that.

He kept pointing out, with infuriating regularity, how it was just as foolish to take the carriage out in such inclement weather as it was to go walking and reminded her of what happened the last time she had embarked on such a trip.

She knew he was right, but it was decidedly frustrating. Not just that it meant she had to wait almost a week before she could put Beatrice and James together, but also because it was always annoying to have to admit her brother was correct.

Now the evening of the ball was finally here and every nerve in Alice's body was fizzing with excitement and anticipation.

While her lady's maid dressed her hair, she stared at herself in the looking glass.

Tonight she would see James again.

She frowned at her reflection. No, tonight James and Beatrice would finally meet. That was what tonight was about. That was why she was so jittery.

Everything hinged on tonight's meeting being a success. Beatrice's very happiness depended on their hearts quickening when they first gazed at each other, for fate to embrace them and for it to be immediately apparent to them both that they were destined to marry.

And it had to happen that quickly. One whole week had passed; only one remained. No wonder she was such a bundle of nerves. 'Is the style not to your liking?' her lady's maid asked.

Alice realised she was still frowning, deeply. She forced herself to smile.

'No, it's lovely, Minnie.'

She patted the sides of her hair, which was styled slightly more ornately than she usually wore it but was still designed to be practical rather than decorative and attention seeking.

'Perhaps you could try that style with the little ringlets around the side of the face,' she said, making small circular motions around her ears.

Minnie smiled. 'Good idea, miss. That style will be so much more flattering on you.'

Alice smiled back as Minnie went to work with comb and curling tongs.

Not that she was being vain, Alice told herself. She merely wanted to make a special effort tonight. After all, the New Year's Eve Ball was one of the highlights of Ferndale's social calendar.

Her desire to look her best had nothing to do with wanting James to see her in something other than that drab brown dress she had been stuck wearing over Christmas. And a simple bun would never do for such an important occasion.

Minnie helped her into the pale pink ballgown she had selected for the evening. She'd worn it during the Season and was certain it was her most flattering.

As she stood in front of the full-length looking glass and surveyed her appearance, her mood deflated. It was the same gown she had worn on the evening Baron Hogmore had declared her the worst of a rum lot. If she couldn't impress a man like him, how could she possibly think she could impress anyone, especially James Marlowe?

She pulled back her drooping shoulders, stood up straight and reminded herself to stop being so foolish. Tonight was all about Beatrice and James. How she looked mattered not one little bit, which was good because Hogmore was right; she *was* the worst of a rum lot.

But Beatrice was not. She was everything that would attract a man like James. That was what Alice would focus on tonight, that and nothing else.

Thanking Minnie for her work, she walked downstairs to join her brother in the drawing room.

Beatrice and her aunt had already arrived and were chatting happily with William. Despondency gripped Alice once more as she looked at her friend and felt even frumpier than she had when observing herself in the looking glass.

Dressed in a stunning soft champagne-coloured gown, with pale pink lace around the neckline, her thick blonde hair piled high on her head, Beatrice was exactly what a debutante should be: young, fresh, pretty and demure.

How could James possibly not fall for a young woman who looked every inch a future countess?

Alice pushed away an inexplicable twinge of ridiculous jealousy and smiled at her friend.

She had no reason to be jealous. She had never been a vain woman, never compared herself to other women and certainly did not compete to be seen as the most attractive. What would be the point in taking part in a competition which you were destined to lose?

Despite the effort she had made, Alice knew that no man would have eyes for her when she was beside her beautiful friend, including James.

That was as it should be, she reminded herself as she crossed the room to kiss her friend's cheek, all the while ignoring the burning sensation in her stomach.

'You two ladies are sure to be the belles of the ball,' William declared, gazing admiringly at Beatrice but hardly looking at his sister.

That was high praise indeed and confirmation that Beatrice was looking magnificent, as her inattentive brother was usually oblivious to woman's fashions.

Alice said hello to Beatrice's aunt and noticed she was sipping on a rather generous glass of port.

She frowned at her brother. Was he trying to sabotage this evening? The last thing they wanted was for the aunt to get tipsy and have to leave early, taking her charge with her.

Her father, Widow Harcourt and the Vicar were

also sipping generous glasses of port, and their reddened cheeks suggested this was not their first glass.

'Oh, we've decided we'll just let you young people go off and enjoy yourself,' Beatrice's aunt said. 'Us oldies would prefer to stay here where it's nice and warm. William can chaperone you.'

The other *oldies* nodded their agreement and went back to whatever it was they were discussing before Alice had entered.

'Shall we?' William said, holding out both arms.

This was most irregular for Beatrice to not have a chaperone, but Alice supposed it did not matter and no impropriety was likely to happen at a ball where almost everyone knew everyone else.

Despite the short distance to the village hall they took their carriage, and wrapped themselves up warmly in hats, coats, scarves and gloves.

Soft light from the multitude of candles spilled out from the hall as they pulled up in front. William helped Alice and Beatrice down the carriage steps and onto the carpet that had been laid to protect the ladies' dancing slippers from the damp ground and snow.

They entered the ballroom and pride washed over Alice.

The simple village hall had been transformed, and it had all been thanks to her, the other local ladies and their servants. A chandelier suspended from the roof sent light twinkling over the guests below. Ferns, pots of winter roses, along with holly and ivy, decorated the room, and the dance floor had been polished to a high gloss. It was the epitome of an elegant Society ballroom.

In the corner a string quartet was tuning up and the room was filling up with members of the local gentry, all of whom were dressed in their finery. The room was alive with happy chatter as everyone circulated, greeted each other and wished each other the best for the coming New Year.

Alice beamed with pleasure, knowing that everything about tonight signalled the ball was going to be a great success. She was still smiling when the excited conversation faded and every head turned in the direction of the entrance. Alice followed their glances and saw James standing at the door, handing his hat and cloak to the servant, but retaining hold of his cane.

At the sight of him, her heart seemingly stopped beating, then it pounded back into life, pulsating so loudly she was sure it must be heard over the sound of the musicians tuning up.

He looked magnificent in his black swallow-tailed evening jacket and cream waistcoat, with his white shirt and tie contrasting with his olive complexion. The cut of his jacket appeared to accentuate his wide shoulders, but Alice alone knew that it was not the expertise of his tailor that gave him such a masculine appearance. Underneath, he was all hard muscles. She had felt them when he had taken her in his arms and kissed her.

She swallowed to try to relieve her dry throat and wished she had not thought of that kiss.

He looked around the room. His eyes locked onto hers and he walked towards her, his progress followed by everyone present.

At that moment she really could believe she was the belle of the ball and she had captured the attention of the most handsome and most eligible man in the room.

His gaze shifted to William. He nodded politely and reality came crashing down. She forced herself to breathe and scolded herself for harbouring such silly fantasies, even if just for a moment.

Of course he headed towards her. She and William were the only people in the room he knew.

He was not singling her out for attention. He did not hold her in special regard. He simply knew no one else in this room full of eager strangers.

'Miss Lambton,' he said with a formal bow.

'My lord,' she replied with equal formality, pleased her voice betrayed nothing of what she had been thinking.

He turned to William, who introduced him to Beatrice.

They politely greeted each other and Alice watched for that spark to ignite. She could see no evidence of it. Perhaps such things did not happen immediately.

As it had never happened to Alice, she had no way of knowing.

Hopefully James would ask Beatrice to dance and it would be at that moment their romance would begin. Or perhaps over supper. However it happened, it had to happen tonight as time was starting to run out.

And once it did happen, Alice would be able to forget all about that strange, unsettling reaction she'd had when first seeing him again.

As if drawn to the light, the locals were moving towards him, closer and closer. That was a problem. James would be expected to meet everyone present and would not be able to dedicate every moment to Beatrice.

'Allow me to introduce you to the other guests,' William said and led his friend off towards the expectant locals.

'He's rather handsome, isn't he?' Beatrice said.

'Yes,' Alice replied on a sigh, watching James as he chatted to the local squire, who was puffed up like a peacock, revelling in the attention of the local aristocrat.

Then she fully registered what Beatrice had said. There *was* an attraction, at least from Beatrice's side. This was good. Very good.

The band struck up a waltz for the first dance and the two men returned.

'Miss Beatrice, would you do me the honour?' William said, bowing in front of her friend.

Alice glared at him, a glare that William returned with a conspiratorial smile and a quick wink.

Hadn't she made it clear to William he was not to indulge in a passing flirtation with Beatrice? He'd promised, on his honour, he would do all in his power to save her from a loveless marriage. So what was he up to?

Then it dawned on Alice and she smiled back. William was not as feather-brained as she thought. Of course asking Beatrice to dance was a deliberate move. Men were by nature competitive. If James thought there was competition for Beatrice he would see her as a more desirable prize.

That had certainly happened at her Season, and had been another point in her disfavour. Once she had retreated to the wallflowers' corner, no man had seen her as worth having, so in the wallflowers' corner she remained.

She took back all her criticisms of her brother and sent him a silent thank-you for knowing better than her how to play a game at which she had never been successful.

'You look lovely tonight, Miss Lambton,' James said, pulling her attention away from her brother.

'What?' She stared at him, unsure she had heard correctly.

'I said you look lovely tonight.'

'Oh, yes, thank you,' she mumbled, aware that colour had exploded on her cheeks and certain it was not a pretty flush of pink, but unattractive blotches of red. She really had to get her nerves under control. Tonight was too important to be sidetracked by any silly attraction she shouldn't have for James.

'It is so good that you came tonight,' she continued, hoping she did at least *sound* completely in control. 'The local gentry will be delighted you made the effort and I do hope that you take the opportunity to dance with as many of the women present as possible.' *Especially Beatrice.*

Her voice not only sounded like she was completely in control, but had somehow tipped into absurdly stilted, as if she and James were meeting for the first time and had to make polite conversation.

'I believe my dancing days might be over,' he said, tapping his leg with his cane. 'But what of you, Miss Lambton? Do you intend to dance the night away?'

'Me?' She gave a forced laugh. 'No, I have far too much to do this evening.' She looked around the room for something that needed her immediate attention.

'It appears to me that the ball is running smoothly.'

'Hmm, well, yes, at the moment, I suppose, but, well… Anyway, I'm sure you should be dancing. The local ladies will expect the new earl to dance with them at least once, and no one's going to mind if you've…' She looked down at his cane.

'So, if you insist that I should dance, perhaps you will do me the honour,' he said, interrupting her embarrassed ramblings.

'What?' she all but squeaked. 'But you said your dancing days were over. Your knee, and all that,' she added, contradicting what she'd just said.

'If you promise to be gentle with me, I'm sure we will manage.'

The last thing Alice wanted right now was to be in James's arms. Maintaining her composure when they were merely standing together was hard enough. How was she going to cope when he was holding her close?

But she had no choice. To refuse would be beyond rude.

James handed his cane to a passing footman, took her hand and led her out onto the dance floor.

James *had* thought his dancing days were over. He had thought much of his life was over when he injured his knee and when Clara and he had parted. But it seemed he was wrong.

He placed his hand on Alice's waist and tried to tell himself he had asked her to dance because she was right; it was his duty to dance with as many of the women present as possible. He also tried to tell himself that dancing with Alice was a safe option, a chance to test his knee with someone who understood.

But neither of those reasons were the truth, and he knew it. He simply wanted to feel her in his arms one more time.

He placed one hand on her slim waist, took her hand in his and she tentatively placed the other on his shoulder, as if wary that she would get burned.

They moved off together in time to the music, and he was pleased to discover his knee gave him little pain. He was also delighted to discover that Alice was a gracious dancer, although that should not surprise him. When she walked it was always with admirable grace and elegance.

It was an absurd waste that she had not danced the night away during her Season. He was certain if men had seen her on the dance floor she would never have been relegated to the wallflowers' corner.

Now that they were dancing, he knew he was expected to make polite conversation, but what could he say? Something inane about the ballroom? He could mention the weather perhaps, ask how she had passed the last week, but he did not want to talk. He just wanted to enjoy this moment.

His hand slid slightly further around her slim waist. She followed his lead and moved slightly closer to him. Closer than propriety perhaps allowed, but who cared, not him. He wanted to feel her against him, just as he had when he'd kissed her under the mistletoe. The memory of that kiss had entered his mind more than he chose to admit over the last week.

He stared down into her grey eyes, sparkling in the candlelight, reminding him of the wings of a gentle dove catching the sunlight, or storm clouds brewing on the horizon, promising something wild and passionate.

And didn't that sum up the two sides of Alice Lambton? The soft, friendly, always smiling woman she presented to the world and the other Alice she kept hidden, the one he'd had tantalising glimpses of.

His gaze moved to her full lips, parted slightly. Soft lips that he had kissed. Lips that had kissed him back.

He had told her she looked lovely tonight, but that had been an understatement. She looked beautiful. It wasn't that she was in a ball gown rather than that plain brown dress. It wasn't that her hair was coiled and pinned in an elaborate manner, revealing the soft skin of her neck. There was something about her tonight that he could not name, something that made her so desirable she had captivated him the moment he walked into the room.

And he knew he wanted to do so much more than just gaze at her beauty. Once again his hand slid further around her waist pulling her in even closer, and once again she followed his lead, her body moulding into his. She was now so close he could almost feel her breasts against his chest.

His hand moved slightly lower down her back, feeling that sensuous part of a woman's body where the buttocks began to swell. She moved slightly closer, so close the tips of her breasts were lightly caressing his chest. He swallowed a groan. Surely that was an innocent gesture. She could not know the effect it was having on him.

He gazed down at her. The colour on her cheeks had bloomed brighter, the flush moving down her neck to her swelling décolletage. Was there ever a more intoxicating sight than the flush of a woman, particularly if it was the result of giving herself over to desire?

Her gaze held his. Her lips parted, her eyes became heavy lidded and a powerful surge of longing ripped through him. He wanted to see her surrendering herself entirely to her desires, to have her naked beneath him, her body ready for him, for him to unleash that passion he knew was simmering under the surface.

He almost stumbled, shocked at where his thoughts had taken him. He should not even think of her in that manner. To do so was unforgivable.

'I'm sorry, is your knee hurting you?' she asked, her voice full of concern.

If she knew how he had just been picturing her, what he had imagined doing to her, she would not be concerned for his well-being. She would be slapping him firmly across the face, as he deserved.

'Yes, perhaps we should stop dancing,' he said, although his reasons had nothing to do with his knee.

'Yes, of course. But if you'll excuse me, while you're resting, I think I will take some air.'

Before he had a chance to lead her off the floor, she all but raced across the room and out the doors at the end of the hall, leaving James feeling ashamed of all he had done and even more ashamed of what he had thought of doing.

## Chapter Twelve

The cold air hit Alice's cheeks like a slap, a slap she needed to shock her out of the bizarre state into which she had tumbled.

If it wasn't so humiliating it would be funny. When they'd been dancing together she had, for one absurd moment, thought he was attracted to her. When he'd looked down at her she had fantasised she was seeing longing in those dark, intense brown eyes.

Longing for her? James Marlowe, the ninth Earl of Thornwood, attracted to her? Plain Alice Lambton, the renowned wallflower whom men ridiculed? It was absurd, not to mention embarrassing, that she could think such a thing.

Thank goodness no one, especially James, could read her thoughts. She could only hope that he hadn't noticed her going all giddy and starry-eyed, or worse than that, registered the way her body had been drawn towards him, desperate to feel his touch. She really was a joke.

She gulped in a few gasps of the cold, crisp air, attempted to regain a modicum of her dignity and bring herself back some semblance of sanity.

She had known dancing with James would be a risk to her composure; she just hadn't realised quite how much. The moment his hands had touched her she had been lost. She had lost her mind and all but lost any connection with reality.

Somehow she would have to face him again and pretend that nothing out of the ordinary had happened on the dance floor. She would have to pretend they had merely shared a waltz, just like all the other couples, just as he should have been doing with Beatrice.

Alice closed her eyes and emitted a small groan. She'd forgotten all about her friend while she had been in James's arms. All she'd thought about was how he made her feel, how she wanted this dance to continue forever and how she wanted him to lean down and kiss her one more time.

She had to be the worst friend in the world, and the most foolish woman that had ever existed.

She'd like to be able to blame William for what had happened. If he hadn't rushed in and asked Beatrice to dance none of this would have happened. Right now James would be flirting with Beatrice, and Alice would be watching on, pleased at a job well done.

But William was not to blame. She was.

She placed her gloved hands on the terrace railing

and looked out at the winter night, at the snow lying on the ground, at the silver frost glinting on the garden wall, and wondered whether she should just walk off into the cold night never to be seen again.

Or perhaps, more sensibly, go home and put an end to this unfortunate night. If she did, then she would never have to face James again, or at least not for some time, and by then she might have forgotten all about what a fool she had made of herself.

She released another groan of despair. Even someone as deluded as her knew that would never happen. She was never going to forget the thrilling way her body responded when he held her, and if she didn't return to the ballroom soon, William was sure to notice. He would worry. He might even enlist James so they could search for her. That would only add to this evening's humiliation and would once again take James away from Beatrice.

She had to go back inside. She had to face the music. But not just yet. She exhaled loudly in frustration, her breath turning white in the cool air.

Despite the freezing conditions, her cheeks were still burning. Until she had completely calmed down she would stay exactly where she was.

She gave a small laugh at her predicament. By the time she achieved the all but impossible task of calming down from her mortifying encounter she would probably have turned into an ice statue.

'Alice, is everything all right?'

At the sound of James's voice Alice's heart stopped. Her breath caught in her throat. It was as if she really had turned into a statue.

She drew in one slow, deep, steadying breath, forced herself to smile, then turned around to face him.

'Oh, yes, everything is quite all right. I was just a bit warm and needed some air. It's so stuffy inside. Don't you think? We really must do something about that before the next ball. I'm sure I'm not the only one finding it stiflingly hot.'

She knew she was prattling, and her jaw was aching from holding her large, fake smile, but what else could she do?

'I'll be back inside as soon as I cool down,' she added, fanning herself and ignoring the fact that she was standing outside during a midwinter frost.

He moved forward and stood beside her.

'It's freezing out here.'

'No, not really,' she said, trying to stop herself from shivering.

'And you're not exactly dressed for the weather in that flimsy gown. If you're going to stay any longer, you'll need to keep warm.'

To her horror he took off his jacket and draped it around her shoulders. This was the last thing she needed. The jacket was still warm from his body. The heat wrapped itself around her, along with his masculine scent of leather and sandalwood, and the hint of his citrus cologne.

'Now you're going to freeze,' she said.

'I'm sure I'll cope.'

She snuggled into the warm jacket. It was as if his arms were wrapped around her, holding her tight. She was being ridiculous, just as she had been on the dance floor, but it felt good, so good.

'I hope it was nothing I did or said that caused you to leave the ballroom so suddenly.'

'What? No, of course not. That's preposterous,' she said and attempted to laugh it off.

What else could she say? And she *was* telling the truth. Nothing he did or said had caused her to leave. But he was most certainly the reason why she had to flee.

She had escaped in a vain attempt to forget all about how much she loved being in his arms. Now he was standing beside her. She was wearing his clothes, inhaling his scent, feeling the warmth of his body seeping into her skin.

If he wanted to torture her, he could not have picked a better method.

'No, I just wanted a bit of fresh air. But that does not mean you have to stay out here.' She shrugged off his jacket and handed it to him.

He took hold of his jacket and placed it back on her shoulders. 'I'm not going anywhere until I know that you are back inside, in the warm and enjoying yourself.'

Damn, why did he have to be such a gentleman? Why couldn't he just leave her to freeze in peace?

'You should go back inside and dance with the other ladies,' she said. 'I'm sure they are all hoping to dance with the new earl and will be terribly disappointed if you don't return to the ballroom soon.'

'Then let them be disappointed.'

Damn again. Why couldn't he just leave her to nurse her mortification all alone?'

'I hope you realise the longer we stay out here together, the more tongues are going to wag,' he said, presumably thinking that would send her scuttling back inside.

'I doubt if anyone even noticed I had left,' she said, something that was a statement of fact, not a display of self-pity.

'I noticed,' he said quietly.

*Read nothing into that.*

Of course he noticed. She had been dancing with him when she had rushed off out the ballroom like a frightened rabbit to take sanctuary on this terrace. Or what had been a sanctuary until he invaded it.

'And unfortunately, whether other people noticed your departure or not, they are sure to have noticed the new earl is no longer in the ballroom,' he continued. 'If we remain out here for too long, or indeed, if we return to the ballroom together, then people are going to speculate on what we were doing during the time we were absent. Alone together.'

Alice's hand covered her mouth. He was right. Everyone would have noticed James leaving the ballroom. No one was likely to miss anything he did tonight, including dancing with her.

'If we stay out here much longer, your health will not be the only thing you put in danger. You will also be risking your reputation.'

He was right again. Not about the damage it might cause her reputation. She cared nothing of that. But they could not be seen returning to the ballroom together. It would ruin James's reputation. If he was seen as a rake who trifled with other women then Beatrice's father would never countenance such a marriage, even if it was with a titled man.

Alice would have ruined everything.

'Well, you go back inside and tell everyone that I have gone home,' she said, panic starting to well up inside her as she desperately thought of a way out of this situation.

'I'll do no such thing. You organised this ball. You should be inside enjoying yourself, dancing the night away. If anyone should leave it is me.'

'No, you can't do that,' she said, placing her hand on his chest then quickly withdrawing it as if it had scorched her fingers. He could not leave. He still had to dance with Beatrice. He still had to fall in love with her.

'You can't leave. It would be such a disappointment to everyone present tonight if you disappeared early.'

'Then it appears we are at an impasse and will have to stay here until we both freeze to death.'

She laughed at the absurdity of their situation and the absurdity of herself for getting them into it. She'd been trying to get away from James and now they were stuck together with no acceptable way out of their predicament.

They both looked out at the frozen landscape. But he was right. They could not stay here indefinitely. Even with his warm jacket wrapped around her she was starting to shiver, and he must be chilled to the bone.

'There's only one thing for it,' she said, determined to take action and solve this dilemma. 'I'll walk round to the front of the hall and go in through the main entrance. You wait here for a few minutes then you can enter through this door,' she said, pointing over her shoulder. 'And no one will realise that we spent a scandalous amount of time alone together.'

'It's a good plan, but there is one major flaw.'

Alice could see no flaw in her plan. But then she had seen no flaw in her plan to marry off James and Beatrice, and yet flaw after flaw kept presenting itself.

James pointed down at her feet. 'You cannot possibly walk through snow in those flimsy dance slippers. Not only will you destroy them but you'll probably end up with frostbite.'

Alice suspected it was worth it if it got them out of this predicament.

'It appears there is only one way round that problem,' he said.

Before Alice had a chance to register what was happening, he reached down and scooped her up into his arms.

'What on earth are you doing?' she cried out, her heart pounding furiously in her chest, her cheeks all but exploding with heat, despite the frigid weather.

'I'll carry you around to the front door. That way you can enter looking entirely presentable, your slippers untouched, and no telltale signs of snow on the bottom of your gown.'

Entirely presentable? There was no possibility of that. Flustered, flushed and breathless would be more apt descriptions. How was she possibly going to appear otherwise, when his arms were encasing her, when she was pressed up against his chest and his arm was under her derriere?

'But what about your knee?'

'Let me worry about my knee,' he said, stepping off the balcony into several inches of snow.

'But people are going to wonder why you have snow on your boots and the bottom of your trousers,' she said, as much as to distract herself from the touch of his hard chest and his muscular arms around her as to any concern about his attire.

'I can say that I needed some air and went for a walk. It might cause people to talk about my odd behaviour, but that will be nothing compared to what they might say if they knew we had disappeared from the ballroom together.'

*Or what they might say if they knew you had carried me, while I was wearing an item of your clothing.* Anyone seeing this would think it was a romantic encounter, not a solution to a problem Alice had created.

He trudged through the snow around the edge of the building, effortlessly carrying her as if she was weightless in his arms.

She knew his actions were just a sensible way out of a difficult situation, and that it meant nothing. At least her mind knew that. Her body was interpreting his behaviour in quite a different manner. Her heart was beating so loudly, she was sure he must be able to hear it. Blood was pulsating through her body and there was no danger of her freezing in the cold weather when she was burning as she had her own inner furnace.

Just as she had snuggled into his jacket, she snuggled into his arms and rested her head on his shoulder. She could feel his heart beating against her, strong and steady, just like him. She closed her eyes, savouring his warmth and letting his intoxicating masculine scent surround her.

It was unsettling, it was unnerving, but oh, it was also so glorious. Never before had she felt so feminine, so vulnerable, as if she had given herself over to him, for him to do with her as he wished. And what she wished he would do was take the opportunity to kiss her again.

Far too soon they arrived at the front door. He gently lowered her to her feet. Was it her fevered imagination or did he deliberately slide her down his body. Deliberate or otherwise, her breasts moved along his chest. Her nipples tightened against the soft fabric of her gown, and she had to fight the temptation to sigh as desire coiled within her.

She glanced up at him. He stared back down at her, his face partly shadowed in the soft light of the pale winter moon. She waited, her breath held, and hoped and prayed he would do what she so desperately wanted: kiss her one more time before they parted.

The sound of people behind the door burst into her reckless fantasies, alerting her to her present circumstances, and she quickly stepped backwards.

To be found together at the front door would be just as bad, if not worse, than being discovered on the terrace. To be seen in each other's arms would be devastating.

She had to think of his reputation. She had to think of Beatrice.

James slipped his jacket off her shoulders. 'Go inside now, Alice, before you get cold.'

She had no option but to do as he commanded. What excuse could she give for remaining? None. So without saying a word, lest her voice betray her, she slipped back into the ballroom.

The moment she entered the warm, noisy room, she exhaled her held breath and leaned against the wall, trying to still her rapidly pounding heart.

She had been right that no one had noticed her departure. No one, that was, except William, who was watching her from across the room, a look of concern on his face.

If William asked about her absence she would tell him she was merely consulting with the servants about something; the supper preparations, the need for more punch, the replacement of burned-out candles, something, anything.

But she could not stay here for the rest of the ball, pinned to the wall, just as she could not have remained out on the terrace. There was nowhere she could escape to, so she would have to do what she always did in awkward situations: keep smiling and stay busy.

With that in mind, she plastered on her sunniest smile and walked towards the supper table, determined to find something with which to occupy herself.

* * *

The moment James had seen Alice safely inside the ballroom, he strode around the side of the hall. Once out of sight of the entrance, he stopped, leaned against the wall and closed his eyes.

What the hell was wrong with him?

He'd gone out onto the terrace to find Alice, to make sure she was alright, and with the intention of apologising or in some other way making amends for his inappropriate behaviour on the dance floor.

Instead he had behaved in a far more inappropriate, far less forgivable manner.

Surely he could have found some other way of avoiding being discovered outside together, one that did not involve lifting her up into his arms and carrying her away like a pirate kidnapping an innocent maiden?

Thank goodness for the cold night air. It was enough to temper even the most fervent ardour. Without it, his reaction to having her in his arms, her body against his, his hand far too close to an intimate area, would be inexcusable.

But that encounter did remove all doubt in his mind. The way he felt on the dance floor was no aberration. He was attracted to Alice Lambton. The question now was, what did he do about it?

He knew what he wanted to do. Keep walking back to Thornwood Hall, back to his refuge from the world, but he could not do that. Apart from it being the action of a coward, there were people inside expecting to spend time with the new Earl of Thornwood. He had duties to perform. He was not his brother. He would not shrink from what was expected of him for selfish reasons.

Although in the case of his brother, those selfish reasons involved wine, women and song. In James's case it would involve trying to avoid a woman.

He gave a low, empty laugh at his predicament. He had hoped burying himself in this remote part of England would help him recover from one woman; now he had become entangled with another.

But any feelings he had for Alice had to be put aside. He would not go down that path again. He had let his guard down once. He was not about to let history repeat itself.

The only women he would be involved with from now on were those who enjoyed uncomplicated relationships that went no further than fun in the bedroom. That was not Alice Lambton.

He drew in a deep breath, peeled himself off the wall, walked around the edge of the village hall and picked up his abandoned cane, then re-entered the ballroom. As expected, the majority of those present looked in his direction. A few cast glances down to the cuffs of his trousers, sodden from the snow, but he suspected none would be so bold as to ask an earl to explain himself.

He looked around for Alice and saw her talking to a footman beside the supper table. He'd prefer to see her dancing, but at least she was inside. They could now commence ignoring each other for the rest of the evening.

William appeared at his side with a sweet young woman on his arm. Beatrice Chigwell, that was her name. She was the one that Alice had tried to convince him would make an excellent countess.

'What on earth happened to you?' William asked. The other guests might be too polite or too reserved to ask an earl to explain himself, but it seemed his childhood friend was not.

'I needed some air, and I'm afraid I stepped off the terrace and into a drift of snow,' he said, looking down at his damp trousers and scuffed shoes, and hoping that excuse would suffice.

'Right,' William said, stretching out that word as if he did not entirely believe his friend. Or was James's guilt making him see accusations where none existed.

'Miss Chigwell, would you do me the honour of the next dance?' he said to the young lady on William's arm before his friend could ask any more uncomfortable questions.

She sent him a polite smile, curtsied, released William's arm and took his.

'While you two are dancing I'll go and find my sister. I'm curious to know whether she too felt the need to throw herself into a snowdrift.'

With that, William departed and walked across the room.

James wanted to follow him and explain that none of this was Alice's fault. But with Miss Chigwell on his arm, he was in no position to do so. Nor could he think of any credible explanation as to their joint absence. He could only hope William did or said nothing to make Alice uncomfortable or would raise any question about her unblemished reputation.

'My lord, I think the dance is about to begin,' Miss Chigwell said, so he led her onto the floor.

They lined up for the quadrille, and James made the requisite polite conversation with his partner, but his gaze never left William and Alice. If William was displeased with his sister, it was not apparent in his actions. Instead of admonishing her, he removed a plate of food from her hands which she was about to place on the supper table, a job that surely one of the servants could have done, took her arm and led her onto the dance floor.

Good, she should be dancing, just not with him. They walked in his direction.

This was not good. William was leading his sister towards them, with the intention of making up the fourth pair for the quadrille.

James rebuked himself for his foolishness. He was being absurd. It was a quadrille, not the waltz. There would be no contact more intimate than a light touch of the hand, or perhaps a guiding hand on the small of the back. And he was not such a depraved lech that he would react to such innocent contact.

The music started, the couples stepped forward and circled each other and once again James was struck by Alice's grace and elegance. She was such a beautiful dancer, one who moved with poise and fluidity, gliding across the floor in total harmony with the music.

And once again he could not believe buffoons like Hogmore would ever disparage her. If that fool had seen her on the dance floor he would have appreciated that she was exquisite, and James was certain she would not have spent her Season sitting beside the potted ferns, as she had jokingly described it.

He released his partner's hand and stepped forward to take Alice's. His eyes locked onto her. Raw desire shot through him, its intensity taking his breath away. This was unlike anything he had experienced before. Even Clara, who he had considered the most beautiful woman he had ever seen, had never affected him to this extent.

He wanted Alice. He wanted to explore her body. To kiss, caress and taste every inch of her. To make love to her and ignite the fire he knew was smouldering inside her. He wanted to make her burn.

He released her hand and stepped back, as the dance required, closed his eyes and breathed slowly and deeply, as if forcing himself to shake off the effects of a potent, intoxicating drug.

This would not do. It would not do at all. He had been right when he told himself he must have nothing to do with Alice Lambton. The way he was thinking of her was wrong, so wrong.

For the rest of the torturous dance he avoided looking at her. When her hand was in his, he controlled his thoughts, concentrated on anything other than the warmth of her touch or her beguiling feminine scent.

Finally, not a moment too soon, the dance came to an end and he escorted Miss Chigwell off the floor.

Rather than join Alice, William and Miss Chigwell as they chatted on the edge of the dance floor, he turned to the nearest woman and asked her for the next dance.

It was Mrs Stratford, the woman Alice had told him he must compliment, but not within the hearing of Mrs Crawford.

He stifled a smile and gave a quick look around. Mrs Crawford was not within hearing distance.

'Mrs Stratford, you are quite the belle of the ball tonight, and you must be the envy of every woman present.'

Mrs Stratford preened like a young lady and sent a withering look in Mrs Crawford's direction, proving Alice was right, and he made a mental note to dance with Mrs Crawford before the night was over. It would not do to cause any ructions within the local community.

For the remainder of the evening, he did what Alice had asked him to do: he danced with as many of the ladies present as time allowed. He even had a second dance with her friend Miss Chigwell and made the effort to engage her in polite conversation.

He could say he was doing his duty and making the acquaintance of members of the local community. He could even pretend he was doing it to make Alice happy. There was some truth in both these claims, but they would be half truths.

As long as he was occupied he could try to dismiss the way Alice affected him and avoid any further unfortunate incidents where he was gripped by his baser instincts.

He was pleased to note that she too danced with numerous partners, and chatted amicably with each one, as if they were old friends, which he assumed they would be. She was just the type to befriend everyone she met, from the lowest servant to those with the highest title, and everyone in between.

Finally, the ball came to an end and James was grateful that he could say his goodbyes. With much jubilation, everyone poured out into the night air, chatting and laughing loudly, and made their way to their waiting carriages, including Alice and her friend, who were escorted by William.

James watched them drive away and climbed into his own carriage. It was over. He had survived. Now he could put everything that had happened tonight behind him.

## Chapter Thirteen

'A dinner party? Tonight?' Alice stared at her smiling brother, certain that he had gone completely mad. 'I can't possibly organise a dinner party for tonight. I've only just finished organising the ball. You should have given me more notice.'

'Don't worry, Ali. It's all been organised.'

'By whom?'

'Me,' he said, as if that would provide Alice with even the slightest bit of reassurance. 'Well, me and Beatrice.'

That helped somewhat, but Alice still had her doubts about her brother's plan.

'Do you know how much goes into organising a dinner party?'

How could he? He'd never organised a dinner party in his life.

'The invitations have been sent out. Everyone's accepted. You and Cook ordered in so much food and wine for the holiday season there's enough to get us through till next Christmas, so there's plenty in store for tonight's party. I informed Cook of my intentions and she was delighted with the idea, especially when I said I'd leave the menu up to her.'

'Invitations? Who have you invited?'

'You.'

She all but rolled her eyes. 'Yes, I assumed I'd been invited, even if you did wait until the day of the event to tell me. Who else?'

'Father, of course, who thought the whole thing a grand idea.'

This time Alice did roll her eyes. Father had even less awareness of what went into arranging a dinner party than William had.

'Beatrice, her aunt, Widow Harcourt, the Vicar, and James. All the people who came to Christmas dinner, along with the two absentees.'

'I see,' Alice said, trying to take in what this meant. Two things immediately jumped to mind. One, she would be spending another evening with James, which elicited all that now-familiar tangle of emotions. Two, Beatrice would also be spending the evening with James, which was what Alice wanted, even if that too elicited a wide range of unsettling emotions she had to fight to not acknowledge.

'Beatrice and I decided it was a shame you missed out on Christmas dinner here at Rosetree Manor,' William continued. 'So we decided to re-stage it for you.'

'That's very kind of you,' Alice said, her hesitant voice not disguising her uncertainty.

'I also wanted to prove to you that I can be a responsible brother, despite what you might think. And I intend to continue in that vein and show you there is none more responsible than I.'

Alice stared at her decidedly jolly brother. He was always in good spirits but this evening he seemed even more so, as if organising a small dinner party was the most fun he'd had in a long time.

'I suppose it will help with my plans for Beatrice's future marriage,' Alice thought out loud.

'Exactly,' William declared. 'As I said, I'm becoming so much more responsible. Now, off you go, sister dear. All that is required of you with regards to preparation for tonight's festivities is to go upstairs, change into your favourite gown, do whatever it is you do to your hair, then enjoy yourself.'

Alice looked around, certain there must be something she was expected to do, some emergency that only she could deal with, something William had overlooked.

'Off you go,' he said, putting his hands on her shoulders and turning her towards the door. 'The guests will be arriving soon. You don't want to be tardy, do you?'

Reluctantly following his instructions, Alice headed upstairs and called for her lady's maid. When Minnie arrived it was apparent she was aware of the party, even if Alice hadn't been, as she came armed with warmed curling tongs and Alice's dove-grey gown draped over her arm, the one she had intended to wear on Christmas Day.

'Shall we style your hair in the same way we did for the New Year's Ball?' Minnie said, tongs at the ready.

'Yes, I suppose,' Alice said, still trying to come to terms with the idea of a party being held at her house where nothing was required of her. She sat down on the embroidered bench in front of her dressing table while Minnie set to work. This was such a novelty, and Alice was not sure if it was a pleasant one.

She liked being busy. When guests were coming, she would usually rush through her dressing so she could hurry back downstairs and oversee all that was happening in the kitchen to ensure everything ran smoothly. Then she would inspect the drawing room and dining room, checking every detail to make certain all was as it should be

She rather wished she was doing that now. It would stop her thoughts from straying to places she'd rather they did not go. Constant activity would take her mind off the thought of seeing James again, and the possibility that after tonight he might be courting Beatrice.

But that would be a good thing. She rebuked herself for harbouring even the hint of a thought that it could be otherwise. James had already shown some interest in Beatrice. He had danced with her twice at the ball; that was a good sign.

Maybe that was why William and Beatrice had decided to host tonight's dinner party. It was not because they wanted to have the Christmas dinner that Alice and James had missed out on. It was so Beatrice and James could get together again, and they could give him the push needed to begin his courtship.

William was right. He really was becoming much more responsible and she should give him some credit. He had finally come to the realisation that it was important for Beatrice to marry, and could see the virtue in Alice's plan to make her the next Countess of Thornwood.

That was all for the best. She just wished she could be happier about the prospect. She knew she was being ridiculous. Nothing would change for her.

Since the end of her first Season, Alice had known she would not marry. So what if she found James attractive? It mattered not. Nor was it of any import that she adored so much about him. That, she supposed, was inevitable. How could any woman who met him not fall immediately under his spell? Just as it seemed Beatrice had done. It was just something Alice would have to cope with.

If Beatrice was already developing feelings for James, it was rather surprising she had not told Alice, but then, neither had Alice told Beatrice much either.

Although that was more understandable as the way Alice was feeling should surely be listed among the things best kept to oneself.

'Miss, I'm finished,' Minnie said, standing back and admiring her work.

Alice looked at her reflection in the looking glass and realised she had completely drifted off.

'That looks lovely. Thank you.'

Minnie had done the best she could with what was available and had turned Alice's usually straight, somewhat limp hair into a voluminous chignon adorned with decorative combs. It did look lovely, but Alice was under no illusions. Minnie could curl, plait and backcomb her hair until the end of days, and still not turn Alice into the type of woman who could attract a man like James. Not that it mattered. She didn't want to attract a man like James, not when he had to marry her friend.

Minnie helped her into her corset, chemise and gown, and once she was dressed Alice descended the stairs to the drawing room, where Beatrice and her aunt were already waiting. Lady Chigwell was chatting to her father, and Alice was vexed to see William had poured her a generous glass of port. Did he want to get the woman tipsy again? Was that his definition of behaving responsibly?

She greeted the aunt then turned her attention to Beatrice, who looked radiant tonight. There was no other word for it. She appeared to be glowing with an internal light and Alice doubted she had ever seen her friend look happier. The prospect of becoming the next Countess of Thornwood was obviously delighting her, and looking the way she did tonight Alice could not see how James could possibly resist her.

'I hope you don't mind William and I taking it upon ourselves to organise tonight's dinner without consulting you,' Beatrice said, taking Alice's arm and leading her towards the settee across the room. 'We wanted it to be a surprise and didn't want to put you to any effort.'

Alice smiled, not wishing to put a damper on her friend's happiness, but being put to an effort was what Alice lived for. It was her role in life; without that, what was there?

The footman opened the door to announce another guest. The temperature in the room appeared to shoot up several degrees and the lack of air suddenly made breathing more difficult.

Alice stared at the door, her body tense.

Widow Harcourt entered with much bustling of skirts, followed by the Vicar, who greeted everyone in his usual jovial manner.

Alice's heartbeat settled down. She released her held breath and resolved to have a word with the footman and ask him not to put quite so much wood on the fire.

Widow Harcourt and the Vicar joined Lady Chigwell and her father beside the fire and were soon involved in an animated conversation. Alice tried to focus on what Beatrice was saying, something about the New Year's Ball, but her attention kept straying to the door, waiting for the last remaining guest to arrive.

Perhaps he wouldn't come. He'd turned down the invitation to dine at Rosetree Manor in the past; perhaps he would again tonight. That would be a disappointment, but it would be so much easier on Alice's nerves. She relaxed into the settee, feeling comforted by this prospect.

But hadn't William said all the invitations had been accepted?

Her nerves fizzed back into life and she sat up straighter. She'd like to think her anxiety was for Beatrice's sake, that she was a bundle of nerves because so much rested on deepening the romantic attachment that had sparked between Beatrice and James at the New Year's Ball. But she knew that was not true. She was simply anxious about being in the company of the man she had been thinking about constantly for the last two days. She would see the man who had carried her in his arms, who had kissed her under the mistletoe, who had caused her body to feel things she had hitherto not known it was possible to feel.

The footman opened the door again and Alice froze, almost as surely as she had done when they were alone on the terrace, while incongruously, her temperature also shot up.

James entered the room, looking sublimely handsome in his black evening suit, and those brown eyes looked straight at her. Her body reacted, just as it had when he kissed her, as if every nerve end was alive. She tried to look away but couldn't. It was as if she was imprisoned by his gaze.

William proved to be her unintentional rescuer, approaching James, warmly greeting him and drawing his full attention. This was followed by everyone else in the room calling out their greetings, although Alice's was a muted response made with a strained smile.

*Focus, Alice, focus. Forget all about yourself— focus on making sure Beatrice shines in James's eyes.*

With that in mind, she turned to her friend and could see she too was looking in James's direction and the smile on her face was easy to interpret.

She was bedazzled by the Earl, just as surely as Alice was. At least half the battle had been won. Alice just had to ensure that by the end of this evening, James felt the same way about Beatrice.

And to do that she had to stop being so self-centred. She had to stop caring about her own feelings and put all her energies into the happiness of her friend. Too much depended on Beatrice finding a husband her father would approve of.

And that started now. Drawing in a strengthening breath, she turned to Beatrice.

'Shall we join the men?' she said.

'Oh, yes, let's,' Beatrice responded enthusiastically, standing up and offering her arm for Alice to take.

Arm and arm they strolled across the drawing room. James and William's conversation came to a halt and the two men watched them walk in their direction.

Under James's gaze, Alice became ridiculously aware of her body, of the way her hips swayed as she walked, of the rise and fall of her chest as she gasped in quick breaths, of the softness of the silk fabric of her gown stroking her stockinged legs.

After what seemed like an interminable walk they reached the men. James bowed to them both and everyone exchanged greetings, while Alice racked her brain for something she could say about Beatrice that would pique James's interest.

'Beatrice was just saying how much she'd love to see Thornwood Hall while she is visiting the area,' Alice said.

Beatrice sent her a quick, questioning look before politeness took over and she smiled at James. 'William tells me it is a magnificent house with a wonderful garden.'

'Then you and your aunt must visit before you return home.'

That was good. Very good. Alice should have

thought of that before. Put the two of them together at Thornwood Hall, with only the aunt as a chaperone, and maybe give the aunt a nice glass of port to occupy her, just as William kept doing, while James and Beatrice got to know each other.

'And William also said that you two have been friends since childhood,' Beatrice continued. 'I believe we must have met on some occasion when I was visiting Ferndale, but I confess I don't remember.' She laughed and looked at William. 'Although I do remember William teasing me when I got upset over some tadpoles the two of you caught.'

William laughed. 'You were such a crybaby.'

'Well, I wasn't much more than a baby,' Beatrice said, joining his laughter.

'You said they would miss their mothers,' William added. 'Tadpoles do not miss their mother.'

'How do you know? Are you an expert on tadpoles?'

While they were laughing at something that was surely not that funny, Alice and James watched on. This was not going as well as Alice would have liked. Beatrice should be laughing with James, not with her brother, but perhaps this was how Beatrice dealt with nerves, which she surely must be feeling in James's presence. Alice knew all about distracting oneself when nervous. Right now, she wished she could be organising something, anything, but it would be an insult to William and Beatrice if she tried to take over the management of the dinner party. And unfortunately nothing appeared to need doing anyway.

The footman entered and informed William that dinner was served.

William thanked the man and turned to the guests.

'Before we go into dine I have an announcement to make,' he said in a loud voice, cutting through the chatter, then looked at Beatrice. 'Or should I say, we have an announcement to make.'

Beatrice moved to William's side and the two of them smiled at the assembled guests.

Alice looked on with apprehension. What on earth was her brother up to now? William had said he was becoming responsible. She should have known better. This did not bode well for her matchmaking. Alice braced herself, hoping whatever he was about to do or say did not ruin Beatrice's chances with James.

'I would like to share with you that this beautiful, wonderful, enchanting woman has agreed to marry this humble, unworthy man.'

Beatrice laughed and put her arm through William's.

Alice stared at them in disbelief. What on earth did William think he was doing? Beatrice's father would never agree to such a marriage, and now he had ruined any chance of her marrying James.

'We already have Lady Chigwell's blessing,' William added, raising his glass to Beatrice's aunt, who raised her own glass in response before taking another sip. 'I have written to Beatrice's father, and as soon as we have his blessing, we can begin making plans for our wedding.'

With that he took Beatrice's hand and kissed the back. She giggled in response like a delighted school-girl.

The older people cheered, James congratulated his friend and shook his hand, while Alice stood star-ing at them in a state of bewilderment, trying to take in the ramifications of this change in circumstances.

'But Beatrice's father already had someone in mind for her to marry,' Alice said, shaking her head and certain she was the only one in the room who was forgetting the facts of the matter. 'He will never give his consent.'

Surely her brother could see that. While Beatrice's father was sure to give his blessing to a match with an earl, would he do so for a barrister? Alice doubted it.

'I hope we do get his consent, but if we don't, well, Gretna Green is just over the border,' William said, causing Beatrice to giggle again and the other ladies in the room to sigh.

'You'd elope?' Alice said, completely aghast at the prospect

'I'd do anything if it meant that Beatrice would be

my wife,' William said, causing another gush of sighing from the ladies.

'I hope you don't have to do that,' the Vicar said with a laugh. 'I wouldn't want you young people putting me out of a job.'

This was greeted with much laughter from everyone except Alice, who was still trying to grapple with this unexpected announcement.

'Now I believe we should go through to the dining room,' William continued. 'My sister would never forgive me if I let the food go cold.'

William took Beatrice's arm to lead her down the hallway to the dining room, James took Alice's, and her father took Widow Harcourt's, and they were followed by Lady Chigwell on the arm of the Vicar, everyone chatting happily about this news. Everyone, that was, except a stunned Alice.

'Can I assume from your reaction that you knew nothing of this?' James asked her.

'Yes, that would be a correct assumption.'

'And can I also assume that you are not happy?'

Alice stared at him. 'No, yes, no, of course I'm happy.'

Alice was unsure why she was not ecstatic. This was the best possible outcome. Beatrice was saved. William would have the ideal wife, and she would acquire a sister-in-law. She had every reason to be delighted.

The only flaw in what was an excellent if unexpected turn of events was how did that leave her and James? Well, she knew how it left them: exactly where they were, where they had always been. Nowhere.

But where did it leave her?

All those feelings she had been trying to suppress, all that attraction she had been fighting to deny, were churning just under the surface wanting to be released. It was so much easier when she had her friend's future happiness to concentrate on. Now all she had to focus on was her own turbulent emotions, and she didn't even have a dinner party to manage.

They took their seats. The sound of cheerful chatter surrounded her.

'So how long have you been...?' Alice asked William, not sure how to finish that sentence.

'The moment I saw her on Christmas Day I knew she was the one,' William said, looking at Beatrice with what could only be described as misty eyes. 'As soon as she walked through the door I was smitten. Hopelessly lost.'

Beatrice gazed back into his eyes and smiled, the sweetest smile Alice had ever seen. How had she possibly missed this? They were in love. They looked so different, as if they were glowing from an internal light. That was why her friend looked so radiantly beautiful tonight.

This truly was wonderful. Alice's confusion died

and she smiled at them, a genuine smile full of warmth for two of the people she loved the most in the world. Two people who were now ecstatically happy.

The Vicar asked a question and drew William's attention, and Beatrice turned to Alice. 'It's rather funny really, isn't it?' she said quietly. 'William told me you were hoping to match me up with the Earl and were annoyed with him for not making him come to Christmas dinner. He said that was why you went over to visit the earl and then got stuck in that sudden snowstorm. In doing so you left me alone with William, and I discovered what a wonderful man he is and we had room for our love to blossom. It all worked out for the best, even if it wasn't in the way you expected.'

'Yes, it did,' Alice agreed, casting a quick look in James's direction and hoping he hadn't heard about her machinations.

He raised his eyebrows slightly, making it clear he had heard every word.

'Your matchmaking worked out better than you expected,' William added, not bothering to lower his voice the way Beatrice had. 'I believe we are going to have to return the favour.'

'Well, I'm just pleased that the two of you are happy,' she said briskly before William could say anything more embarrassing. 'This consommé is delicious,' she said to everyone seated around the table, hoping someone, anyone, would talk of something else.

Thankfully, Widow Harcourt started to discuss how her cook made a wonderful mock turtle soup, while Alice sat stiffly beside James, hoping and praying he did not question her about her matchmaking and nobody made any further references to extending the same courtesy—or was that discourtesy?—to her.

# *Chapter Fourteen*

'So you were matchmaking, were you?' James said, intending to tease Alice. 'I would never have guessed.'

The blush on her cheeks made it clear she did not find it funny.

'I'm sorry about that,' she said quietly, while conversation buzzed around them. 'It's just that Beatrice's father had arranged a marriage for her to a frightful man and she would have been so miserable. I thought marriage to an earl, well…' She shrugged. 'I'm sorry.'

'You made your intentions in that regard blatantly obvious. I'm afraid subterfuge is not one of your strengths and sometimes you can be as subtle as a sledgehammer.'

She sent him a questioning look which caused him to smile. Did she really not know how blatant her matchmaking had been? Her lack of artifice really was rather adorable.

'You were singing your friend's praises on Christmas Day, telling me what an ideal countess she would make. I believe you even mentioned her embroidery skills. That is a sure sign that someone is trying to matchmake.'

Alice gave a small, awkward laugh. 'Oh, yes, I did, didn't I?'

'Perhaps you have the makings for your next book right here,' he continued. 'One where a misguided Lambsie attempts to marry off the gentle bunny rabbit to the big bad wolf but is thwarted when the clever owl swoops in and saves the day.'

She laughed again, this time without the embarrassment. 'They are rather like a sweet bunny and an owl, aren't they?' She looked at him. 'Not that you're a big bad wolf or anything like that.'

'No, I'm a stubborn mule, if I remember correctly.'

She bit the edge of her lip. 'It looks like I really shouldn't have tried to interfere. I believe I am more like Emma Woodhouse than I thought I was. And like Emma I should have left well enough alone.'

'There's no harm done,' James said, although he was unsure if that was entirely true. Spending time in her presence had certainly harmed his equilibrium and destroyed his determination to spend as much time as possible in solitude. 'And just like in your children's books this entire adventure has ended happily.'

They both looked at William and Miss Chigwell.

'Although I think they more resemble doves, billing and cooing, than a bunny and an owl,' Alice said, her voice full of affection. 'They really are so in love, aren't they?' she added with a sigh.

An inexplicable churning gripped his stomach as a burning sensation ripped up his throat. What on earth was that all about? He couldn't be jealous of someone else's love, could he? That would be completely irrational, but weren't emotions often irrational? That was why it was wisest not to give in to them.

He continued to watch William and Beatrice, a couple whose uncomplicated affection for each other was obvious. Yes, what he was feeling was definitely envy, possibly jealousy, and with a harsh sting of regret on its tail.

He envied the ease with which they could give themselves over to happiness, and their ability to surrender completely to love, and he regretted ever thinking such simple, joyful emotions could be his.

He suppressed a snort of disbelief at his previous gullibility and resumed eating his meal. He'd once thought himself to be in love and had thought himself loved in return, but it was a love that was untested, and not one strong enough to withstand the storms of misfortune.

He hoped Beatrice and William's affections were of a stronger nature and were not based on foolish romantic dreams the way his had been.

He looked over at Alice, who was smiling and nodding at something her future sister-in-law was saying.

Tonight she looked particularly lovely, with her grey eyes matching the colour of her gown, her skin glowing and her hair curling in such a flattering manner around her face. He hadn't noticed before how it was not light brown as he had first thought, but contained streaks of honey blonde and soft caramel that caught the light when she turned her head.

It was such a temptation to pull out the pins holding her hair in place and watch it tumble around her shoulders, but that was something he would never do. To do so would lead to places he would not go with a woman like Alice Lambton.

She laughed at something William said, causing him to smile.

He had to admit, there was so much he admired about her. The way she cared about others, the way she had such an easy manner with people from all classes, was truly commendable. And he would admit to a certain respect for her intelligence and wit. It was unusual for any woman to make him laugh, for *anyone* to make him laugh, for that matter, but she was capable of doing so.

But love, never. Clara had taught him a valuable lesson about love and he was not so addle brained that he required further instruction before that harsh truth sank in.

He watched the two young women talking and laughing together. Love might not exist for the likes of him, but he had to admit, it was making Alice's friend's eyes sparkle and her skin glow. He'd hardly noticed her before, but tonight she did look very pretty. His gaze turned to Alice, whose eyes always seemed to sparkle with happiness and affection for all around her.

How did she manage that? Unlike himself, she did not envy her friend and brother's happiness. There appeared to be no regret that she had not married and would not have children. For many young women, facing the prospect of life as a pitied spinster would make them resentful of other's happiness. But not Alice.

He supposed she was truly a good person, which was rare indeed. And such a good person deserved to have the contented life they wanted. Maybe that meant being married to a good man and surrounded by a gaggle of children. Or would that be a flock of children in Lambsie's case?

He smiled to himself, then the smile faded. But that man would have to be someone completely different from him. It would have to be a man who could give himself completely, a man who was not disillusioned about love. A man who was more like a loyal and good-natured Labrador than a big bad wolf.

He smiled sardonically at the ridiculous image of him becoming a contented, domesticated pet, curled up in front of the fire.

He wasn't and never would be a lapdog, but he was

aware he should not be spending this evening buried in introspection. He should be making an effort to be more congenial. He turned to Lady Chigwell and exchanged a few pleasantries. Then he turned to each member of the party and made the requisite polite conversation.

In that manner, the meal passed amicably, with him doing his best impersonation of a man who enjoyed nothing better than company, and not one who'd arrived in this county with every intention of secluding himself away in his estate.

When the meal came to an end. Alice stood up and tapped her fork on the side of her glass to draw everyone's attention.

The babble of voices came to a halt, and all stared in her direction.

'I know it is customary for the women to now leave the men to their port or brandy, and what I am about to do goes against all protocol,' she said, smiling at everyone at the table. 'But you all know me and when have I ever given a fig for protocol?'

This caused everyone to laugh knowingly.

'I just wanted to express what everyone in this room is feeling, a great, abiding happiness that two such deserving people have found love.'

Everyone else might be feeling that, but James had no desire to point out that there was one cynic sitting at the table.

'I also have to say how happy I am that two people I love so much should have found each other.'

'Hear, hear,' the other guests called out.

'But it wasn't always so obvious that they were made for each other,' she continued. 'When I told William that Beatrice was visiting her aunt, all he could say was "Isn't she that annoying little girl with long blonde plaits?"'

This caused a ripple of laughter, while Beatrice made a mock frown at William, who smiled and apologised profusely.

'And Beatrice remembered William as that horrid boy who was always covered in mud.'

'He was,' Beatrice said above the laughter. 'I don't think I ever saw him without mud all over his trousers and shirt.'

'But now the little girl with plaits and the grubby boy have turned into these lovely, warm-hearted and might I add mud-free couple who have fallen in love and wish to spend the rest of their lives together. They were perfect alone, but together I know they will be even stronger, and I'm sure their love will grow deeper with each passing day.'

She smiled at everyone around the table. 'So let's raise our glasses to toast the loving couple.'

'To William and Beatrice,' everyone at the table chorused together.

James joined in the toast, all the while looking at

Alice. He should be reacting to her words in his now-familiar cynical manner, but as she talked of love and happiness a strange sensation welled up inside him, one stronger than anything he had felt before, one that contradicted his belief that he could never love again. And that terrified him.

Everyone smiled at Alice, and William thanked her for her kind words. She took her seat, knowing she had meant every word.

She also knew there were a lot of things she had left unspoken, and that they would remain that way, particularly how this courtship had changed everything for her. From the moment William had made his announcement, she had become acutely aware how she had been pushing away her feelings for James, often not very successfully.

Now that she no longer had Beatrice as a reason to squash those feelings down it had become blindingly obvious what she was feeling for James was not just attraction, but something far stronger. She was falling in love with him, or perhaps more accurately, she *had* fallen in love with him.

Even when talking to someone else, she was forever aware of his presence, and constantly thinking of him when not in his company. The way she felt when he smiled at her or laughed at something silly she said was unlike anything she had felt before, akin to a melting sensation. And that was nothing compared to how her pulse raced whenever she was near him, and how the desire to touch him and be touched by him possessed her. It was all deeply unsettling yet undeniably thrilling.

But unlike William and Beatrice, this was not a mutual feeling. She had fallen in love with a man whose own romantic experiences had left him disillusioned, a man who had confessed to having been in love with the most beautiful woman in New York.

How could she, Alice Lambton, ever expect a man like him to return her feelings?

If she had to fall in love, it would have been much more sensible to have fallen for a man who was not so handsome, a man who could have any woman he wanted. She no longer had to deny her feelings because of loyalty to her friend, but she still had to deny them if she was to avoid wasting her life yearning for something that could never be hers.

That would certainly be easier if they did not live in the same area. She would have to continue seeing him, all the while tormented by these absurd unrequited feelings.

She sat up straighter. Perhaps she needed to find another woman who would make him an ideal wife. That would protect her from the danger of ever doing or saying anything to reveal the depths of her feelings.

She shook her head slightly. When something had

failed once, only a fool would attempt it again. And while she was a fool, she wasn't that much of one. No, she would have to find some other way of dealing with her inner torment.

'Ladies, it's time we adjourned to the drawing room and left the men to their port and brandy,' Beatrice said, standing and performing the role of lady of the house, a role that Alice would have taken if she had not been once again distracted by thoughts of James.

With much rustling of silk and satin, the ladies all stood, then paraded back down the hallway to the drawing room. Alice reminded herself that tonight was William and Beatrice's night. It was time to put away all thoughts of James. If that was possible.

Once they were settled in the drawing room and coffee was served, all the women leaned forward towards Beatrice, desperate to hear more of their love story.

'He asked for permission to court me during the New Year's Ball,' she said to the group. 'During the first dance I knew he was wanting to say something but he was so tongue-tied,' Beatrice continued, laughter in her voice. 'I was so hoping it was a proposal, but the dance came to an end and he'd said nothing.'

Everyone shook their heads and smiled at the folly of men, including Alice.

'Then during the second waltz, I decided to prompt

him. I told him if he was to suggest he was interested in courting me then I would be amenable.'

The ladies all gave small claps of approval.

'And he said yes,' Beatrice's aunt answered for her.

'No, he lifted me up in the air, swung me around and caused quite the stir in the ballroom.'

'The second waltz?' Alice asked, trying to bring it to memory. 'I thought the only dance you had with William was that first waltz, and then the quadrille, I suppose, although James partnered you for that.'

'It was while you were outside taking the air,' Beatrice said, with a wry smile. 'About the same time the Earl was out walking in the snow.'

Alice gasped. Beatrice had noticed. If both William and Beatrice had noticed, how many others had? Then she relaxed somewhat. Her objection to anyone knowing she was alone with James had been in case it ruined his chances with Beatrice. That no longer mattered.

Widow Harcourt and Lady Chigwell started chatting together, discussing courtships during their own time as debutantes, and the interest they'd had from men since their widowhood, including Alice's father's towards Widow Harcourt, and surprisingly from the Vicar towards Lady Chigwell.

Alice decided she would prefer not to hear this conversation—in particular she did not want to hear about the romantic antics of her father, or the Vicar for that matter—so she turned her full attention to her friend.

'I was not outside for that long, and if James was outside at the same time that was purely coincidental.'

Beatrice leaned forward to speak confidentially. 'William and I knew exactly what was happening at the ball.'

'What? You mean about my attempt to match-make?' Alice gave a small, embarrassed laugh, hoping that was what her friend was referring to. 'Yes, I was being needlessly meddlesome, wasn't I? I should have not tried to interfere and let the two of you meet and fall in love rather than try and engineer a match between you and James.'

'Especially as it wouldn't have worked if you had managed to get the Earl and me together on Christmas Day.'

'No, I suppose not. You would have only had eyes for William.'

'Just as the Earl only has eyes for you.'

Alice nearly spluttered on her coffee in a most unladylike manner. 'What? No. You're… He doesn't… No.'

Beatrice made that wry smile again. It seemed now that she was in love and heading towards the altar she thought she knew everything.

'I've seen the way he looks at you, Alice. It's much

the same way William looks at me, although in the Earl's case it's all broody and intense.'

'No,' Alice said, no other word being capable of coming out of her mouth.

'Oh, you must have noticed it when we walked across the drawing room before dinner. James was staring at you as if you were a rare and precious treasure he just had to possess. William and I both noticed it.'

Alice stared at her friend, remembering her physical reaction to his gaze. Was that why her body came alive when she had walked towards him? It had been as if he had been caressing her with his eyes, but she had assumed that was all due to her own overactive imaginings.

'And then there's the way the two of you were behaving at the New Year's Ball,' Beatrice added, still with that knowing smile. 'No one would miss the way you two were acting, like magnets that can't help but be drawn together no matter how much they try and resist the attraction.'

'No, I was still matchmaking, trying to get you and James together.' Even Alice could tell she was sounding defensive.

Beatrice laughed as if this was a jolly lark. 'He followed you out onto the terrace, Alice. *Followed you*. Then the two of you spent an inordinate amount of time absent from the ball. That is hardly a judicious way to matchmake, I must say.'

'But…'

'And then you came in with your face all flushed, despite the freezing temperatures, and then James appeared a few minutes later, looking equally discomposed, with snow on his shoes.'

Discomposed? James? Surely those two words were a contradiction.

'The question now is, what are you going to do about it?' Beatrice said, her eyebrows raised.

'Do?'

'Yes, do. I had to gently, and not so gently, manoeuvre William into making an offer for my hand. I think it might be time for you to do the same with the Earl.'

Alice could no more imagine manoeuvring James into a courtship than she could imagine manoeuvring a ship into a harbour, and she had an equal amount of experience at both.

But Beatrice had given her something to think about. Was there some attraction on James's side? That was surely too absurd to be possible. But he *had* kissed her, albeit under duress. He *did* dance with her at the New Year's Ball, and he *had* carried her through the snow.

Once again she experienced that strange melting sensation at the thought of him picking her up as if she was as light as a feather, of him holding her in his arms against his warm, hard chest.

The men entered the room to join the ladies. Alice looked in their direction. James was staring straight at her, just as he had done when he arrived this evening.

Could it be true? Could James be feeling for her the same emotions she was feeling for him? It was unfathomable, but if William and Beatrice had noticed, then maybe, just maybe…

No, she was surely seeing what she wanted to see, rather than what was real, just as her friend and William were. He was James Marlowe, for goodness' sake. The handsome, dashing, debonaire Earl of Thornwood. She was plain old Alice Lambton.

Beatrice gently nudged her arm. 'Manoeuvre him into doing what he obviously wants to do,' she said quietly. 'It's the only way,' her friend added with the new-found authority of a woman engaged to be married. 'If you don't, you will always regret it.'

## Chapter Fifteen

Alice woke the next morning still no closer to knowing what she was supposed to do about James. She'd spent the rest of the dinner party all but speechless, watching him for any of the signs of what Beatrice had described. Apart from that one long, lingering look he had given her when he'd entered the drawing room, she had seen nothing that could suggest he was in any way feeling the same emotions she was.

If anything he appeared to be avoiding her. Despite what Beatrice had said about the behaviour of magnets she was sure that was something a smitten man would never do.

As they'd said their goodbyes, Beatrice had leaned in to kiss her cheek, but instead had whispered in her ear. 'I expect to hear all about what actions you have taken regarding the Earl when we next meet.'

And that was all she said. Her friend could have at least given her some instructions on what these actions should be. Fluttering the eyelashes? Making suggestive gestures with one's fan? Flirting? Flattering? These were among the instructions given during her training for the Season. They were supposedly tried-and-tested methods of attracting a man's attention. They'd all seemed somewhat ridiculous to Alice at the time and she had dismissed them immediately, never bothering to master the techniques.

Now it was surely too late. And if she started such behaviour in front of James he was likely to think she had gone completely mad. That might get his attention, but for all the wrong reasons, and would definitely not encourage him to act on any feelings he may or may not have.

Finding herself no wiser as to what she was to do, she joined William for breakfast. While watching him eating his eggs on toast and perusing the morning paper, Alice wondered whether he might have the answer to her problem.

Beatrice had been no help, but it might be a good idea to get a male's input on this subject. She bit into her toast and dismissed that idea. Apart from the very thought of such a conversation being far too embarrassing, William had been the manoeuvred one, rather than the manoeuvrer, so he was unlikely to be any help.

'As the weather has cleared, I think I'll go for a walk,' she informed him, while buttering another piece of toast then smothering it with marmalade.

'Good idea,' he said, looking at her over the folded newspaper. 'Would you like me to accompany you?'

'No, thank you. I'm sure you'd like to pay Beatrice a visit.'

A slow smile crossed his face. 'Yes, that had been my intention.'

'Good, then I shall go for a nice brisk walk and perhaps dedicate the afternoon to writing my next book. I'm going to be occupied all day, so don't hurry home. Presumably Father will be spending the day with Widow Harcourt, so feel free to stay as long as you wish over at Beatrice's house.

Alice suspected it was going to take most of the day to work out her manoeuvring strategy, not to mention putting it into practice, so she needed to give herself plenty of uninterrupted time.

Still smiling, William went back to his paper.

Once breakfast was over, Alice collected her hat, gloves and woollen shawl and set out in the direction of Thornwood Hall. It was about a mile's walk across the fields. That was surely distance enough for her to decide on a plan of attack if she really put her mind to it. The carriage trip along the winding country lanes would take longer, but 'a nice brisk walk' might help her think more clearly.

After a few dozen steps she halted. Would a mile's walk really give her enough time to solve this perplexing conundrum?

No. What she needed to do was take the somewhat longer and more circuitous route along the river. And maybe the sight and sound of flowing water would be just what she needed to clear her mind of all her anxious musings. Then she would be able to rationally work out what she was to do.

To that end, she walked purposefully in the opposite direction until she reached the gently flowing river. The willows, stripped of their foliage, still bore a slight dusting of snow. The path was somewhat damp underfoot from the recent snow, but it mattered not. This was just what she needed. Nothing soothed the soul better than a nice walk in such an idyllic setting. There was a pleasant chill in the air, which would surely blow away all the cobwebs, allowing her to think clearly.

She strode along the path, but her mind did not clear. If anything, the thoughts whirled around and around at a faster pace, never settling and never allowing her to develop one single idea on what she was to do or say when she arrived at Thornwood Hall.

Other women seemed to know instinctively how to act in such circumstances. She considered herself a reasonably intelligent woman; surely she too could work out how to let a man know how you felt about him.

Flirting, flattery and eyelash fluttering had all been dismissed. She could just tell him how she felt. But that was the problem. Such an action would require words and she was unsure what words she could use. She also suspected, even if she could think of a clever or poetic speech, they would get stuck in her throat the moment she looked at him.

She released a loud, despondent sigh as she crossed an arched stone bridge, noticing that the river was no longer a gentle stream, but had widened and was now flowing with greater force.

She stopped and looked around. While she had been grappling with her tangled thoughts she had walked past the turn-off that would have taken her to Thorn-wood Hall, and had carried on, further and further away from her destination.

Had that been deliberate? Was she trying to avoid seeing James again? She knew the answer to that. Of course she was. The idea of exposing how she was feeling was far too disconcerting. Beatrice might think manoeuvring was the answer, but that was easy for someone like Beatrice to say. She was pretty, petite and perky. Any man would be more than happy to be manoeuvred by such a woman, but that was not Alice.

She looked back down the river and sighed once again.

No, it would be much better to just give up this plan before it had even been formulated, return home and bury herself in her writing, just as she had told William she would.

Maybe she could write the story James suggested, where Lambsie tried to match the bunny up with the wolf, only for the smitten owl to swoop in and save the day. She smiled, imagining the drawings, then frowned. She could also add a few pages with silly Lambsie thinking that she could marry the wolf herself, only to come to the realisation that such a pairing was absurd.

No, she most certainly would not be including that. Even children, who could accept a bunny and an owl falling in love, would not be so naive as to think sensible Lambsie would be foolish enough to set her sights on a wolf, and would never believe that a wolf could have the slightest affection for a lamb.

She continued her walk along the river, determined to forget all about James, plots, plans and manoeuvres and focus instead on her next book.

It didn't take long for thoughts of small animals involved in mischievous adventures to fill her mind and drive away all other thoughts, just as they always had. She smiled as she walked, pleased that her imagination hadn't failed her, and had once again provided her with the safe refuge she often sought from the world.

She rounded another turn in the river. The damp ground pulled at her boots, drawing her attention away from thoughts of farmyard animals. She looked down at the boggy path, at her mud-splattered boots, the heel stuck in the clinging muck, and at the grubby bottom of her skirt, then up at the path ahead, which had turned into a quagmire of puddles.

It was time to return to Rosetree Manor.

With some hesitation she took a step back along the path, trying to avoid a particularly boggy patch. She placed her foot on solid ground, or what looked like solid ground. Her mistake was evident when the earth sucked at her boot, pulling it down.

She grimaced as mud flowed over the top of her boot and down onto her stockinged feet.

To the accompaniment of squelching, she dragged her boot out of the mud's grip.

Stepping backwards and balanced on one foot, she looked for firmer ground to place her foot. Puddles surrounded her, and what looked like solid earth could be deceptive, as she had just discovered.

There was nothing for it.

Trying to ignore the slimy feel of water and mud squishing around her toes, she placed her foot onto another boggy patch, her boot descending to a greater depth.

This was more than unpleasant. She was in danger of getting stuck. It was imperative she get off this path.

To that end, she reached up and took hold of a tree branch to steady herself. Pulling hard and gripping the branch firmly, she pulled on her boot. The mud slowly released its captive. Still holding the branch, she stretched out her leg towards the grassy embankment, the only area that had remained relatively dry and stable.

Balanced on one foot, she focused on extricating the other boot. It slowly came out, accompanied by a slurping gulp. With a sense of relief she released the branch and jumped towards the embankment. Her foot slid on the wet grass, down the embankment back to the puddles.

Her arms windmilling, she reached out for the branch. It slid through her fingers and she fell backwards, landing heavily on her bottom and sending muddy water spraying in every direction.

Several words that should never pass a lady's lips were shouted, loudly, as mud coated not just her derriere, but most of her blouse and a substantial part of her shawl.

Pushing on the ground and coating her gloves in the process, she hoisted herself up in what could only be described as an ungainly manner, and found herself back in the same predicament, with both boots stuck in the mud.

Those unladylike words escaped her lips once more.

She was going to have to repeat the whole procedure again, although at least this time she would not be trying to keep clean as she attempted to free herself.

'May I be of service?' a voice said from the top of the hillock. She closed her eyes and her body clenched. She knew that voice. It was James. She had thought her predicament could not get any worse. She had been wrong.

She looked up to the top of the embankment. He was watching her from astride his horse, looking extremely clean and in control. Before she could say *No, I don't need any help, I know exactly what I am doing*, he dismounted and climbed down to the path.

'Give me your hand and I'll pull you out.'

She started to remove her gloves, which were covered in mud.

'Don't worry about that, just give me your hands.'

She did as he said, embarrassed that she had now muddied his riding gloves.

'Just relax and I'll pull you out.'

Relax? That was easy for him to say. He wasn't the one who was filthy, stuck in an undignified position, feeling completely gauche and looking ridiculous.

He pulled on her arms. Her boots made a wet, sucking sound that only added to her mortification.

'Thank you,' she said when he pulled her up onto the dry embankment.

'Allow me to give you a ride home.'

'No, I couldn't. I'm filthy,' she said, determined to flee as quickly as possible.

'I'm out riding. I'm not exactly concerned about a little mud.'

*A little mud? Had he seen her behind? She was caked in mud.*

'No, no, I'd much rather walk,' she said.

'You can't walk in that state. You need to get home and get cleaned up.'

She could see the sense in what he was saying, but was unsure which would be worse, to be seen walking through the village in this state, or to ride home with him. No, that was an easy question to answer. Being mortified in front of the villagers was far preferable.

'No, no, everything is absolutely fine,' she said, which was such a blatant lie as to be almost comical.

'I insist,' he said in his most insistent voice.

She didn't move, wondering what else she could say to make him leave her alone to nurse her humiliation in private. But once again the elements were not on her side. The heavens opened up, sending down a deluge onto the mortals below.

Not waiting for her to come up with any reason why she wanted to walk home in the pouring rain caked in mud, he took her hand and all but dragged her up the hillock to his waiting horse.

'But I—'

Before she could finish, his hands were on her waist. He lifted her up and settled her sideways on the saddle. In one quick movement, his foot was in the stirrup, his leg swung over the horse and they were in motion.

The leather of the saddle creaking under her, her skirts billowing out around her, they rode through the trees along the path that took them towards Thorn-wood Hall. She wanted to tell him she'd much prefer if he took her back to Rosetree Manor, but she found it impossible to form coherent sentences, not when the man she adored had his arms around her, holding her steady, his warm, hard body pressed up against her, and that heady scent of sandalwood and citrus enveloping her.

And even if she could find the words, with the icy rain pelting down and the sound of the horse galloping across the soft earth, she doubted he'd hear her any-way. But one thing she knew for certain: any fanci-ful notions of manoeuvring him into a declaration of affection, or attempts to convince him she was exactly what he was looking for in a future countess, had just been drowned in a large puddle of mud.

They rode up the gravel driveway leading to Thorn-wood Hall, and James directed the horse around the side of the building to the stables. The hooves clat-tering on the cobblestones, he came to a halt in the courtyard. He quickly dismounted and lifted Alice down. There was no slow descent from his arms, as had happened on New Year's Eve. This time it was all business.A stable boy raced out to greet them and James handed him the reins.

'You're shivering,' he said to Alice, pulling off his jacket, draping it around her shoulders and leading her out of the rain to the shelter of the stables.

'Find some clothes for Miss Lambton to change into,' he called to the stable boy.

'But—' the boy protested.

'Anything will do as long as they are dry, and bring some water and a sponge for her to remove the mud from her hands and face.'

*Her face? She had mud on her face as well?*

Before the young lad could protest again, James rushed her into the brick building. Compared to outside it was warm and thankfully dry with no mud in sight.

'You're soaked through to the skin and you're freezing cold.' He looked towards the house, then back at the stables. 'You need to get out of those wet clothes immediately. You'll have to change in that empty stall.'

She looked towards where he was pointing. The wooden half door provided a modicum of privacy, but still, it was an open area designed to house a horse, not a changing room. She looked around. Several horses' heads were poking out the other stalls, all looking in their direction as if this was the best entertainment they'd had for some time.

'But—'

His hands landed on her shoulders and guided her into the enclosure, which bore that earthy smell of straw, leather and horse. 'If you don't want to catch pneumonia you'll do as I say.'

Alice stifled her objections, remembering pneumonia was exactly what brought about his brother's untimely death, and entered the stall.

He turned his back, and she assumed she was supposed to strip. She did no such thing, but remained standing in the middle of the stall, dripping on the dry straw.

The boy arrived with a pile of clothes and handed them apologetically to James, placed the bucket and sponge beside the door to the stall, exchanged an uncertain look with Alice, then departed.

Could this be any less dignified? She'd gone from resembling a muddy urchin to now being treated like a horse.

Without looking in her direction, James hung the clothing over the stall door. 'I will wait for you outside,' he said and strode away.

There was nothing for it. She took the sponge and wiped off the worst of the mud from her hands and ran it over her face. As stables did not provide looking glasses, she had no idea what sort of job she was doing. She then held up the clothing the stable boy had provided her: a pair of dark grey trousers, a long flannel shirt of indeterminate colour, faded from constant washing, a rough woollen brown jacket and a flat cap.

Not exactly haute couture but James was right. She was shivering with cold; even her jaw was starting to tremble. She needed to get out of her dress and into this warm, dry clothing as quickly as possible.

Without haste, she pulled off her dress, chemise and corset and pulled on the woollen trousers, giving thanks that they were loose fitting and made for a man at least as tall as herself. She shrugged herself into the flannel shirt, donned the jacket and attempted to tuck her hair into the cap.

Feeling decidedly silly, she stepped out of the stall into the centre aisle of the stable.

'What do you think?' she said to the watching horses.

Several whinnied, although she wasn't sure whether that was in approval or with amusement or because, dressed as she was, they expected her to start pitching hay.

She looked towards the entrance. Now all she had to do was compose herself, lift her head high and like a proud show pony strut out to the courtyard with as much dignity she possessed, which unfortunately, was very little.

## Chapter Sixteen

Under the eaves out of the rain, and with the help of the stable boy, James removed the saddle from his horse, brushed off the mud, threw a blanket over his back and waited until Alice was finished dressing so they could stable him.

He did not have to wait long for her to walk out, a sheepish expression on her face, her damp clothing piled up in the bucket she was carrying.

He smiled to himself. She should look ridiculous. The woollen trousers were too big for her, but they did show off just how long and slim her legs were, something that was difficult to gauge under her usual voluminous skirts. The trousers were held up by a thick leather belt, and it was now obvious her slim waist was natural and not due to the tight lacing of a corset. The worn shirt, tucked into the trousers, billowed out above the leather belt, and the heavy woollen jacket, which should have looked inelegant, gave her a certain rakish charm.

She'd even donned a cloth cap, her loose, damp hair peeking out from beneath and several locks falling around her shoulders.

She stared at him with a look of defiance. 'Do not say a thing.'

'I was just going to say I've never seen you look prettier,' he said, which was not entirely a jest.

He signalled to the stable boy to take the horse into the stables and he took the bucket of sodden clothes from Alice's hands. Removing the damp sponge, he lightly rubbed it across her cheek, removing the last of the mud.

'There you go,' he said. 'As good as new.'

She gave a small, slightly embarrassed laugh.

Keeping to the eaves to avoid the still falling-rain, they skirted around the house and entered the down-stairs doorway that led to the servants' quarters.

A surprised footman was instantly on his feet, his newspaper fluttering to the floor beside the warm stove. His expression betrayed a flicker of surprise at Alice's appearance before he adopted the blank mask of a well-trained servant.

'Can you please make sure these are brushed down and dried?' he said, handing the man the bucket of sodden clothing.

'Yes, my lord. There is a fire in the blue drawing room. Shall I arrange for tea to be served?'

James nodded, shrugged off his oilskin riding coat

and handed it to the footman, then led Alice out the servants' quarters, up the backstairs and into the drawing room.

'Oh, lovely,' she said as soon as she saw the blazing fire, rushing over and warming her hands.

James stood near the door and watched her. As she leaned towards the fire, the vent at the bottom of the jacket parted, exposing her shapely behind to his gaze. He almost groaned as he imagined clasping those round cheeks as he held her close to him.

She turned towards him. His eyes moved up her body. The jacket was parted in the front, the material of her shirt clinging to her full breasts, the nipples pointing through the soft fabric.

He swallowed another groan and forced his eyes to move to her face, away from places they should not have strayed. They held each other's gaze for a moment, then she turned back to the fire.

*Make polite conversation.* James admonished himself. *Do not think of her buttocks encased in those loose-fitting trousers, or her legs, waist, breasts or any other body part on display in her mannish costume. And certainly do not think of how much easier it would be to strip her of her clothing, now the countless buttons, laces and heaven knows what else that women encased themselves in, had gone.*

*Make polite conversation,* he repeated to himself, but nothing would come to mind.

This was absurd. He was never uncomfortable in a woman's presence. Even as an adolescent he had never faltered when hoping to charm and disarm.

Such awkwardness did not happen to him. Until now. Was it because of the way she was dressed or was it because he should not be trying to charm or disarm her? Or was it something else? Even in Clara's presence he had not felt this unsettled, as if something he kept tightly wound inside himself was unravelling.

'William looked happy last night,' he said, pleased he'd finally found something appropriately innocuous to say, and indicating she should take a seat.

'Oh, yes, wasn't he?' she said on a sigh, lowering herself to the settee beside the fire. She did so in the manner all women did when restricted by corsets and bustles, her back ramrod straight, her hands moving to her side to sweep up her skirt.

'My, things are so different and so much easier when wearing trousers.' She stood up again, plonked herself back down and gave a little laugh. 'When you're wearing, well, what women wear, you're so restricted. This is so much more comfortable. I might start a new fashion and begin wearing trousers.'

James thought perhaps it would be best if she didn't, not when he could see the shape of her legs outlined against the fabric and could easily imagine the long slim calves and thighs underneath.

He took a seat next to her on the settee, judging that

it would be better if he was not sitting across from her in sight of those long legs.

He looked down. Damn. It made little difference, and now she was sitting beside him. What on earth was wrong with him? He *was* acting like an awkward adolescent boy, all because of a woman in trousers.

A maid knocked lightly and entered carrying the tea.

'Don't be shocked by my appearance, Mary,' Alice said, standing up and doing a little twirl. 'I fell in some mud, then got soaked through in the rain, so the stable boy kindly found me some old clothes to wear.'

Mary's eyes grew wide then she giggled. 'I think they might be Jethro's. He often leaves a change of clean clothes in the stables in case he gets invited to dine with us servants. He gets so grubby when he's out doing whatever it is that gamekeepers do.'

Mary placed the tea service on the table and continued to address Alice as if he was not present. 'There's some Christmas cake and those mince pies you enjoyed so much, miss.'

'Oh, lovely, my favourite,' Alice said, causing James to smile at her expected reaction. 'Thank Cook for me, won't you?' she added as she poured the tea.

Mary bobbed a quick curtsey and departed, and Alice handed him a cup of tea. Had he not noticed before how long and slender her fingers were? Just like the legs he was to neither think about nor look at.

He took the cup and placed it on the nearest table.

'William is paying a visit to Beatrice today and I suspect he will be there all day,' she said as she placed a slice of cake on her plate. 'Especially if he can encourage her aunt to indulge in some port and she becomes distracted. He really is wicked.'

'Are you not jealous?' he asked, remembering how he had felt last night as he watched the happy couple looking at each other as if there was no one else in the room.

'Jealous? No, why should I be jealous?'

He chose to say nothing.

'Oh, you mean because I'm an old spinster and my friend is to become a happily married woman.'

'That was not what I meant and you are hardly old. What are you, twenty-three? Twenty-four?'

'Twenty-four. Well, a young spinster then,' she said with a laugh and took a bite of the Christmas cake. She closed her eyes and all but purred with pleasure. He wanted to yell at her, *Do not do that. Not when it makes me imagine how you would look if I was the one to be giving you that pleasure.*

'No one could describe you as a spinster. Not the way you are looking now,' he murmured, not entirely sure if he'd said those words out loud.

Her eyes opened. She blinked repeatedly, then her eyes narrowed. 'Are you teasing me?'

'Of course not. Alice, you are a beautiful woman.'

Her grey eyes remained narrowed, her body guarded.

'Do not let anyone ever tell you differently. Do not let anyone ever make you feel as if you are anything less than enchanting.'

Her eyes grew wider as she stared back at him. He expected her to make a joke or some flippant remark and both hoped she would and wouldn't.

'You think I am beautiful?' she asked quietly.

He removed that jaunty cap from her head and stroked a still-damp lock back from her cheek. 'I think you are the most beautiful woman I have ever met.'

She gave a small gasp, her red lips parting. In invitation? Before he had time to consider whether that was the case, his lips were on hers.

Alice's plate clattered to the floor. He had called her beautiful and was now kissing her. In her wildest dreams, and her dreams had become increasingly wild since meeting James, she had never expected this to happen.

But oh, how she wanted it. She closed her eyes and gave herself over to the sensation of his lips on hers, his rough cheeks against hers, his strong arms encasing her. He tasted so wonderful, smelt so glorious, felt so heavenly.

She parted her lips wider to take in more of that sublime masculine taste. His tongue ran along her bottom lip and Alice was certain she would swoon in his arms at such ecstatic pleasure.

But it didn't stop there. His tongue continued to tease and torment her increasingly sensitive lips and to her surprise entered her mouth. She had thought the kiss under the mistletoe had been exciting and exhilarating but this kiss was different. It was thrilling. It was frightening and it was charged with a level of sensuality that sent heat racing through her as if a fire had been ignited deep in her body.

Then she found herself kissing him back with a hunger that surprised her, as if a wild, carnal animal who had been locked up inside her had finally been released. She wanted to taste him, caress him, stroke him, and desperately wanted him to do the same to her.

Copying his movements, her tongue lightly stroked his lip, loving the feel and taste. Her hands wrapped more firmly around his head, her fingers burrowing into his hair. This was wonderful, but her greedy body wanted more, much more.

Taking his hand, she guided it to her breasts, their aching need letting her know that was what she had to have. A moan escaped her lips as he cupped one breast, his fingers moving over the tight nub, causing pleasure to ripple through her that was almost painful. Still kissing her, his hand caressed the other breast, his fingers tormenting the sensitive bud until she was all but writhing underneath him.

'Yes,' she murmured. In encouragement? In appreciation? In blissful surrender? She neither knew nor cared, just was certain that this was what she wanted.

His hand left her breasts and a bubble of panic welled up inside her. He could not leave her like this, burning with such a desperate need for his touch, a hunger for him to take her where her body wanted to go.

He undid the buttons of her shirt. She sighed with relief. He was not finished with her yet. He parted the material, exposing her breasts to his gaze. This should have felt uncomfortable, even embarrassing, but it was neither. Instead, she lay back on the settee, arching herself towards him, giving herself to him.

'You are so beautiful,' he murmured. And that was exactly how she felt, beautiful, desirable and cherished.

He leaned down and kissed each nipple, as if in worship. Alice gasped, in surprise, in wonder, in ecstasy. She didn't know and didn't care; she just wanted more. Her gasp was stifled when his lips found hers again and he kissed her harder, as if he wanted to consume her. His hand once again cupped her breast, his fingers teasing the increasingly sensitive bud. She kissed him back, her tongue now confidently entering into the sensual dance, while her body pulsed with growing urgency as if she was teetering on an edge, waiting to tumble into the unknown.

His kisses moved to her neck, nuzzling the tender skin. Her rapid breathing turned into cries of pleasure as his kisses moved lower, stroking across the top of her chest.

'Oh, yes,' she murmured, either to herself or out loud, she was unsure. But it expressed exactly what she was feeling as his kisses moved across the mounds of her breasts. She needed to feel his lips on those tight, sensitive buds, for him to once again kiss those demanding peaks.

When he took one nipple in his mouth, she cried out in blissful pleasure, hardly able to believe such intense sensations were possible.

'Oh, yes,' she murmured again on a gasp as his tongue and lips took her higher and higher, until she was unsure she could bear such intensity.

Her body on fire, the coiling and pounding between her legs reaching fever pitch, she reached down and undid her belt, opened the buttons of her trousers and guided his hand to where it had to go.

His lips still teasing and tormenting her nipple, his hand moved between her legs. She lay back and gave herself over to him, over to these sensations, certain he would know what to do to relieve her of this all-consuming pulsating intensity.

With each stroke of his hand, with each caress of

his nuzzling lips, the intensity built inside her, until she was no longer in control and all she could do was feel the pleasure he was giving her, feel the raw, carnal ecstasy that consumed her.

Just as the boundary between pain and pleasure blurred completely, a wave of rapture crashed over her, starting from his stroking hand and flooding through her entire body, leaving her shuddering in its wake.

Her pounding heart started to slow. She opened her eyes to find him staring down at her. 'You are so beautiful, my love,' he whispered before kissing her gasping lips.

*My love.* Alice closed her eyes, cherishing those words.

She had seen the fire of uncontrolled desire burning in his eyes, desire for her, desire for the woman he called *my love*. A surge of power gripped her. She opened her eyes, reached up to him and undid the buttons of his shirt, just as he had done to her. The shirt slid open, exposing to her gaze those hard muscles she previously had only felt.

Her hand moved over the smooth, taut skin, her fingertips tracing the line of his chest and around the firm muscles of his back.

'Alice, you're tormenting me,' he whispered.

'I want to torment you,' she murmured back. 'And I want you to torment me again.'

She knew enough about what happened between a

man and a woman to know there was more than what she had just experienced and she wanted it all, everything this glorious man could give her.

To that end, she reached down and pushed at the top of her trousers, trying to free herself from the restriction keeping James from her.

'Are you sure?' he murmured in her ear before once again nuzzling her neck.

Of course she was sure, and if she wasn't, the touch of his lips once again on her sensitive skin would have convinced her.

'I'm sure,' she murmured back.

He sat up and took hold of the top of her open trousers. She lifted her buttocks off the settee to make it easier for him to pull them down over her hips. Still helping him, she pulled one leg out of the trousers.

His hand slid between her legs, and that now-familiar pulsing beat erupted back into life. She lay back on the settee and closed her eyes, knowing now what sensual pleasure was about to be unleashed within her and anxious to surrender herself once again to his experienced guidance.

'Yes,' she said, as he parted her folds and pushed his fingers insider her. 'Take me,' she murmured as much to herself as to him. 'Take my virginity.'

As if hit by lightning, he jumped back and stood up. 'Oh, God. What on earth am I doing?' he said.

Alice could explain to him what he was about to

do—he was going to make love to her—but she suspected that was not the real question.

'I should never have done any of that,' he said, returning to the settee. 'Can you ever forgive me, Alice?'

'Forgive you?' she said, her voice little more than a croak. 'There's nothing to forgive.' She wanted to add the only thing that needed forgiving was him stopping and leaving her in this state, desperate for him to finish what he had started, desperate for him to relieve the coiled tension once again gripping her body, desperate for him to show her what it was like when a man made love to a woman.

He placed his head in his hands. 'Alice, you deserve so much better than this.'

*There was better?* She doubted that very much.

'You need to save yourself for the man you marry.'

He ran his hand through his hair, then looked over at her, his face contorted as if in agony.

'I don't care,' she whispered in response to what her body wanted but not sure if her mind was in agreement.

He had told her to save herself for the man she would marry, and all but said that man would not be him. Yes, she wanted more than just his kisses and caresses. Yes, she wanted him to love her, not just make love to her, but with her mind fuddled with desire she could not think of that now.

'I don't care,' she repeated, louder than a whisper.

'You know what I am like, Alice,' he said, almost as if he was talking to himself. 'You deserve to be with a man who can offer you what I can't. Love, happiness, a future.'

He leaned towards her and she hoped he had decided to forget all this nonsense and kiss her again, but she doubted that was the case, and it wasn't. He pulled her shirt together to cover her breasts, as if they were an unwanted distraction, then attempted to pull up her trousers.

In a reversal of what had just happened, she lifted up her buttocks to once again make it easier for him.

'I should never have kissed you. I should never have caressed you,' he said as he pulled the opening of her trousers together and with fumbling fingers attempted to do up the buttons.

'You did nothing except what I wanted,' she said, taking over the job and fastening the belt.

'But you are an innocent. I should never have taken advantage of that.'

'You did not take advantage of me,' Alice said, sitting up and doing up the buttons of her shirt. 'And don't worry, I'm not after a proposal of marriage or anything.'

'I didn't mean—'

'We've had our fun,' she said with a nonchalance she did not feel. 'Maybe you should go and see if my clothes are dry.'

'Alice, I—'

'I'd like to go home now, and I'll need my clothes if I'm to do that.'

He nodded, rose from the settee and left the room. The moment the door closed Alice's head fell to her hands, in much the same way James's had when he expressed his regret for what they had just done.

He might have his regrets, but that was not what Alice was feeling. After such a tempestuous day, she wasn't certain what she was feeling, but knew regret over what they had just shared was not among the chaotic emotions swirling inside her.

## *Chapter Seventeen*

James paused outside the door and drew in a deep breath. What had just happened? He shook his head. He did not need to ask that question. He knew what had happened; the real question was *why* did it happen? But he knew the answer to that as well—because he couldn't resist her.

But that was something he had known he had to do. Hadn't he repeatedly told himself she was not for him?

And yet he had kissed her, and once he felt those soft lips on his, he had lost himself completely. All he'd wanted to do was kiss her deeply, caress her, then bury himself inside her and make her his own. But he had no right to do so, no right to even think of doing so, and he certainly should not have let things go as far as they had.

To say it was because he desired her was no excuse. There was no excuse and no justification for what he had done.

Thank God she had mentioned she was still a vir-

gin. If she hadn't, he was certain he would have ignored all sense of what was right and wrong and taken
what he so desperately wanted, all to satisfy his own
needs.

There was no denying it. He was a selfish cad and
somehow he had to make this right with Alice. He had
to find a way to make amends, to make her see he was
genuinely sorry for what he had done, and hope she
really did forgive him.

But first he needed to get her out of those clothes.
He groaned. Why did he have to think of that? Now
the memory of how he had stripped her of her clothing re-entered his mind, of how he had feasted on the
sight of her naked body, of how she looked lying back
on the settee, her legs parted, those luscious breasts
exposed to his appreciative gaze. He was going to
have to forget the touch and taste of her naked skin,
and the memory of how she looked when she reached
the peak of ecstasy.

He knew that would be a challenge, if not an impossible demand, but he would have to try if he was
to avoid making such a fatal mistake ever again.

Guilt still nipping at his heels, he walked down
to the servants' quarters. Alice's dress and chemise,
minus the mud, were hanging on a drying rack suspended over the coal range.

'Miss Lambton would like to leave now,' he said to
the housekeeper. *Or at least I want her to leave now*

*before I disgrace myself any further.* 'Are her clothes dry yet?'

'Yes, I believe so, my lord,' she replied, unwinding the rope holding the drying rack in place and lowering it to the ground. 'I've managed to get most of the mud off, but Miss Lambton's lady's maid will have to thoroughly launder them. Shall I take them up to the guest bedchamber for her to change?'

James nodded. 'And please ask the coachman to prepare a carriage to take her home.'

With great reluctance he walked back up the stairs and along the hallway. He paused outside the drawing room door, knowing there was only one way he could put right what had happened between them and undo the damage he had done.

He entered the room and found her sitting demurely on the settee, but the blush that exploded onto her cheeks as he entered showed she was just as uncomfortable with what had just happened as he was.

'Your clothes are dry. You can change in the bedchamber you were in before and I've organised a carriage to take you home.'

'Thank you,' she said, standing up.

'No, Alice, wait. We need to discuss what just happened.'

The colour on her cheeks intensified but she sat back down, while he racked his brain for something to say.

'I'm so sorry.' He knew those two words, which he had already said, were woefully inadequate.

'Are you sorry for what happened or for what nearly happened but didn't?' she asked, her burning cheeks contradicting the boldness of that statement.

'Both,' he said in all honesty before he had time to think. 'What I did was unforgivable. What I wanted to do even more so, and you have every right to expect a proposal from me.'

She laughed, a small, embarrassed laugh. 'I believe you told me once that you had no desire to marry anyone.'

He shrugged. 'Yes, but this has changed everything.'

She said nothing, just looked down at her hands, clasped together in her lap.

'Alice, I am so sorry for what happened between us. I should have used more control but, well, I didn't, but we both know that under such circumstances a marriage proposal is the only way that things can be put right between us.'

He paused but she still said nothing, just clasped her hands tighter in her lap.

'You are a lovely young woman and would make any man an excellent wife. But you deserve to be with a man who treats you with respect, not one who...' He pointed towards the settee, indicating what a better man would never have done.

'You deserve to be married to a man who can love you in the way you should be loved, a man who can make you happy.'

'I see,' she said, not looking at him, and he wondered if she truly understood what he was saying to her.

'I am not that man, Alice, and never can be, given all that has happened in my life. I am not the man I once was. But if it is what you wish, then of course I will marry you.'

'I see,' she repeated.

'I would be honoured to make you my wife,' he added, as an afterthought.

She made a small, derisive laugh at that statement, then drew in a deep breath and turned towards him. 'I can see that you feel obliged to atone for what happened, but there is no need.'

'That's not what I—'

She held up her hand to stop his words. 'No one knows what happened between us and as long as neither of us discusses it with anyone else, then my reputation remains untarnished.'

'Of course I would never—'

'I'm still a virgin, so in the unlikely event I do meet someone who wishes to marry me then, as you said, I will have still saved myself for that man.'

'Alice, I am sure—'

'I appreciate your offer of marriage, given how

much you don't want to marry anyone including me,' she continued, a certain hardness entering her voice that cut James to the quick. 'But I was a willing participant in everything that occurred between us and you owe me nothing.'

'But I am honour bound—'

'You are not bound by anything. I appreciate that you want to do the right thing, but I do not want to marry you, James.'

He stared at her, uncertain he had heard correctly. *She didn't want to marry him.*

He knew he should be feeling relief, but that was not the emotion coursing through his body. The hollow sensation in the centre of his chest was more akin to that deep loneliness he often felt as a child, and that gnawing sense of abandonment was the same one that had followed him through his childhood and into his adult years.

Strangely, he was tempted to plead with her, to convince her they had to marry, but that was surely not what he wanted, and it was obviously not what she wanted either.

'I'm so sorry,' he repeated, wondering if he was sorry for what had happened, or sorry for himself, or sorry that she had rejected him.

'Right, now that has been settled,' she said in a light-hearted tone which he was certain had to be forced. 'I believe it is time I got out of these clothes.'

James cringed and she gave an embarrassed laugh. 'I mean, I should change back into my dry clothing.'

She stood up and James got to his feet. What did he do now? Did he kiss her goodbye? After what they had just exchanged that would seem the most appropriate thing to do. It was certainly what he would do with any of his previous lovers. But Alice was not his lover. She was a woman he should not have touched, should not have kissed and most certainly should not have started to make love to.

And if he did kiss her again, he knew he would not be able to resist doing so much more, proving what a cad he was and the extent to which she deserved a man better than him.

She remained standing, as if she too was unsure how to end this.

'Goodbye, James,' she finally said and walked out the room.

The moment she left he sank back to the settee, certain that no man had ever felt more wretched than he did right now.

Alice walked up the stairs towards the bedchamber in a dreamlike state as if no longer tethered to the real world. She could hardly believe anything that had happened since James discovered her sitting in that muddy puddle beside the river.

She stopped at the top of the stairs and gripped the

banister, trying to make sense of all she'd just experienced. James had kissed her, he'd caressed her in the most intimate of places, he'd taken her to heights of sensual pleasure she had hitherto not known existed and he had even proposed, albeit in a begrudging manner.

She had left the house this morning determined to formulate a plan which would reveal any affection James might harbour for her and had even secretly hoped he might wish to marry her. Beatrice had told her men needed manoeuvring, and it looked like she had unintentionally manoeuvred James into doing and saying everything she wanted. But it was all askew and she now had another conundrum to grapple with.

She had discovered that Beatrice was right. It was hard to believe but the magnificent, magnetic and intoxicating James Marlowe was actually attracted to her. The proof of that was still tingling on her body in every place that his hands and lips had caressed.

She gripped the banister even tighter. And the way that he had looked at her provided even greater proof. It was so intense, so full of desire, even affection. She placed one hand over her heart as she recalled the image of his face as he gazed down at her while he took her closer and closer towards that wonderful peak of pleasure. At the time she had almost convinced herself it was the look of love she saw in his eyes. Now she knew that was merely wishful thinking.

It was definitely desire, maybe even affection, but love? No. That half-hearted proposal was born of guilt, not love. She loved him—of that she was certain—and if he loved her in return then yes, marriage to him would be bliss itself, but he did not love her. It was only his sense of honour that made him ask for her hand, and she would not force him into something he did not want. A marriage made out of duty and guilt rather than love was doomed.

But there was no denying there was desire, intense, passionate desire, and after what he had shown her today, how could she not want more from him? Her other hand left the banister and covered her heart. When she'd left home this morning, she would never have thought that she was about to learn so much about her own body. Who would have thought such pleasure was possible?

Her finger gently stroked along her still-sensitive bottom lip, remembering the touch of his lips and his tongue. Lips that had also touched the skin of her neck and her breasts, hands that had caressed every part of her. She squeezed her legs together at the memory of his caressing hands, closed her eyes and sighed lightly.

Such pleasure was a revelation, and she wanted to experience that pleasure again and again. How could she possibly return to her old life after what she had just experienced? She could not live the life of a spinster when she knew what rapture a man could provide her.

She'd set off this morning trying to solve a conundrum of how to find out how James felt about her. Now she at least knew he was attracted to her. But she was presented with another conundrum. What were you supposed to do when a man was attracted to you, didn't want to marry you, and didn't want to do anything to compromise your reputation so you were free to marry another man—but that other man did not exist and never would?

She walked down the hallway towards the bedchamber, hoping she had better luck trying to figure out her latest problem than she had when she set out for her walk this morning. Perhaps he merely needed to see that no further harm would be done. They'd already transgressed and there was no going back, so what did it matter if they transgressed again and again and again?

None, but an awful lot of pleasure would be achieved, and surely there was no harm in that.

She entered the same bedchamber in which she'd slept at Christmas time to find Mary waiting for her, with a pile of relatively clean but much dryer clothing.

'Looks like no harm has been done,' Mary said as if she could read Alice's thoughts. 'Getting caught in the rain has certainly put a bloom on your cheeks.'

'Oh, I see,' Alice said, biting her bottom lip so she didn't laugh.

Mary helped her into her clothing and tied her dishevelled hair back into a tidy bun.

James had certainly put a bloom on her cheeks but had left her mind, not to mention her body, reeling. Somehow she had to convince him that even though she had no wish to become his wife she did want to become his lover.

The question was, did she have the confidence, the brazenness to ask him outright? She did not know the answer to that question. But another question was, after what she had just tasted, how could she not go back for seconds? And the answer to that was clear. No, she could not.

## Chapter Eighteen

The following day James once again found himself staring out the large windows that overlooked his estate, just as he had on the day before Christmas. The scene before him was just as bleak as it had been on that day, although this time he was unlikely to see a red-cloaked figure walking up the driveway. After what had happened between them, he suspected he would never see Alice again, at least not at his home and never alone.

All night he had debated whether he should go over to Rosetree Manor and apologise yet again. But how many times and in how many ways could he say sorry? He could offer to marry her again, although that too was certain to be pointless. She had made her feelings clear on that issue. But a woman like her should be married. She was made to love and be loved and to fill her home with happy children.

His hands clenched at his side. That man better make sure he was worthy of her, that he did treat her with the love and respect she deserved or he'd have James to answer to.

He looked back at the empty drawing room and sighed. That man better love her in a way in which he knew himself incapable of doing and make her happy, something else he lacked the ability to do.

She did not deserve to be stuck in this gloomy mausoleum of a house, where the misery of his family seemed to cling to the walls. Nor did she deserve an equally gloomy husband, one with a shattered knee and scarred face, along with a shattered heart and scarred soul. She deserved a man who could love her, wholeheartedly, without the restraints of physical and emotional wounds holding him back. That wasn't him and never could be.

He sighed deeply, but he was going to miss her. If he'd just kept his hands off her, she could have still been in his life; they could still be friends. He'd still be able to hear her laughter, her teasing, her joyfulness. But if she was in his life, would he be able to resist the temptation to kiss her again, to hold her again, to make love to her? When he was in her company it was impossible to not contemplate the pleasure of taking her to his bed.

By God, she really did deserve a man much better than the cad he had become.

The crunch of gravel under carriage wheels drew his attention back to the window.

Alice.

She was coming back to him.

Shouldn't she be trying to keep as far away from him as possible? Perhaps she had decided he was right. She had come to the realisation he *was* now obliged to marry her. If that was what she wanted, then it was a fate he would accept, although strangely it was not one that was filling him with the misgivings he would have expected.

His only real misgiving was that it would be wrong for Alice to enter a loveless marriage, but if that was what she wanted, then that was what would be.

He left the drawing room and went out to the entrance to greet her, an unexpected lightness of spirit taking hold of him, and he even found himself smiling. Then his smile dissolved and that heaviness descended back onto his shoulders.

The carriage travelling up the driveway was not the Lambtons' as he had first thought. This was a modern, highly polished vehicle, the four black horses bearing plumes and braiding, and he could now see the coachman and footman were dressed in unfamiliar livery.

His heart sank. More visitors. That was the last thing he wanted. He had no desire to entertain any passing aristocrats, not when he was dealing with the turmoil caused by yesterday's visitor.

The coach drew closer and his heart sank even further. On the side, he could now see the Duke of Brimley's crest. What the hell that man wanted with him James had no idea, but he suspected this was not going to be a pleasant visit and one James intended to do everything in his power to end as quickly as possible.

The footman jumped down from his platform at the rear of the vehicle, opened the door and lowered the stairs. Clara stepped out.

That was to be expected, he supposed. The Duke would be travelling with his new bride. But why had he brought her to Thornwood Hall? To gloat? To rub James's nose in his victory? That was the most likely explanation.

James gritted his teeth together and approached the vehicle. This most definitely would be a short visit, and the two of them would be on their way as soon as a modicum of propriety had been observed.

He bowed formally to Clara. 'Miss Waverly, or should I say Lady Brimley, this is unexpected.' He looked up to the carriage and waited for the smug Duke to descend.

'It's just me and my lady's maid,' Clara said as a shy young lady appeared, her eyes lowered.

He waited for familiar emotions to swamp him. The excitement of seeing her again, for his breath to catch again, the way it did whenever he caught sight of her beauty. Nothing.

'The Duke and I are travelling around the country,' she continued. 'We're staying in Carlisle with some of his cousins. I told him I wanted to visit a relative of my mother's, and because she's rather impoverished meeting a duke would be far too overwhelming for her.' She laughed lightly, her shoulders moving delicately in that flirtatious manner he knew so well. 'It's naughty of me, I know, but you always rather liked that naughty side of me, didn't you?' she added and tapped his arm with her bejewelled hand.

That should have provoked a reaction. Again nothing.

'I heard you had inherited a title and an estate in this area and I had to see it for myself.'

'So you have left your husband behind and are travelling alone?'

How long had they been married? It couldn't be more than a few months.

'Yes, but the Duke won't mind. He had some boring men he wanted to talk to anyway, about sheep or something. And I'm not alone.' She turned to her lady's maid. 'Go down to the servants' quarters. I'll call you when I need you.'

Her eyes still lowered, the maid bobbed a curtsey and she scuttled off around the side of the house. James had to wonder whether Clara even knew the young woman's name. Probably not. And it was even less likely that she knew anything about her family or circumstances. And even unlikelier still that she would provide the family with soup and mince pies when the mother was poorly.

'So, are you going to invite me in?' Clara said, smiling at him, a smile that had once had him entranced. Had there always been something slightly false about it? While those full red lips were pulled into a perfect smile which revealed even, white teeth, it did not reach her eyes. Those big blue eyes, surrounded by long, thick black eyelashes he had always compared to silken fans, were not smiling, but seemingly observing him closely to measure his reaction. Had she always looked at him like that, or was this something that had developed since she became a married woman?

'Yes, of course,' he said, gesturing towards the house.

She took his arm, her body so close it was touching his. 'I'd been told you still walked with a cane.'

'Yes, I did while I was recovering.'

James had hardly noticed but he rarely used the cane now. When had that happened? He had not needed it when he danced with Alice at the ball, nor when he had carried her through the snow, and he had all but run down the stairs when he thought it was her carriage arriving, oblivious to any pain his knee might be giving him.

'That's good. You don't want to look like an infirm old man hobbling along. It's not exactly the most desirable image to present to a lady,' she said with a teasing laugh.

A twinge nipped at his knee, something that hadn't happened for some time, but then, it had been some time since he had thought about that accident that had cut open his knee and face.

'And your scar is not as bad now.' She sent him another of those beaming smiles. 'In fact, it gives you a rather dashing look. You should tell people you got it in a duel over a lady's honour.' She laughed and gave his arm a light squeeze.

He led her through the entranceway and informed the footman to serve tea in the drawing room.

'Coffee, darling,' Clara said. 'I can't abide all this tea drinking that goes on in this country.'

The footman bowed and departed.

'This house is rather grand, isn't it?' she said, looking around as they entered the drawing room. 'Who would have thought that you would become an earl and I would become a duchess.'

She walked over to the settee and patted the seat beside her. James recoiled as if he'd been struck. He did not want to join her on the same settee that only yesterday he had taken Alice in his arms and all but made love to her.

However, he did not want to appear rude, so took a seat on the settee when Clara again motioned for him to sit beside her.

'It seems things have changed for both of us since we were last together.' She smiled, but once again that smile did not reach her eyes. 'Do you remember the last time we were together? Before...' She waved her hand in the direction of his knee. 'I certainly do, and if the Duke knew what we had done I very much doubt he would have offered for my hand.' Her smile grew wider and she gave a coquettish wriggle of her shoulders.

'So how is married life?' James was not going to discuss their time together and he doubted the Duke would give a damn about anything that had happened between them. All he would have cared about was Clara's generous dowry.

'Are you enjoying being a duchess?'

He might not know the answer to the first question, but he certainly knew the answer to the second. Clara had now been elevated to the highest rank in Society, and it suited her well. She looked every inch the duchess. Her clothes, as always, were immaculate. He doubted Brimley could keep her in the latest Paris fashions, but she presumably still received an allowance from her generous father. Randolph Waverly would be very pleased with his daughter, who had now well and truly served her purpose by reaching such a lofty social position, and he would be more than happy to continue supporting Clara in her customary manner. Her self-confidence, which was never in short supply, had seemingly increased, and everything about her suggested this was a woman who saw herself as above all others, which indeed she now was.

'It's not as I expected, I must admit. I'd expected grand balls, theatres, glittering soirées with the fashionable set. All Brimley wants to do is spend my dowry on repairs to his crumbling houses and rundown estates. That's about all we've been doing. Travelling from one estate to another so he can organise roof repairs and other such trivia.'

She smiled at him, a slow smile that had once made him helpless with desire. 'But once this journey is over, he promises me we can return to London. I assume you have a London town house and will be down there for the Season.'

'I fear not. Like your husband I have a lot to do to improve this estate and intend to remain here.'

'Surely not. You can't possibly want to be stuck out here, in the countryside, away from civilization.' Once again she sent him that smile designed to melt his resolve. 'We had such fun together in New York. I know you loved every minute of our time together, as did I. You don't have to hide away now that you're no longer a cripple.' She nodded towards his knee. 'Your scar is barely noticeable. There is no reason for you to avoid Society any longer.'

'There is still much that needs doing on this estate that requires my presence.'

She frowned in disbelief. 'Why not pay someone to do that? An estate manager or something. That's what Brimley plans to do.'

And that was exactly why so many aristocrats were in such dire straits they had to marry American heiresses to save them. That was how his brother and father behaved, and it was not an example he would follow.

'I wish to remain on my estate. I want to take responsibility for ensuring it is well run.'

She stared at him as if he was speaking a language she did not understand and he realised everything he said was true. Thornwood Hall *had* provided him with a place to hide away, but now it was providing him with a purpose in life. He had loved his time with Clara in New York; it had been non-stop fun and laughter and he'd been bedazzled by her wit, intelligence and confidence. That had been why he thought himself in love with her, but if they had married they would have soon come to regret it. It was not a life that could sustain him forever, but making a difference to the lives of people on his estate and in the village, that was a life worth living.

He stared at Clara as a realisation dawned on him. Somewhat ironically his accident had saved them from making a terrible mistake.

'But we did have fun such together, didn't we?' she said.

'Yes, we did,' he admitted.

More fun than he'd ever had before in his life, and that was why he had wanted to marry her. But Clara could never be with a man who did not provide her with endless gaiety. That was why he pushed her away after the accident. That was why it would have been a mistake to take her as his wife. And that was why he now knew it had never really been a true love.

'We could still have fun together,' she said with a smile that could only be described as saucy.

'I have my own town house in London. Father bought it for me.' She reached over and gave his hand a small squeeze. 'I've met some other American women married to British aristocrats during our travels and they have all taken lovers. They say it's almost expected of them.'

James too was well aware of this unspoken but accepted practice, particularly in arranged marriages that remained loveless. The men often retained a mistress, and once the wife had provided the required heir then she too was sometimes given the freedom to take a lover, provided she was discreet.

'Oh, James, darling, are you going to make me spell it out? We had fun together. We can continue to have fun together. I'm offering to become your lover.'

James took hold of her stroking hand and lightly kissed the back. 'I'm sorry, Clara, we now live in very different worlds. This is the world I wish to live in.' It was bizarre but it was true. He did not want to return to Clara's glittering world.

'I can see you're still angry with me. I should never have left you when you…' She nodded towards his knee. 'I'm sorry, let me make it up to you.' She moved even closer to him, her breasts almost against his chest.

He shook his head slowly. 'You have nothing to be sorry for, Clara, nothing to make up.'

'But you must regret losing what we had. I certainly do, and we could have it again. We should arrange to meet in London,' she whispered, as if they had reached an agreement. 'Brimley won't care and it will be just like old times, but even better as we'll no longer have to worry about chaperones.'

'Clara,' he said, still gently clasping her hands. 'We will not be becoming lovers.'

Her forehead furrowed and her lips pinched tightly. James suspected this was the first time in her life Clara had not got exactly what she wanted, and it was obvious she did not like it.

'But I'm sure you'll find the life you seek in London,' he said, trying to console her. 'As a duchess you're at the very pinnacle of Society in both England and Europe. You will attend the most lavish balls and dinner parties. You'll even be able to mix with royalty. *And if it's a lover you want, you are sure to find one*, he could add. To his amazement he realised that thought did not cause the agonising pain it should.

She continued to stare at him in consternation, as if still trying to comprehend that he had not accepted her offer.

'I do hope you find happiness in the life you have chosen, and I feel certain that you will, but your future life will not include me.'

Once again he lifted her hand to his mouth and lightly kissed it while she frowned at him.

The footman entered with the coffee on a tray and coughed lightly. 'My lord, Alice Lambton has arrived. Shall I show her in?'

'No, I'll—'

He was not fast enough. As was her way, Alice had followed the footman in and not waited to be announced.

'James, I—'

Her words died. She looked at Clara and James together on the settee. He dropped her hands, stood up, his body clenching, his mind numb as he struggled to find the words to ease the anguish he saw etched on her face and explain a situation which must surely damn him even further in her eyes.

## Chapter Nineteen

To stop herself and the room from reeling Alice grabbed hold of the edge of the doorway. She wanted to look away from the sight before her but couldn't.

This had to be Clara. James had said she was the most beautiful woman in New York Society, and the woman seated beside him, the woman whose hand he'd been holding to his lips, was definitely the most beautiful Alice had ever seen.

Everything about her was perfect. Her pale skin was flawless and would surely be described as resembling fine porcelain. Those large cornflower-blue eyes that were staring at her in curiosity were surrounded by the longest, darkest eyelashes Alice had ever seen. Her golden blonde hair, styled in an ornate manner, appeared to glisten, even in the weak sunlight of the winter's day.

And her clothing far surpassed anything Alice had seen during the Season. The light-peach-and-cream-coloured dress showed off a figure that was both slender and curvaceous. Alice was sure she possessed the tiniest waist in existence, and the tucks in the bodice, along with the delicate silk flowers at the neckline, couldn't help but draw attention to her most feminine of qualities, which she possessed in annoying abundance.

Alice had no doubt this woman would have shone in New York Society, and if she had attended London Society, every other woman present would have faded into her shadow.

It was easy to see why James had fallen in love with her. How could any man not be dazzled by such a woman?

Alice emerged from her state of bewilderment and the absurdity of her situation hit her like the sting of salt in an open wound. For one ridiculous moment she had absurdly thought she had a chance with James Marlowe. A man who had been in love with this vision of loveliness.

It was worse than laughable. It was pathetic. If anyone had known she had come over to Thornwood Hall to suggest to James they become lovers they would have laughed themselves senseless. Thank goodness no one knew and she could put that ridiculous notion away.

James remained standing, staring at her, looking as shaken as Alice was feeling. And understandably so. If the woman he loved knew what had happened on the very settee on which they had been sitting she would be horrified.

'Alice, Miss Lambton, may I present Clara, the Duchess of Brimley,' he said, his voice choked.

The vision tilted her head and smiled, a smile that was of course extremely pretty and made with sweetly shaped Cupid's-bow lips.

Heaven help her, Alice was going to have to curtsey, and to make it a low one as etiquette demanded when meeting one's superior. And that was what she was, Alice's superior, in every way, not just her title. She was not only beautiful, but she possessed that confident grace and elegance that Alice would never be able to achieve, even with hours of rigorous training from the most dedicated of tutors.

This was a woman who was obviously used to being the centre of attention, just as Alice was used to being shunted off to the periphery. Perhaps she should now find herself a potted fern to sit beside as she'd done throughout the Social Season. Either that or make a hasty retreat. There were no potted ferns so it would have to be a retreat, but if she was not to look even more the fool she would have to engage in a moment or two of polite exchange.

So she made her curtsey and hoped in her distraught state she did not fall flat on her face and look like the buffoon she felt.

'Your grace,' she mumbled.

The duchess nodded her immaculately coiffured head then turned her attention towards James. 'I can see you are already attracting the attentions of the locals.'

Of course she had a beautiful, well-modulated voice. Her American accent had a musical lilt to it that was charming and she spoke with a confidence that suggested she was used to getting anything she asked for. And from the way she was looking at James, it was obvious it was him she wanted. Alice imagined when the Duchess wanted a man, any man, all she had to do was click her fingers, and he would come to heel.

'Alice, won't you please take a seat? I'll call for another cup,' James said, indicating a chair across from them and signalling to the footman.

'Oh, no, I don't want to interrupt,' she said, acutely aware that her own voice did not sound confident, nor did it have a lilting, musical quality and it would certainly not bring any man to heel.

'You're not interrupting, and the Duchess was not planning on staying. She has a husband to get back to.'

That caused those finely shaped eyebrows to rise.

Interesting.

Perhaps this exquisite creature wasn't getting everything her own way after all.

Alice remained standing just inside the doorway, suddenly torn as to what to do. She did not want to stay and witness something between James and the

Duchess that was sure to be excruciating. On the other hand, she did want to know exactly what was going on between him and this woman.

She crossed the room and took a seat.

'Alfred, please bring another cup for Miss Lambton,' James said.

Rather than take his seat next to the Duchess he walked over to the fireplace and leaned against the mantelpiece.

'So I take it you *are* a local,' the Duchess said, those big blue eyes flicking up and down Alice's clothes, the slight frown making it clear she found Alice's appearance rather provincial.

Before walking over to Thornwood Hall, Alice had taken more care with her appearance than was usual. Rather than a sensible grey skirt and plain blouse which would be more suitable for the weather and for walking, she had picked a pretty pale blue day dress with cream lace around the neck and cuffs. That was, she had thought it pretty when she left the house.

Now it felt as if she was trying far too hard and failing dismally, like a scarecrow donning a lace bonnet then preening and primping as if transformed into a lady and no longer a ragged scarecrow.

'Yes, I live not far away in Rosetree Manor. My brother, William, and…' She paused. 'And James have been friends since we were children.'

Once again those arched eyebrows rose slightly.

Alice had hesitated before using James's given name, then thought better of it. If this woman now knew she and James had reached that level of informality, then so be it. And being on a first-name basis was nothing compared to the level of informality they had reached on the very settee where her no-doubt-perfect rear end was now sitting.

'How delightful,' the Duchess said, her voice dripping with insincerity. Was there a hint of jealousy in her arched tone? Surely she had nothing to be jealous of.

Alfred entered with another cup and a plate of Christmas cake and smiled at Alice. 'Cook thought you might like some cake.'

Alice smiled back at him. 'Cook thought correctly, but I'm sure I'm not the only one who wants to sample this delicious cake.'

The Duchess waved her hand in front of her face. 'No, some of us like to watch our figure.'

'James?' Alice said to the man scowling from beside the fireplace.

He too waved his hand, but Alice doubted that had anything to do with wanting to keep his figure in trim and more to do with wanting this exchange to end as soon as possible.

To prove to everyone she did not give a fig about her own figure she placed two slices of cake on her plate, then shrugged and added a third. The Duchess once again flicked a gaze up and down Alice, and she knew what she was thinking. With a figure like hers why would she bother watching it?

Alice took a defiant bite of the cake.

James smiled at her. 'Can I assume it is still your favourite?'

Alice swallowed and nodded. 'It gets better with every passing day.'

The Duchess looked from one to the other. 'You've had cake here before?'

'Oh, yes,' Alice answered before James could say anything. 'James and I celebrated Christmas Day together.'

There. *While I chew on this delicious cake, you can chew on that*, Alice thought with a certain smugness.

The Duchess tilted her head at James, as if for an explanation.

'It was quite the impromptu celebration that neither of us had planned,' he said, then smiled. 'But I believe we made the most of the situation,' he added, using one of Alice's favourite maxims.

Alice smiled back at him in thanks. He could have explained about the snowstorm that had stranded her in the house and that she was an unwanted guest who had invited herself. Alice was certain the Duchess would revel in hearing how he had tried his best to rid himself of her. But he chose not to. Did that mean the Duchess now meant nothing to him? Or was that wishful thinking? Yes, of course it was wishful think-ing. He had told her he was in love with this woman and had wanted to marry her. And just look at her, for goodness' sake. Of course he was still in love with her. And if there was any jealousy, it was all on Alice's part; her uncharacteristic snappiness was proof of that.

Her cake suddenly tasted like ashes in her mouth. She forced it down and took a sip of her coffee.

The Duchess continued to appraise Alice, those big blue eyes growing colder, those red Cupid lips taking on a hard edge.

A little shiver of fear moved up Alice's spine. Per-haps she should have done nothing to provoke the duchess. A woman such as her would never expect someone like Alice to challenge her supremacy.

'I'm so pleased James has found a way to entertain himself, stuck out here in the countryside, away from sophisticated company.'

'As I have said, it is where I wish to be,' James said, cutting through any response Alice could give, which she was sure would have been inadequate, as the Duchess was correct. He *was* stuck out here, and there was nothing particularly sophisticated about Ferndale.

The Duchess turned her smile on James. 'But it's nothing compared to what London can offer you,' she said, her voice almost a purr. Alice could not help but suspect there was a hidden message in that statement.

James said nothing, and Alice suspected that silence spoke volumes.

'I see,' she said, placing her cup on a nearby table. 'Well, if you prefer what this unsophisticated backwater can offer, then I suppose there's nothing more for me to say.'

Alice looked to James, waiting for him to respond to what was obviously an insulting barb. Again he said nothing.

'Miss Lambton, may I offer you a ride back to your home?' the Duchess asked.

'Oh, um, no thank you. I was planning to walk.'

'Yes, I suspected you were the sort of athletic woman who enjoyed a hearty walk in the countryside, but I insist. You wouldn't want to damage that lovely dress—' her eyes flicked up and down Alice '—any more than you already have.'

'In this unsophisticated backwater you quickly learn that getting a bit of mud on your clothes is not always a bad thing,' James said to the Duchess, then smiled at Alice.

Heat rose up Alice's cheeks. Was that another hidden exchange? One just for her? Was it a reference to what they had shared on the settee? This was all too convoluted for Alice. It was so much easier when people said what they meant.

'And if Alice wishes to remain then she is most welcome to do so,' he added.

The Duchess looked slowly from one to the other then back again, her pinched expression making it clear that she was not used to being contradicted.

'Well, I don't know what happens in the country-side, but surely it would be inappropriate for an un-married woman to remain in a man's company without a chaperone,' the Duchess said, her voice terse.

Alice wanted to inform her that they had been alone in each other's company on several occasions, but she suspected the Duchess cared not the slightest about Alice's reputation and her offer to take her home was about something else entirely.

'But I can wait until you've finished eating all that cake.' She stared at Alice, as if planning on watching her as she ate the three pieces of cake on her plate.

'Yes, perhaps I should be returning home,' Alice said reluctantly. 'Thank you, it is very kind of you to offer to take me.'

'Good, and we can have a nice chat on the way. Just us girls.' With that she swept across the room and gave James a kiss on the cheek. 'I hope I will be seeing you again soon.'

'Give my regards to your husband,' James said.

The Duchess merely laughed as if James had made a joke.

He turned his focus to Alice, his steady gaze holding hers. 'And I hope to see you again, Alice. Soon.'

Before Alice could respond, the Duchess took her

arm and led her out the room, down the stairs and to the waiting carriage.

Alice had seen it parked to the side of the house when she had arrived but had hardly registered its presence. If she had paid more attention, if she hadn't been entirely focused on what she was going to say to James, she would not have been so oblivious to her surroundings and would have noticed the carriage did not bear the Thornwood crest.

'It was so wonderful to see Jamie again,' the Duchess said as soon as she had settled herself on the well-padded velvet bench and pulled a fur blanket over her knees. 'We did have such fun in New York and I must admit I do miss him.'

Alice merely gave what she hoped was a polite smile, not wanting to hear a word about that fun.

'I can hardly believe he is happy to remain out here in the countryside,' Clara continued, leaning forward as if to reveal a confidence. 'Of course, just between us, I would not be surprised if he has taken a lover.'

Alice stiffened, and her smile became rigid.

The Duchess gave her a long, appraising look and Alice tried her hardest to reveal nothing, but suspected she was failing dismally.

'I shouldn't tell secrets, but James is such a virile man. I know he would not be capable of going too long without a woman to warm his bed. There is bound to be some giddy lass in the area who thinks she's the luckiest girl alive to find herself being bedded by such an experienced man.'

The duchess shook her head slightly and gave a despondent sigh. 'As long as the little fool doesn't think she has a hope of becoming the next Countess of Thornwood. With rakes there's always two types of women, those you bed and those you wed.' She laughed as if this was the wittiest of jests.

'Isn't it the folly of women that we can't help but be attracted to the rake, even if we know they are bad for us? Although I am pleased to say that when James was courting me, he put all that aside. He was completely loyal and loving and dedicated all his affections entirely on me. But now that I am out of his life, I'm sure he's returned to his old ways and is chasing any willing chit that comes his way.'

She resumed smiling at Alice. 'Although as you and James appear to be good friends, I'm sure none of this is news to you.'

Alice forced herself to return the smile. Her first assumption was correct. What she was witnessing was jealousy. It was almost impossible to believe it, but this stunningly beautiful woman was jealous of her.

Alice had never been on the receiving end of jealousy before but knew it could make one act in a cruel manner, and the duchess's words were certainly designed to hurt. But that did not make what she was saying any less true.

'Oh, here we are,' the Duchess said when the carriage pulled up in front of Rosetree Manor. 'What a delightful little house.'

Alice chose not to point out that after Thornwood Hall, it was the biggest house in the county, certain that would only bring about another cutting comment about life in the unsophisticated provinces.

Alice said her goodbyes and climbed down from the carriage, her heart shattered, all her foolish dreams destroyed.

The carriage drove away and Alice finally let go of that agonising smile. She exhaled slowly, in a failed attempt to blow out the tension that had gripped her body from the moment she walked into the drawing room and saw James and Clara together.

She walked up the path towards her home at a slow pace as she tried to make sense of all that had happened. The conversation at Thornwood Hall had convinced her that Clara no longer meant anything to James, but unfortunately that loathsome conversation in the carriage had opened her eyes to some further distressing truths.

James *had* loved Clara. He did not love Alice. He *had* wanted to marry Clara. He had offered to marry Alice, but only because he felt duty bound to do so. He had made it clear he did not really want to marry her or anyone else, but the Duchess was correct; she too could not imagine a man like James going long without a woman in his life, and in his bed.

She reached the doorway and halted under the portico, the cheerful Christmas wreath on the door seemingly mocking her.

When Alice had set out towards Thornwood Hall it was after coming to a firm decision. Even though James did not love her, even though he did not wish to marry her, she wanted to become his lover.

Clara was right.

Alice, who had always considered herself to be a sensible, intelligent woman, had become a giddy lass, all because a handsome, virile man had paid her some attention. She was now that silly little chit who was eager to warm James's bed.

She leaned against the brick wall and placed both hands on her stomach in a futile attempt to ease her torment.

When she'd been walking towards Thornwood Hall she had thought herself the bravest woman in the world. She was going to tell James what she wanted. She'd imagined him admiring her daring spirit, taking her in his arms, leading her upstairs to his bedchamber and making her the luckiest girl alive, because she was being bedded by such an experienced man.

She really was a fool. That was not what she wanted, but it had been what she was prepared to settle for. What she really wanted was for him to love her the way she loved him. What she was prepared to take was second best. At least, that had been what she had been prepared to accept until Lady Brimley had opened her eyes and made her see things as they really were.

She could not become James's lover. The devastation when he moved on to someone else, someone he really did want to wed not just bed, would be more than she would be capable of enduring. As much as she wanted to ignore the truth, she couldn't anymore. Lady Brimley had shattered all those romantic dreams with which she had deluded herself.

She placed her hand on the doorknob, still uncertain about so many things, but knowing one thing for certain. She could not remain in Ferndale, not when she knew James was just a short walk away, not when she knew how easily she could cease to be a sensible, intelligent woman, and be reduced to a silly chit.

With that firmly in mind, she walked into the house and down the hallway to the drawing room.

'How was James?' William said.

Beatrice was sitting beside him, and from their flushed cheeks she deduced it was not just a pleasant chat beside the fire that she had interrupted.

'Yes, how was the Earl?' Beatrice added, her words laden with expectation.

'He was as he always is,' she responded, certainly in no mood to discuss anything that had just happened at Thornwood Hall, or that humiliating conversation she'd had with Lady Brimley on the way home.

'But I have some news,' she added, causing her brother and friend to smile and lean forward as if that news could be nothing but good.

'I've had a letter from my publisher. He wants me in London, urgently. There's some problem with the latest book and he wants to discuss it with me in person, immediately. So I had better travel down to London on the next available train. I'm assuming it will be all right if I stay in your town house?'

'Of course,' William said, his brow furrowed. 'But—'

'I better hurry if I'm to make the afternoon train,' she said and rushed out the room before either William or Beatrice could ask questions she neither wanted to think about nor answer.

## Chapter Twenty

James had watched the two women depart, then remained standing at the window, with the whole scene playing over and over again in his mind.

Clara had turned his world upside down when they'd first met and he'd instantly fallen in love with her beauty and sparkling personality. During their time together, he'd changed from a serious young man who was escaping a miserable family life, into one who could enjoy all the pleasures of a charmed existence.

But he was no longer the man who had danced with Clara at balls and attended endless soirées. That man had died when his knee had been crushed under a runaway carriage.

The man who had returned to Thornwood Hall was not the man Clara had loved. Nor was he the man who had believed himself in love with Clara. The wedding vows included 'in sickness and in health' and his accident had made it clear his love for Clara and her love for him could only exist during times of health, happiness and wealth.

When they parted his heart had been crushed just as surely as his knee, and it was his wounded heart that had made this remote refuge so welcome. But he'd been right to push her away, and she had been right to leave him.

And it was in this remote refuge that he had healed, both physically and emotionally.

He smiled to himself as he remembered his reaction when he'd seen that red-cloaked figure at the end of his driveway. He'd been so gruff and determined to drive her away, and yet it had not been able to dim her spirits or her kindness. While Clara's beauty had hit him like a lightning bolt striking on a clear day, Alice's beauty had gently unfolded the more he got to know her, perhaps because her beauty was not superficial, but shone from within and was reflected in everything she did and said. James had never seen any woman move with Alice's elegant grace. That had been the first thing he had noticed about her. When she'd walked around the drawing room on Christmas Eve, looking for something to occupy her time, he had immediately found himself drawn to the way she moved, which was more elegant because it was without artifice but suggested a level of self-possession that was full of quiet dignity and composure.

While it was the first thing that had attracted him

to her, it certainly was not the last. Each time they met he discovered more about her that enchanted. Her eyes sparkled with humour and warmth and contained greater depth of colour and hue than mere grey as he had first thought. Her lips smiled so readily and yet were also enticingly sensual.

Clara was right when she said Alice was the type of woman who enjoyed a hearty walk, but that was nothing to criticise. With her cheeks flushed from exercise she always looked vibrant, like a summer sunrise, full of energy and warmth.

Nor did she need the artifice of the world's most expensive and exclusive couturier to make her look desirable. She was stunning in a simple unadorned gown, and even more so in a workman's trousers and shirt. He smiled again at the memory of how she had looked when she emerged from the stables, wearing that perky cap on her head, and those baggy trousers and faded shirt.

But it wasn't just her physical beauty that had slowly revealed itself to him. The more time he spent with her, the more aware he was of her inner beauty, which seemed to glow with even greater intensity. Her kindness to everyone, from the lowliest servant upward, her dedication to spreading happiness throughout the community, her self-reliance and unselfishness—these were all qualities she possessed in abundance, and these were the qualities that made her the woman he had fallen in love with.

He continued smiling as that thought settled in his mind.

*The woman he had fallen in love with.*

He had fallen in love with Alice Lambton.

How could he not have realised that before? Of course he was in love with Alice, deeply, overwhelmingly, with all his heart and soul. She was a woman he could imagine weathering all life's storms with. A woman who would give him strength to face times of despair, and with whom he could share all life's pleasures.

And yet he had pushed her away, just as surely as he had done with Clara, but while he'd done so with Clara for all the right reasons, with Alice it had been for all the wrong reasons.

He dragged his hands through his hair. How could he have made that insulting marriage proposal to her? The magnitude of his arrogance hit him like a punch to the stomach. It was all but inconceivable that he be so reckless with her feelings and it had to be put to rights.

He had to tell her that marrying her would never be a duty. It would be an honour, one greater than anything he deserved.

He rang for the footman to tell the coachman to ready the carriage then thought better of it. He could not stand around waiting. He needed to be moving or he was sure he would burst out of his skin in agitation. He had to tell Alice how he felt.

To that end, he rushed out the drawing room, past a bewildered Alfred and down the stairs, and commenced running towards Rosetree Manor, minus his coat and gloves but hardly noticing the winter air.

As he ran across the fields he tried to think of what he would say to her, but all that came to his mind was *I love you*, and that was hardly adequate to express all that needed to be said. He raced up the path that led to her home, still with no idea what he would say to her.

He paused in front of the door to catch his breath and to try to think. What on earth was wrong with him? He was never lost for words but he had no idea how to express the depths of his feelings, could think of no words strong enough to describe how much he loved her, and had no idea how to beg her to see him as someone she might love in return.

He knocked on the door and the maid showed him into the drawing room, where William and Miss Chigwell were deep in conversation.

Still trying to catch his breath, he stood at the doorway, aware of his pounding heart and his laboured breathing.

'I'm so pleased you're here,' Miss Chigwell said. 'William and I were just about to walk over and see you on a matter of some urgency.'

James stepped forward, his senses on high alert, and looked from Miss Chigwell to William, who was frowning at his future wife.

'No, Beatrice, sweetheart, we hadn't yet agreed as to what we are to do. I still think it is none of our—'

'Of course it's our business. If it's not our business, then whose is it?'

'Well, I think—'

'It's what she would do for us. We're all family now and of course it is up to us.'

'Whoever's business it is, can you please tell me what is going on,' James said, becoming ever more frustrated with this discussion.

'It's Alice,' Miss Chigwell said, turning back to James, her expression so grave it stole the air from his lungs.

'What? What's wrong?' he gasped, fear tightening like a steel trap around his chest.

'She's gone to London to see her publisher,' William added.

The panic subsided. That was hardly a catastrophe. So why was Miss Chigwell acting as if this was some sort of disaster?

'She has not gone to London to see her publisher,' Miss Chigwell said to William while frowning, adding further to James's confusion. 'Well, she has gone to London, but not to see her publisher. Her publisher is on holiday in Scotland until the end of January.'

'Please, will someone tell me what is going on?' James said. 'We've established she's gone to London. It matters not who she has gone to see. What I need to know is when will she be back?' He had stated that clearly enough for anyone to understand, if a bit too loudly, and hopefully he would now get some equally clear answers.

Miss Chigwell shook her head and released an exasperated sigh. 'You men are so foolish. How you ever got to rule the world I'll never know. Alice has not raced off to London in such a hurry because of her book, or because she was summoned by her publisher. She was running away from you.'

'Me?' Had he done something so outlandish that it would drive a woman out of her home? There was that kiss, but she did not object, and didn't flee to London at the time. Had Clara's presence upset her? Yes, that unfortunately was very likely. He should never have allowed them to travel in the carriage together.

'Oh, for goodness' sake,' Miss Chigwell said, cutting through his muddled thoughts. 'Alice is in love with you. I don't know what happened between the two of you today. I tried to get some sense out of her before she fled but it was all a garbled mess. Something about some other woman you are in love with. All I know is you have broken her heart and she's gone to London to get away from you and to recover.'

'Love? Broken heart?'

'Yes, love, broken heart,' Miss Chigwell said, crossing her arms and glaring at James. 'And if you feel anything for her, I suggest you go and resolve the mess you've made.'

'That's what I'm here to do.'

'Well, she's gone. And if you want to catch her before the train leaves for London you're going to have to make haste.'

'Yes, yes, of course,' James said, rushing out the house without saying goodbye.

He ran down the path and came to a halt. Why on earth had he left Thornwood Hall without waiting for his carriage? He could not possibly run all the way to the station, and even if he did, he would never make it in time before the afternoon train left for London.

A cart came around the corner, laden high with hay and straw. He rushed up to it, waved his hands and brought the driver to a halt, which wasn't hard as the cart was being pulled by a stout but slow moving Clydesdale horse who appeared to be in no hurry.

'I need to get to the train station,' James said.

The man merely stared at him as if he had no idea what he was talking about.

'Can you please give me a lift to the train station?'

'Ah need t' feed sheep.'

'Yes, I know but I will pay you handsomely for your time.'

While the man was still contemplating this offer,

James climbed up onto the wooden bench beside the driver, emptied his pockets and handed him everything he had.

'Train station it is then, aye reckon,' the man said, pocketing the money. With a flick of the reins they moved off, the horse travelling at a pace only slightly faster than James could run.

'Can you make that horse go any faster?' James said, leaning forward as if urging it on.

'Empress dunn' like to be rushed.'

James reached back into his pockets and pulled out his fob watch. 'I'll give you this if Empress can get me to the station before the London train leaves. It's gold.'

With that, the man flicked the reins again. 'Gee up, lass, we've nae time to waste.'

At a steady trot they travelled through the village and arrived at the station. Before the cart had come to a halt James handed the man his watch then jumped down from the bench and raced up the stairs to the platform.

The train was still in the station, but the volume of smoke puffing from its stack and the hiss of steam from its engine suggested it was about to leave, as did the stationmaster, who was vigorously waving his flag and blowing his whistle.

James wove his way past the milling throng on the platform, and jumped onto the train through the only door the porters had not yet shut, mere seconds before it pulled out of the station.

He looked around at the crowded wooden benches, packed with men, women and children, along with luggage and baskets of food.

It was apparent he had entered through a door to the third-class compartment. Stepping over feet, bags and rather surprisingly, a cage of clucking chickens, he made his way out of the carriage and through to the second-class compartment, where the seats were less crowded, bags were stowed away and there wasn't an animal in sight.

Finally, he made it to first class, and walked along the corridor, looking through windows into each packed compartment, desperate to find Alice. Just as he was about to give up hope, certain that she must have caught an earlier train, he saw her seated in the last compartment, looking out the window at the passing scenery. Unfortunately, like everywhere else on this train, this compartment was full, with five other passengers, all reading newspapers or books or, like Alice, staring out of the window.

James had not considered this. In fact, he had not considered anything when he had rushed after the train. Not only did he not know what he was to say to Alice, but it seemed he would have to say it in front of an audience.

He looked back along the corridor. Perhaps he

should find himself a seat and wait until they disembarked in London before he made a speech that was surely going to be the most important of his life.

He looked back into the compartment. She turned to face him, stared at him for a moment as if not even registering it was him, then gasped.

There was nothing for it. He was going to have to tell Alice why he was on this train, how he felt and how much he loved and adored her. That was daunting enough, but he was about to do it in front of a compartment full of bored strangers.

## Chapter Twenty-One

For the second time that day Alice felt as if the floor was moving under her feet, and it wasn't just because she was travelling on a rocking train.

She blinked several times in case she was seeing things. James was looking at her through the window in the door, a strange expression on his face, unlike any she had seen before. She could almost describe it as vulnerable, uncertain, but these were not qualities she would ascribe to James Marlowe.

Her gasp had not been missed by the other passengers, and they too were looking in his direction, but with the disinterested curiosity of people who had nothing better to do.

He opened the door, stepped inside and stood there, still with that unfamiliar, awkward expression on his face.

'I think you'll find that this compartment is full,' said a stern-looking man sitting across from her, a man with the largest walrus moustache Alice had ever seen.

James turned to face him. 'Yes, I'm sorry, but I need to talk to Alice.'

'Well, whatever you have to say, it's going to have to wait.'

'It can't wait. I have waited too long already.'

'Well, I never. Young people today, they've no manners whatsoever.' The man huffed his annoyance, flicked his newspaper and disappeared behind it.

'Why are you here?' Alice asked. 'I didn't know you were travelling to London.' She swallowed and closed her eyes briefly. Hadn't Lady Brimley mentioned something about London?

'As I said,' he began, and pointed towards the man behind the newspaper, 'I need to talk to you.' He still wore that expression she would describe as embarrassed if it was anyone other than James, but embarrassed was as unlikely as awkward when it came to James.

'Talk to me? About what?'

He looked around at the passengers. All of them, except the man reading the newspaper, were staring up at him. His gaze returned to her. It became even more distressed, then it softened.

'Alice, I am in love with you.'

She gasped, along with the other women in the compartment and at least one male. Even the man with the walrus moustache lowered his newspaper, suddenly interested in what was happening.

James took a step inside the compartment.

'I adore you, Alice,' he added, staring at her as if now oblivious to the fact that they were not alone. 'You are the most beautiful woman in the world and I love everything about you. Your smile, your laugh, your sparkling eyes, your equally sparkling wit, your...' He paused and looked around at the five other people watching him. 'Let's just say I love everything about you.'

As one, all five heads turned to Alice, who was staring up at James, still unsure if this was real or a dream.

'You love me?' she said, her voice choked. 'But what about Clara?'

The five heads turned in James's direction.

'Seeing Clara again only made me realise that what I am feeling for you is love, true love, eternal love, love that would last, love that comes not just from the heart but from the soul.'

The women in the compartment, and that one man, all sighed again. The women placed their hands over their hearts and everyone turned in Alice's direction, breaths held as they waited for her response.

'Alice, I want you to be my wife,' he said, causing all heads to snap back to James then slowly turn to Alice.

'Young man,' Walrus Moustache said, rustling his

paper in agitation, 'I believe it is customary for that to be said when the man is on one knee.'

Five sets of legs instantly pulled in, giving James room to do as the walrus-moustached man said.

'No, James,' Alice cried out, causing everyone in the compartment to gasp again, and James to take a step backwards, his expression crestfallen.

'I don't mean no to the marriage proposal. I mean no to you getting down on one knee.' She looked around the compartment. 'He had a terrible accident. He was saving some children from a runaway carriage and he hurt his knee badly.'

The women's hands quickly returned to their hearts and even Walrus Moustache nodded his approval.

'Where's your cane?' she added. 'Did you travel all the way here without your cane?'

James looked down at his hand and appeared surprised at not seeing that familiar object. 'I must have left it at Rosetree Manor. When I heard you were taking the train to London I was so desperate to catch you before you left I must have raced off without it.'

'Oh, your poor knee.'

James smiled at her and it was as if everyone else in the compartment faded away. All she could see was his smile and his eyes focused entirely on her.

He moved back into the compartment, took her hand and lowered himself to one knee without a flicker of hesitation, his eyes still fixed on hers.

'Alice, I know I have not shown myself in the best light since we met. I have been morose, bad-tempered, ill mannered and, well, someone I for one would not fall in love with.'

Alice wanted to disagree with this assessment of his character, but with her breath caught in her throat she was unsure she could say anything.

'When you came into my life, I should have known immediately that you were the one, the one I could love with all my heart. Like a fool it took me far too long to realise what a beautiful woman you are, that you have a beautiful heart, a beautiful soul, a beautiful face and, well, other beautiful parts as well.'

Alice bit the edge of her lips to stop herself from laughing with joy.

'If you would consent to be my wife, I promise I will show you every day of my life how much I love you, how much I need you and how lucky I am that you came into my life. Alice, will you do me the honour of becoming my wife?'

'Yes,' she said quietly, which was greeted with loud clapping from her fellow travellers. 'Yes,' she repeated, slightly louder to be heard over the cheering. 'Yes,' she said for a third time.

'For goodness' sake, kiss her,' Walrus Moustache said, his loud voice cutting through the hubbub of the excited passengers.

James pulled Alice to her feet and did just that.

He kissed her deeply, oblivious to all present and the cheering that filled the compartment. She sank into his arms and the noise disappeared. All she could feel was his lips on hers and his arms around her; all she could think was she was to marry James Marlowe and this would be what the rest of her life would be like.

'Tickets, please,' a voice even gruffer than that of the walrus-moustached man broke through the web of desire and happiness that had wrapped around them.

James broke from Alice's lips and looked at the conductor.

'And we'll have none of that behaviour in here, if you don't mind, sir, miss,' the conductor added.

'They're getting married,' Walrus Moustache said, followed by sighs from the ladies present. 'He's just proposed. A man's got a right to kiss the woman who just accepted his offer of marriage.'

'Very good,' the conductor said in the same gruff tone. 'Now, let's be seeing your tickets.'

They all handed their tickets to the conductor, including Alice, and he clicked each one, then stared expectantly at James.

'I don't have a ticket,' he said.

'Then you best pay up.'

James reached into his pocket, then frowned. 'I gave all my money to the owner of Empress so he'd make her go faster.'

'Empress?' Alice asked.

'The horse. Her owner was taking straw to feed the sheep.'

It seemed getting married was making James incoherent.

'Here,' Walrus Moustache said, handing several notes to the conductor. 'I'll pay for your ticket. You can count it as my wedding present.'

'Thank you,' Alice and James said together.

'But let's get off at the next stop anyway and return to Ferndale,' she said. 'After all, I now have a wedding to plan for.'

'Well, make up your mind,' the conductor said.

'We'll be getting off at the next stop and returning to Ferndale,' James said. 'Because we have a wedding to plan for.'

The conductor sighed in an officious manner and handed some change to Walrus Moustache just as the train pulled into the station.

James took her hand, and still accepting congratulations and best wishes from everyone in the compartment, they made their way off the packed train and onto the platform.

'Thank you, Alice,' he said, taking hold of both her hands and gazing down into her eyes as they stood in the middle of the crowded station. 'Thank you for making me the happiest man alive. Thank you for showing me what true love really means. Thank you for being you.'

With that he took her in his arms and, oblivious to the array of stares, shocked looks and smiles of approval, he kissed her again, deeply and lovingly, and Alice was certain she too was the happiest woman alive.

# Epilogue

A great deal of discussion took place regarding the Lambton weddings, with everyone insisting that their wedding should be first. In the end it was decided that all three would take place on the same day at the same time and in the same place.

Alice's father still wanted to walk his daughter up the aisle. The solution was, he would do so, then take his place at the altar and wait for Widow Harcourt to join him.

The Vicar's intentions towards Lady Chigwell did add an extra complication, but the man put duty first and agreed to conduct the three weddings and put off his own to a later date.

While all the preparations were taking place and days were being selected that suited everyone and worked in with the Vicar's busy schedule of other weddings, Alice was starting to wonder if, while she had been inadequately matchmaking, half of Ferndale had paired up with the other half, and with no help from her whatsoever.

But the wedding day did come around, and within a few short weeks she was dressed in a beautiful ivory silk gown trimmed with delicate lace and embroidered in silver thread depicting the spring flowers that would soon be arriving.

On her father's arm she walked up the aisle of the local church towards James and William, with Beatrice following behind on the arm of her father, and Widow Harcourt, the woman who would soon be her step-mother, on the arm of her eldest son.

The local ladies had excelled themselves and the church looked magnificent. Garlands of evergreens had been strung between the pews, dotted with white winter roses and bouquets of snowdrops. Soft winter light filtered through the stained glass window, sending gentle colours dancing over the altar.

Behind the brides walked six bridesmaids, two for each bride, and Alice of course chose the two good friends she had met during her Season sitting beside the potted ferns, Primrose Fairburn and Margaret Whitmore.

Her father handed her over to James and took his place at the altar. Alice looked up at her husband-to-be and her heart swelled as he smiled down at her.

James looked magnificent in his dove-grey morning suit and ivory waistcoat, a sprig of snowdrops in his lapel. And this magnificent man was soon to be her husband.

'You look so beautiful,' he whispered as he took her hand, and they turned to face the Vicar.

All through the service his hand lightly caressed hers and she could hardly hear what the Vicar was saying, until it came time to make their vows, to which they both replied with a resounding 'I will.' Then they had an interminable wait while the Vicar repeated the same words to the other couples, before he finally said, 'You may kiss your bride.'

And he did. Alice kissed him back, her husband, the man she would be spending the rest of her life with, and even greater happiness filled her heart, body and soul.

To the pealing of bells the three couples made their way out of the church, where it seemed the entire village had congregated to see the happy couples and shower them with rice.

After weeks of rain and snow the sun was shining as if the weather itself was giving its blessing. On the steps of the church James kissed her once again, to the cheering of the crowd.

'I can hardly wait to steal my wife away and get you to myself,' he whispered in her ear, sending shivers of anticipation through her and letting her know she was wrong. While she was happy now, there was an even higher level of happiness waiting her in the days, nights and years to come.

Primrose and Maggie joined them, and both kissed Alice on the cheek.

'We are so happy for you,' Primrose said. 'And I don't believe I've ever seen a more dazzling bride.'

'And he's so handsome,' Maggie added quietly while James was distracted talking to the local squire. 'You lucky thing.'

'And to think not long ago you declared emphatically that you would never marry,' Primrose added.

'Well, sometimes even I can be wrong,' Alice said, laughing and linking arms with her two friends. She wanted to say she hoped they too would meet someone as wonderful as James and experience the same joy but knew how that would be received. In the same dismissive manner Alice would have reacted just a few months ago.

'So when do you move into your new town house?' Alice asked Primrose.

'Any day now,' she said, smiling with delight.

Primrose had inherited a London town house from a maiden aunt and an income to ensure she was able to support herself.

'You are both so lucky,' Maggie said. 'Neither of you will have to endure another Season. I have no choice but to go through another. My fourth.'

Alice winced for her friend.

'I believe my mother will be dragging me along to balls, soirées and parties until I'm well into my dotage and will still be thrusting me in front of every eligible man like a hawker trying to sell goods nobody wants.'

Alice and Primrose both patted Maggie's arm in support. She really did have a terrible mother who made the horrors of the marriage mart even worse than they already were.

'Hopefully you'll meet a nice man at tonight's wedding breakfast,' Alice said in her most optimistic voice, which caused Maggie to raise her cynical eyebrows. 'You never know. Stranger things have happened. Who would have thought I would become the Countess of Thornwood.'

Maggie lowered her eyebrows at that and had to agree, and after kissing her cheek one more time, the two young women wandered off to give their best wishes to the other two couples.

James finished chatting with the squire and once again wrapped his arm around her shoulder. 'Why are you looking so despondent? Anyone would think this was a funeral not a wedding.'

'I'm sorry. It's just I worry about Primrose and Maggie. Primrose intends to bury herself away from Society, with only her rescued animals for company, and Maggie is about to face yet another Season, this time without even Primrose and me for company. And her mother is, well, to put it bluntly, absolutely ghastly.

Even when men do show an interest in Maggie, her mother manages to drive them away by the force of her desperate enthusiasm.'

She looked up at James. 'Do you know any men who might make suitable husbands?' Before he could answer she looked over at her brother, who had his arm around Beatrice and was surrounded by joyous guests. 'Or maybe William has a couple of suitable friends he can introduce them to.'

'You're not planning on matchmaking again, are you?' James said, giving her a small squeeze. 'Because the last time you made a foray into that area it worked out so well, didn't it?'

'Yes, I believe it did.'

'You're right, it did indeed. It worked out perfectly,' he said with a laugh. 'You managed to match me up with the one woman in the world I was meant to be with,' he added, and took her in his arms to kiss her again.

\* \* \* \* \*

*Whilst you wait for the next instalment
of Wayward Wallflowers, why not
read Eva Shepherd's
Rakes, Rebels and Rogues miniseries*

A Wager to Win the Debutante
A Widow to Defy the Duke
A Marriage to Scandalize the Earl

*And why not check out her
Rebellious Young Ladies miniseries*

Lady Amelia's Scandalous Secret
Miss Fairfax's Notorious Duke
Miss Georgina's Marriage Dilemma
Lady Beaumont's Daring Proposition

# MILLS & BOON®

Coming next month

## A MARQUESS TO REMEMBER
### Jenni Fletcher

Florence's nostrils flared, as if she were restraining her temper with an effort. 'I still think there has to be a way out of this marriage.'

'There isn't.'

'So that's it?' She stared up at Leo with an appalled expression. 'You're just going to give up?'

'Yes.' He sighed, feeling very tired all of a sudden. This whole argument seemed to have been revolving around his head for weeks. Ironically, tonight was the first time he'd involved her in the discussion, but every time, he'd come to the same disheartening conclusion, that there was no way out. The marriage trap had well and truly closed around him. 'Now I think that's enough of a tour for tonight. I suggest that we both retire and get some sleep.'

'Well, that explains it.' She rose slowly to her feet, her gaze still fixed on his. 'That's why you look at me like so coldly, like you despise me. It's because you do.'

'What else did you expect?' He didn't deny it. 'This marriage isn't what I wanted.'

'Me neither, no matter what you think.' She wrenched her shoulders back. 'All I know is that there has to be some reasonable explanation for what happened and I'm going to find out what it is.'

He looked her up and down, impressed despite himself. With her chin in the air and a fierce glare on her face, she looked magnificently, almost regally defiant. If he weren't still so angry, he thought he might have been tempted to reach out and haul her against him, to stop her mouth with his own.

'Then I wish you luck.'

*Continue reading*

## A MARQUESS TO REMEMBER
### Jenni Fletcher

*Available next month*
millsandboon.co.uk

# COMING SOON!

We really hope you enjoyed reading this book.
If you're looking for more romance
be sure to head to the shops when
new books are available on

## Thursday 18th December

To see which titles are coming soon, please visit
**millsandboon.co.uk/nextmonth**

---

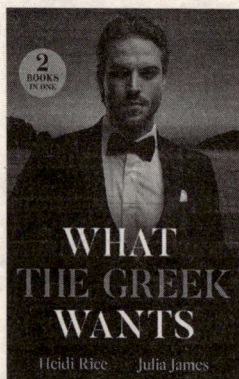

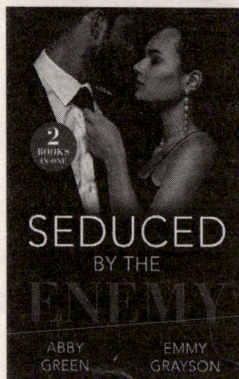

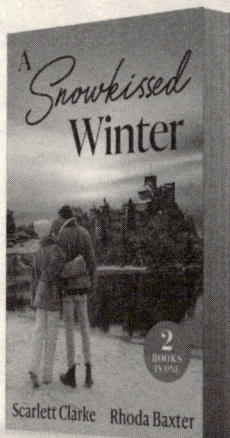

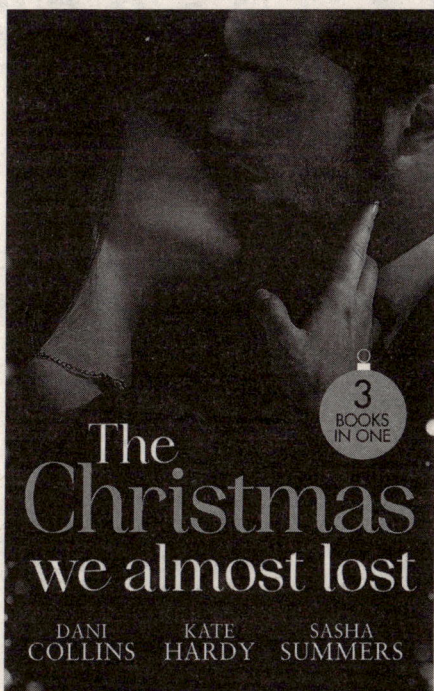